## WHEN TH[E]
## ABBY WENT TO HER TRUCK,
## THEN PAUSED AND LOOKED UP

Stars dotted the black velvet sky, a crescent moon hung like a sickle, and dew scented the chilly air. In the shelter of the trees, with the soft rustling sounds of small creatures in the underbrush, the nighttime no longer seemed full of menace. Instead, it enveloped them, like Jon and she were the only two people in the wide universe, and it was good.

She'd stayed for his father, of course. But she *had* been thinking of the son, possibly more than was good for her. She'd forgotten how nice he was.

It didn't mean anything, though. He was Roman's son, he was a good guy, and she'd done what any good neighbor would do under the circumstances.

"Do you want to come in?" Jon hesitated, glancing toward the house. "Could I offer you some tea before you go?"

The tentative way he said it tugged at her heart. He looked so forlorn.

Then she heard the dog, throwing himself at the gate. She'd opened the doggy door for him while the EMTs had been loading Roman into the ambulance, so he'd have access to the yard, but the poor animal was desperate for company.

"All right," she said.

Jon threw her a relieved smile.

The smile made something bloom inside her, something that whispered she wouldn't be able to sleep now, anyway, that she had a civic responsibility to be a good neighbor, that he was nice and she was nice and spending a bit more time together might be . . . very nice.

**Books by Roxanne Snopek**

*The Sunset Bay Series*

SUNSET BAY SANCTUARY

DRIFTWOOD CREEK

BLACKBERRY COVE

**Published by Kensington Publishing Corporation**

# BLACKBERRY COVE

## ROXANNE SNOPEK

ZEBRA BOOKS
KENSINGTON PUBLISHING CORP.
www.kensingtonbooks.com

ZEBRA BOOKS are published by

Kensington Publishing Corp.
119 West 40th Street
New York, NY 10018

All Kensington titles, imprints, and distributed lines are available at special quantity discounts for bulk purchases for sales promotion, premiums, fund-raising, educational, or institutional use.

Special book excerpts or customized printings can also be created to fit specific needs. For details, write or phone the office of the Kensington Sales Manager: Attn.: Sales Department. Kensington Publishing Corp., 119 West 40th Street, New York, NY 10018. Phone: 1-800-221-2647.

Zebra and the Z logo Reg. U.S. Pat. & TM Off.

First Printing: January 2019
ISBN-13: 978-1-4201-4424-6
ISBN-10: 1-4201-4424-3

ISBN-13: 978-1-4201-4427-7 (eBook)
ISBN-10: 1-4201-4427-8 (eBook)

10 9 8 7 6 5 4 3 2 1

Printed in the United States of America

*For Ray, the love of my life. I know how lucky I am.*

# Acknowledgments

With thanks to Connie Jones, who helped me sketch out the characters, poolside, with margaritas. Best time I've ever had planning a book. Also to Megan Snopek, who gave me enthusiastic encouragement and feedback on key plot points, Paula Altenburg, who added still more direction and atta-girls, when they were sorely needed, and to Ray Snopek, who told me, again and again, that I could do this. And brought me coffee.

# Prologue

Even from a block away, the heavy bass beat coming from the club drummed in Abby Warren's ears, echoing the thud of her heart. Above the wide door a flickering neon sign proclaiming it LADIES NITE was missing bulbs for the *I* and the *E*.

Lads night, all right.

It was the third place she'd been to in Eugene this evening. Surely Quinn would be here. People gravitated to the familiar, after all, especially in times of stress.

As if there was a time when they weren't under stress.

She jogged across the parking lot, stepping wide over potholes filled with puddled water. Muscle cars and patched-up pickups dominated the lot, giving her an idea of the customer base inside. Good old boys, looking for a good old time. Not too particular about where or with whom they might find it.

At the entrance to the nightclub stood a wide barn-door of a man, the classic image of a bouncer, black with a shiny shaved head, ripped arms crossed over his massive chest, and mirrored aviator sunglasses.

"Looking for someone, miss?" he inquired.

Even though Abby couldn't see his eyes, she felt them assessing her. She wore sneakers, a fleece hoodie, and jeans with mud stains on the knees, hardly an outfit designed for partying. It was an outfit to disappear in. Normally this suited her to a T, but tonight, she'd have to use a different tactic.

"Yes. My sister. Let me pass, please."

"Twenty-dollar cover," he said, without moving. "Payable here."

She'd found that as the night progressed, the bouncers got increasingly more difficult, and her patience was already nearing the breaking point. The upside to being chronically underestimated was that she had the element of surprise on her side.

"Listen, asshole." She held up a picture of Quinn. "This girl is in trouble, underage, and I'm not the only one looking for her."

At the word *underage,* he'd uncrossed his arms and started listening, as she knew he would.

"Everyone gets carded."

"You idiot." She was quaking inside, but didn't let it show. "Ten bucks and a hand job gets you a fake ID. Now, I've been up and down Willamette already so that means the buck stops here. You going to let me get her myself? Or should I call the cops?"

"Make it fast." He stepped aside. "Mouthy bitch."

"You have no idea," she replied as she shouldered past him.

Ignoring the irritation of the patrons around her, Abby pushed her way inside. The music was almost deafening, and multicolored lights flashed on the black walls in time with the beat. People, everywhere. Dancing, laughing, yelling, drinking. The smells of alcohol, perfume, and body odor rushed over her in a heated wave.

The central floor was a crush of bodies, surrounded on two sides by high-top tables and booths. Women stood at the tables, long legs hip-cocked on high heels, looking her up and down with amusement as she approached.

"Look what fell off the turnip truck," called a voice.

She ignored the laughter, scanning the crowd for Quinn's honey-colored hair.

"I think you took a wrong turn at Green Gables, honey," said another woman, with a sneer.

Abby wanted to show them the photograph but doubted that any of them were in any condition to help her out, even if they were so inclined. Plus, the fresh-faced innocence that disarmed men didn't work so well with women. Female weaponry required armor that she wasn't equipped with.

Behind the DJ's booth was another level, she noticed. Higher up, behind a low glass-paneled barrier. Instead of tables and booths, patrons lounged on upholstered furniture, men with their legs outstretched, women perched on the chair arms, or nestled into laps.

There.

For a moment, she caught a glimpse of familiar scarlet fabric and Quinn's golden hair. Then bodies closed in and she was gone. She was wearing the red dress again, Abby realized, the one their mother had left behind. Of course she'd have chosen it tonight. Abby should have thrown the damn thing out when she'd had the chance.

She grabbed the railing atop the glass fence and pulled herself up the stairs, winding between bodies, ducking under martini glasses held aloft, hoping not to cause a scene by spilling someone's drink.

All she wanted was to get her sister and get out of here before someone figured out they were gone.

In snapshots, between bodies, Abby saw Quinn lolling on the lap of a scruffy-jawed man who looked to be in his thirties. His hand was on her thigh. Quinn's blue eyes were vacant, her cheeks flushed, her hair matted and falling around her face, her neckline askew.

"Excuse me," Abby said, again and again. How much alcohol had Quinn drunk? Had someone given her drugs, too?

As she pushed past one person, then the next, she made it to the upper area. One after another, the men began noticing her.

She forced herself between a subset of couples, then climbed over a pair of legs and grabbed Quinn's hand.

"Come on, Quinnie, let's go." She pulled hard but Quinn only laughed and fell back against the older man.

"Hey there, little lady." He looked up at Abby and tightened his arm around Quinn. "This is a private party. Invitation only."

"Then uninvite this one," she snapped. "Come on, Quinn. Enough's enough."

The man's eyebrows went up. "Ooooh, hear that, boys? Bossy little thing, isn't she?"

"That's my sister." Quinn's words slurred together. "Miss Bossy Pants. Like Tina . . . whatshername . . . the funny lady."

Her words trailed off.

Laughter went around the circle. It had an undercurrent Abby recognized and didn't like. But she'd handled worse.

She leaned forward, resting her arms on the back of the couch, her hands on either side of the man's shoulders. She looked him in the eye and gave him a slow smile.

"Listen, honey." She used her throatiest voice and spoke low so his friends couldn't listen in. "You don't want me here any more than I want to be here. I've cut the nuts off bigger guys than you and fried them up with bacon, but I like your face, so I'm going to give you a chance to do the right thing. I just want to take my little sister home before someone gets hurt, so you're going to let that happen. Okay?"

His eyes bored hard into hers as if unsure whether or not to take offense. He'd expected a shrinking violet. He was getting a Venus flytrap. "And what if she and I are having a good time?" he asked, apparently choosing to remain neutral for the moment.

Abby touched his jaw with the back of her knuckle and gave him her sweetest smile. "I apologize if I was unclear. My sister is seventeen years old. Take your fucking hands off her."

He blinked as her words registered. Then his hands flew up, palms out. "Jesus. Shit. Go."

He all but pushed Quinn off his lap and she would have slid onto the floor if Abby hadn't grabbed her.

"I'm nineteen," Quinn protested. "I'm not a kid."

"Shut up and walk," Abby said through gritted teeth. Holding Quinn was like holding a bag of water.

"You ruin all my fun."

Somehow she managed to get them away from the roomful of men, down through the tables, past the dance floor, and outside into the night air. No one wanted jailbait, to Abby's relief.

"Found her, huh?" said the bouncer, his face impassive.

Abby stood in front of him, holding Quinn by the shoulders. "Take a look at this face, okay, big guy?"

Quinn's head wobbled on her neck. "Yeah. Look at my face, big-eye."

"From now on," Abby said, giving her sister a shake, "she's on the no-fly list. Or you'll have me to deal with again. Got it?"

Abby might have lied about Quinn being under eighteen, the age of consent, but she hadn't lied about her being below the legal drinking age. She wanted the man to remember that letting Quinn inside, no matter how old she got, wasn't worth the hassle.

"Whatever." The bouncer crossed his arms. "You two have a nice night."

Abby tightened her arm around Quinn's waist and dragged, pushed, and carried her back to the vehicle. She leaned the girl up against the door while she fumbled with her key, then shoved her onto the seat and fastened the belt over her hips.

"I'm tired of running, Abs." Quinn rubbed her eyes, smearing her makeup. "I just want to be normal."

Normal. Like that had ever been in the cards for them.

"I know. Me, too." Abby reached across and adjusted the passenger seat. "Lie back and go to sleep, okay?"

"I just wanted to have some fun." The petulant tone was gone from her voice. Now it was sad and small and lost. "I wish we could have stayed in L.A. I miss my friends. I miss Carly."

"Stop it, Quinn."

Sniffling sounded from the passenger seat. "I should have helped her."

Not again. "There was nothing you could do."

"You don't know that."

"We've been over this, Quinn. Carly begged you to leave it alone. You don't even know what you saw."

A sullen silence argued otherwise.

"Listen. If they figure out you were there that night, they'll come after you. And not just you. Both of us. Do you understand? If Carly said it was nothing, then it was nothing. We move on with our lives."

Quinn turned her face to the window and shut her eyes.

Abby gripped the steering wheel as waves of fatigue and relief washed over her. Her hands started shaking and tears filled her eyes. Eugene wasn't working.

She had to find a new place, away from city life, where Quinn could find some peace.

Somewhere safe.

# Chapter One

From Abby's notebook:

## BLUEBERRY BUTTERMILK COFFEE CAKE

This is the perfect treat for a lazy Sunday morning, or as part of a breakfast buffet for friends and family.

Cake batter:
 2 cups whole wheat flour
 2 cups all-purpose flour
 3 teaspoons baking powder
 1 teaspoon baking soda
 1 teaspoon salt
 ½ cup butter
 ¾ cup brown sugar
 2 eggs
 1 teaspoon vanilla extract
 2¼ cups buttermilk
 2 cups blueberries

Streusel topping:
 ⅓ cup all-purpose flour
 ⅓ cup bran

⅓ cup chopped walnuts
⅓ cup brown sugar
6 tablespoons butter, softened

Preheat oven to 350 degrees F. Grease and flour a 9 x 13 inch pan. To make the batter, sift together flours, baking powder, baking soda, and salt. Set aside.

In a large bowl, cream together butter and brown sugar until light and fluffy. Beat in the eggs one at a time, then stir in the vanilla. Beat in the flour mixture alternately with the buttermilk, mixing just until incorporated. Stir in blueberries. Pour batter into prepared pan.

To make the topping, combine flour, bran, walnuts, and sugar in a small bowl. Cut in the butter until mixture resembles coarse crumbs. Sprinkle over batter and swirl a knife through, to incorporate some of the topping into the cake.

Bake in the preheated oven for 45 to 60 minutes, or until a toothpick inserted into the center of the cake comes out clean. Cool slightly and serve.


From Abby's notebook:

> *The dormant season may seem uneventful, but plants are resting, gathering strength and energy, preparing for the next season of abundance.*


*Two years later*

At the gate to the old man's property, Abby cut the engine and stepped out of the truck. Tentative late-morning sunlight splintered between the naked trees crowding the narrow, winding road between Sanctuary Ranch and Roman's place, as if not yet strong enough to commit to spring. Heavy evergreens swallowed what was left and the drifting Oregon fog made the dying ticks of the old motor sound like pennies dropped on a wool blanket.

The Byers low sprawling ranch house was hidden from the road, deliberately secluded. But the solitude was an illusion. Creatures small and large, land-bound or with wings, skittered, skulked, and stalked in those misty-green depths. They triggered a heightened awareness dosed with awe and respect, but not fear. Abby absolutely believed that those wild things were more afraid of her than she was of them.

Humans were different. Predator and prey looked alike until experience, and hindsight, offered up the subtle distinguishing clues.

Solitude was safe, though as Roman Byers was learning, not great as a long-term plan.

Trust, for joy, she reminded herself.

Suspicion, for survival, her primitive brain replied.

She walked around the vehicle, reached into the passenger side, and slid a covered basket across the bench seat, wedging it against her hip. Inside were carrots, turnips, beets, and a few parsnips from the cellar, topped with a bunch of fresh parsley that she managed to keep growing year-round in the cold frame.

She came by as often as she could without raising questions. The man's secret was still hidden, so far. But it kept her up at night, eating at her stomach, and every time she arrived to visit, dread quickened her steps. With high season just around the corner, it would soon be even harder for her to keep tabs on him.

Last fall she and Quinn had planted an enormous bulb garden. Snowdrops and crocuses were already up, with daffodils and tulips right behind them. She'd gotten up early this morning to get the beds ready for public viewing but there was still a lot of mulch to spread on the footpaths.

On her way out, Daphne called her to the kitchen and handed her a loaf of oven-fresh bread, a chunk of leftover meat loaf, and an enormous slab of her blueberry buttermilk coffee cake.

"Who knows what that grumpy duck is living on out there?" the cook had asked. "Can't have him starving to death next door, can we?"

No, Abby agreed. Starvation wouldn't do at all.

A rise and slope of wooded hillside, a creek that emptied into the ocean, and a couple of miles of gravel road was all that separated the ranch from their nearest neighbor, but Roman had stayed hidden from them for years. Once found, though, he couldn't be unfound. He was a stray and Sanctuary Ranch collected strays like honeybees gathered pollen.

Lucky for Roman. Until Jamie, Abby's friend and coworker, had happened upon him, he'd been on track to be one of those headlines: HUMAN SKELETON FOUND ON ISOLATED PROPERTY. FOUL PLAY NOT SUSPECTED. Abby bent low to get herself and her package through the rusted metal rungs of the gate, wondering why he still insisted on keeping it up. A sign reading BEWARE OF DOGS listed sideways on a single nail in the wooden side post.

Beware of dogs. Ha!

"Roman, it's me," she called as she rounded the bend leading to his house. "Don't shoot."

It was a running joke with everyone at the ranch, now. When Jamie had first knocked on his door, she'd been greeted with a shotgun. Turned out the gun wasn't the weapon to worry about. Nature had given Roman Byers a tongue as sharp as his mind, a defective brain-mouth filter, and a stubborn streak a mile wide.

Pain had honed those weapons to a wicked edge and loneliness taught him to wield them. Abby recognized what lay behind the attitude. Pity infuriated him. Verbal jousting was the way in.

"Chaos," she called, looking for the man's dog, "I've got a treat for you."

Usually, that was the signal for Roman's beautiful, brilliant and diabolical young Labrador to come pelting toward her.

Nothing. No dog in sight.

She continued up the path, hefting the basket on her hip. The old man preferred to be left alone, but occasionally, when the training sessions he and Chaos took at the ranch went long, Roman joined the rest of the staff in the main house for supper. Daphne loved feeding guests, and always made plenty, just in case.

Over the past winter, however, he'd been forced to ask for help. He'd chosen Abby, and sworn her to secrecy. She drove him to his appointments, physiotherapists, doctors, specialists. More specialists. Usually, if he wasn't hurting too much, they stopped for coffee. Sometimes, they had lunch.

"Roman?" Abby checked the yard, with its mature fruit trees and great mounds of perennials greening up from the black soil. She could see now that he'd neglected them the previous season. As soon as the bulb garden was done, she'd come help him out.

How that must have pained him.

"Hey, old man." *You better not have died on me.*

All those times she'd baited him, and he'd just smiled.

She bit her lip, looking past the fence to the woods. Roman refused to give up his birdwatching walks but Chaos was trained to stick close, help him up if he fell, and lead him home if he got disoriented. Chaos had turned into an excellent helper. He'd also been taught to bring Roman his mobile phone, his pills, the remote control for the TV, and in case of a true emergency, to cut through the wooded hillside to Sanctuary Ranch for help.

Now, she feared Chaos gave him a dangerous sense of self-reliance.

She climbed the wide plank steps to the back porch, pulled open the screen, and rapped on the door. Immediately, the sound of claws scrabbling on hardwood greeted her.

The dog was inside, whining and howling, throwing himself at the door between them.

She tried the knob. It was unlocked. She pushed inside and nearly tripped over the dog, who bolted past her, stopped at the first bush, lifted his leg, and peed and peed and peed.

She dropped the basket. "Roman?"

Chaos hadn't been out in hours and his doggy door was still locked, which meant something had interrupted Roman's usual morning routine.

"Roman?" Abby glanced around the great room. The man wasn't in his armchair or lying on the couch. She pushed through doors, shoved furniture, looked down the stairs to the cellar. He wasn't in the kitchen or pantry or sunroom.

As she ran toward his bedroom, she heard the sound of water trickling.

Oh no.

He was in the bathroom, on the floor, naked and motionless, while water slopped over the edge of the bathtub onto the floor.

*You better not have died on me.*

"Roman!" She reached around him to close the faucet, which was trickling ice-cold water, then dropped to the floor. Her knees slid sideways in the puddle. Her brain stuttered at the scene before her.

Blood feathered from a cut over his eye. He was wet and shivering. The puckered, spotted skin on his back was bluish white and dotted with silver hair, and small circles where bathwater had evaporated.

His thighs were clenched together and quaking, the bones

visible beneath the sagging skin. He'd managed to drag a small towel over his genitals, and clutched it with one clawed hand, a desperate grasp at dignity that broke her heart.

"Roman, can you hear me? Wake up, please. Please!"

He opened his eyes and gave a low groan that ended with an expletive.

"Oh, thank God!" Abby exhaled in a huge rush. He was awake, conscious, and breathing.

"Took you . . . goddamn . . . long enough," she heard him say.

She grabbed a hand towel, folded it, and pressed it against the cut.

"Hold this."

He tried, but his hand was shaking too hard.

She tucked another towel under his head. Under the thin gray stubble, his scalp was damp and oily, his skin ashen, his eyes sunken and wreathed with lines.

"Hang on," she said. "I'm going to get a blanket."

With trembling hands, she yanked the comforter off his bed and ran back to the bathroom where she tucked it around him. Preserving body heat was essential but protecting his battered pride was just as important.

"Can you get up?" she asked, winding her arm beneath his shoulder.

He cried out at the movement. "Bloody . . . hip . . ." he said through gritted teeth. "I can't move."

"How long have you been lying here?"

"How the hell should I know?" he muttered.

It was nearly noon. He'd likely been lying here for hours.

A cold nose nudged her from behind. Chaos, whining at the state of his master, pacing back and forth, not knowing what to do.

Abby knew the feeling.

She patted the pockets of her hoodie, feeling for her

phone. First she called 9-1-1. Then she called the ranch.
Then she called Quinn.

Last, she called Roman's son.

Surely, now, Roman would tell him the truth.


Whitey Irving, editor-in-chief of *Diversion* magazine,
was sitting behind his enormous desk, his hands linked over
his belly, observing him the way a toad might observe a fly.

Jonathan Byers stood in front of the desk feeling like a
truant schoolboy, staring at a spot of dirt on the ceiling,
choosing his words, deleting the ones he knew he'd regret.

"It's a good story—" he began.

Irving waved a hand. "No, son. It's not. But you seem a
little hard of hearing."

"If you let me tell you about it, I know you'll want to
run it."

This story was risky. You didn't accuse a top Hollywood
moviemaker of professional misconduct without bracing for
blowback.

You also didn't do it unless your facts were rock solid.

Jon's were. All he needed was one disgruntled employee,
one duped investor, one harassed woman to go on record and
the rest would follow. It would be a landslide.

"I already know what it's about and I'm not interested."
Irving unfolded his arms and sat forward. "You're a good reporter, Byers. Keen, hardworking, except of course, when
you're taking time off to be with your father in Oregon."

Jon felt his eyes widen as a double whammy of betrayal
hit. His managing editor, who'd always had his back, had apparently been keeping score.

"I've never missed a deadline." His jaw felt tight. "Hal
said as long as I filed my stories and made it back for the
team meetings, it wasn't a problem."

Irving ignored him. "My biggest issue is that you don't seem to understand the power dynamic here."

"Power dynamic? This isn't about me. It's about a story. A huge story that for some reason people here don't want to touch." It was Pulitzer material; he knew it in his gut. Yet they wouldn't even consider it.

Irving looked at him for a long moment.

His story was better than good. It was sensational. It would expose the elaborate cover-up protecting a man who, once this came to light, would go from being a Hollywood darling to an industry pariah, overnight.

"Richard Arondi is dirty, sir, and I've got everything to bring him down. It's a game changer for the whole movie industry, revealing an ugly underbelly that everyone seems to want to ignore. I thought those were the kinds of stories we published. Was I wrong?"

"I thought Hal told you not to follow it—"

"I did it all on my own time."

"I don't care. It's not of interest." He spoke slowly and deliberately. "Are you hearing me this time?"

Beyond the glass of Irving's office, bright-eyed colleagues looked up from blinking monitors, then quickly looked down, an elaborate pretense that fooled no one.

Arondi was said to have a mix of Jamaican, African, Native American, and Polynesian blood, all of which contributed to exotic good looks surpassed only by his charismatic personality and undeniable creative gifts. Arondi broke new ground. He did what he wanted, when he wanted, regardless of naysayers, or market trends or political correctness and his films were legendary. Everyone wanted to be seen with him. Everyone loved him.

Except for those who hated him.

Arondi's predatory treatment of aspiring actresses in particular was well known, and what Jon most wanted to bring out into the open. But standing up to Arondi or speaking out against him meant career suicide for someone trying to break in. Putting up with his lecherous behavior was almost a rite of passage, the cost of doing business.

"I've got quotes, dates, times. It's iron-clad, Whitey. The second I can name names, this is a go." Jon's cell phone vibrated. Without looking, he pulled it out of his jacket pocket and silenced it.

"I do not care." Irving leaned over his desk. "You seem to be laboring under the misapprehension that this is a partnership. It's not. You're an employee. I'm your boss."

"But why, Whitey? What am I missing here? I don't get it. *Diversion* loves to break scandals; we do them all the time."

"Not this one. Not this time. End of story."

There had to be some reason. Jon knew that Richard Arondi's production company regularly bought full-page ads for upcoming movies and could understand Irving not wanting to piss off a major advertiser, but this was a whole different level. This was beginning to sound like something that compromised journalistic ethics, which, even for an entertainment magazine, still counted for something.

He was tired of being stonewalled. Time to play his last card.

"Perhaps it's not right for *Diversion* magazine. But someone will run it and when they do, their sell rate will skyrocket."

It was a wild shot, a huge gamble, but this was a career-making story and he couldn't let it go without fighting for it.

For a moment, it appeared the man was reconsidering.

"Hal doesn't want to fire you. He likes you, Byers, and I can see why. You're a likable guy. Passionate. I admire that. But I'm a numbers man. I watch sales figures, subscription numbers, ad revenue, ratings. I watch profit margins, run cost-benefit analyses. I don't care about articles. And I don't care about you. You're just a number on the payroll."

Jon didn't like where this was going.

"We gave you time to come to your senses, and you didn't. So. Collect your things. You're done here."

"Wait." Jon felt as if he'd had a bucket of ice water thrown in his face. "You're firing me? Over a story?"

Too late, he realized that what he'd taken for calm was merely the calm before the storm.

Jon saw the ice harden in Whitey Irving's eyes. For a fat man, he got to his feet with surprising alacrity. He came at Jon with his stubby index finger stretched out, stabbing at him, his lips curled.

"You idiot. You really don't listen, do you? There's no fucking story here." He inhaled and his nostrils flared as if he smelled something unpleasant. "Hal put his own neck on the line for you but you didn't appreciate that, did you? You don't take orders, you don't work well with others, and you refuse to recognize when you're in over your head. I told you, we're not running the story. Now, get the hell out of my office before I call security."

Tonight, Jon thought as he rode the elevator back down, he'd panic. But right now he was too busy being furious.

When the elevator doors opened, he was greeted by Hal's intern, holding a cardboard box of Jon's things in his arms. The boy gave it to Jon with a frightened look.

"Sorry, man. They told me to, um, give you this."

Jon swallowed his anger. It wasn't this kid's fault. He grabbed his things and slammed out the big glass entrance doors.

His cell phone buzzed again as he was juggling his keys in the parking garage. He tossed the box into the backseat and hit the button to accept the call.

"Jon Byers," he said. "Who's this?"

"It's Abby Warren, from Sanctuary Ranch," replied a voice that sounded vaguely familiar. "It's about your father."

No, Jon thought. No more. Not now.

"He's in the hospital," Abby continued. "How quickly can you get here?"

# Chapter Two

From Abby's notebook:

*Watch the temperature. A soil thermometer will help you know when to plant vegetables. But don't jump the gun. Fragile seedlings do not have the strength to withstand late frosts.*

Abby propped one elbow on the windowsill of Roman's room, and rested her head on her hand. He'd been assessed in the emergency room and admitted. The hospital staff hadn't been surprised to see him; if anything, they acted as if they'd been expecting him. Then again, they knew his secret.

Roman had sent her out of the room while the doctors worked on him, of course, and while the staff threw sympathetic looks her way, no one spoke to her of his condition. She wasn't family.

A muffled grunt came from the bed.

She straightened up and leaned toward him. "Roman? How are you feeling?"

He lifted one hand and beckoned for her to come closer.

"Feeling great, kiddo. They know their pharmaceuticals, these folks."

She took his hand and squeezed gently. "You scared me."

"Sorry about that. Did they give you the four-one-one?"

Abby glanced toward the door. "You've sworn everyone to secrecy on pain of death, so no. You might want to tell them I'm part of the inner circle."

Roman shook his head. "Simpler this way."

"For you." She'd never felt so helpless, so impotent. "Is it . . . progressing?"

Roman sighed heavily and the faint sour smell of his breath drifted toward her, the odor of hunger, illness, and pain. "Same shit, different day. Lost my balance. Gravity took care of the rest."

Abby shuddered. "Roman, this is getting out of hand. You have to tell Jon. You have to figure out a plan. You can't go on like this."

Jon had long wanted to get Roman into an assisted living facility. The two had argued about it numerous times and so far, the older man had held firm. But this wouldn't play well for him. When Jon found out about the tumor, the conflict would escalate to Biblical proportions.

Roman shook his head impatiently. "I told you. I will when I'm ready."

Abby stretched out stiff back muscles. She wasn't used to this much inactivity. She'd been at the hospital all day and the adrenaline had faded from her bloodstream hours ago, leaving her wrung out and quivery. She didn't know how much more she could take.

*Don't die on me, old man.*

She should have said no, right away, when he'd first revealed the extent of his illness; she should have gone behind his back and told Jon anyway.

"You know that appointment you took me to a few weeks

ago?" he'd asked her. Had it only been January? It felt like she'd been holding this for years.

He'd told her he was meeting his physiatrist. She hadn't known much about Roman's original injury only that he had chronic hip and back issues related to an accident many years ago. Physiotherapy and rehabilitation was an every week event for him.

"So many different docs, different therapists." He'd closed his eyes. "So much wasted time."

"You would be in a wheelchair if not for those appointments."

"Most of them weren't physio. Most of them weren't even about my back."

She'd had no idea what he was talking about. "What were they for, then?"

"My head." He chuckled, a rough, gravelly sound like pouring wet cement.

"Your head. I don't follow."

"All those years I worked on my legs, my back, my muscles, and bones, and what turns up to punch my ticket but brain cancer."

He'd said the words so casually, that it took a moment for Abby to recognize that yes, he'd said brain cancer. It still triggered the same sensation inside her chest, as if she was filled with insects trying to beat their way out.

"You can't tell anyone," he'd emphasized. "Not Jon. Nobody at the ranch. I don't want pity or handouts or advice. I don't want Daphne rolling in like a freight train with casseroles and flowers and cards. All that well-meaning shit will kill me faster than anything."

Yes, that had been her chance to force his hand, right then. She could have said no. She should have said no. She should have called Jon up right then and told him the truth.

He'd be so angry.

She looked at the thin figure surrounded by white sheets.

"Roman, it's not fair to Jon, your keeping this from him. It's not fair to me, either. I have a job. Garden season is about to begin and Olivia's counting on me."

"Sorry if my dying wishes are inconvenient for you. Go play with your flowers. See if I care."

"Don't be such a baby." She blew out a breath and looked upward, searching for the right words to convince him. "I'll support you to your dying day. But I'm just one person. You need more than I can give you."

"You're exactly what I need."

"You need your son," she corrected. "Please, please tell him."

He grimaced. "I will, damn it. I told you I would. It's not the kind of conversation to have over the phone."

"Well, then, you're in luck. He'll be here in a few hours."

He glared at her. "I never told you to call him."

"You never told me not to. I didn't say anything about the cancer. I left that for you."

Poor Jon. He'd be prepared for bruises and sprains. Not a glioma tumor.

Brain cancer.

Poor Roman. Poor Jon.

She got up and went to the door. As soon as Jon arrived, she would find some doctors and make them explain everything. Who knows, maybe they'd learn that Roman was wrong, that he needed a second opinion, that Doctor Google had filled his head with too much information and he'd convinced himself he had a disease he did not.

"Sit down, Abby. I'm not telling him, you're not telling him; and the staff won't tell him. Not until I give them the okay."

She realized he was right. On numb feet, she walked back to the bedside and sank into the chair.

Jon would know something was wrong, though. Roman had lost weight. He'd hidden it beneath loose clothing, but he was definitely thinner than he'd been last summer. He'd taken to shaving his head too, but she hadn't thought twice of it until now. Lots of men did that. Bald is beautiful and all that.

When he lifted the plastic glass of water, his hand trembled. A symptom of the tumor? Roman refused to give her details, but she'd read up on glioblastomas. The early signs were subtle, but Roman had them all. The dizzy spell that made him fall was just one more indication that, no matter how he wished to pretend otherwise, he was getting worse.

Roman sipped, coughed, and returned the tumbler to the table. He turned his eyes to the ceiling and sighed again. "I've still got a few months left. Maybe a year. These are hard to predict, I guess."

"A few months." The wings beating against her ribs grew more panicked. "I can't possibly keep this to myself that long."

"I know when the time is right."

"I'll help Jon. We'll look into treatment. We'll figure this out, I promise."

"That's not how it's going to go, Abby." Roman's gaze turned steely. "Jon's going to give me enough of a fight. When the time comes, your job will be to help him understand."

She didn't like the way that sounded.

"Understand what?"

There were no tears, no self-pity or sentiment or fear, just determination. He spoke as if reading from a fact sheet.

"They want to cut open my head. Fire radiation at it. Pour me full of poison. I'm not doing that. None of it. Do you understand?"

"But if surgery extends your life—"

"I'm not letting someone stir around up there with a scalpel. It's not happening. You have to help my son understand that."

"Jon will never understand that. I don't understand it! What if treatment could extend your life?"

Time is all there was. Who wouldn't fight for every second of life they could get?

"A few extra months of shitting the bed and puking my guts out? No way. With any luck, I'll have a nice quiet stroke and go out in my sleep."

Abby put her hands to her ears. "Stop. Stop it. This is wrong. You can't expect me to be okay with this."

Roman shifted his legs beneath the sheets, wincing. As firmly as he'd spoken a moment ago, he now looked uncertain. "You're stronger than you look, Abby. That's why I chose you. Jon will have a difficult time with this."

A laugh burst out of her, mingled with tears. "You think?"

"I mean," Roman continued, "he will fight me, to push for treatment, to argue with doctors, to fly me to the Mayo Clinic or Mexico or wherever for experimental drugs or clinical trials or healing prayers or drum circles. And I don't want that. None of it. I want to die in my own home, with my dog and my garden and my birds. I want Jon there with me. And I want you there too, as much as possible." He paused. "You're good company. Jon's going to need that."

"I'll do whatever I can for him. As long as you tell him the truth. Promise me, Roman!"

"I will." Roman exhaled heavily. "When I'm ready. And not a moment before."

# Chapter Three

The trip from Los Angeles to Sunset Bay usually took over fourteen hours but an accident just outside of San Francisco had shut down the highway for nearly forty minutes.

Standing outside his car in between bouts of rain, Jon listened to the driver ahead of him tear a strip off the poor flag person. Despite his own frustration at the delay, he reminded himself that if fault fell on anyone, it certainly wasn't the young man in Day-Glo orange.

"What's wrong with you people?" the man yelled, punching the air. "Single lane alternating, is that too much to ask? There's no reason for a complete standstill."

He was a little younger than Roman, Jon guessed, but of a similar temperament.

The road worker approached the man. "Sorry for the inconvenience but until I get the go-ahead, no one's moving."

"How long is it going to be?"

"I don't know." Water was dripping down his hooded cape.

The man snorted. "Give me your best educated guess."

"I'm telling you, I don't know. Some guy up there missed the turn and ended up sideways on the road. Traffic's blocked in both directions. It took forever to get emergency crews in."

"Any injuries?" Jon asked, leaning on his open door. Their inconvenience was nothing if people were hurt.

"I don't think so. I saw the driver walking around, talking on his phone."

"Probably what caused the accident in the first place," groused the other driver. "I hope his car is totaled. This road should be better patrolled for stuff like that. This is ridiculous."

There were worse things than being stuck on the road because of an accident. Being a participant in the accident, for one.

"Come on, man," Jon said. "Ease up. This isn't helping."

The flagman threw him a grateful look but the older gentleman wasn't impressed.

"Ah, to hell with both of you." The man swore and stomped around to the other side of his car and lit a cigarette, fuming.

Jon considered engaging the annoyed driver but between worry for his father and the humiliation of being escorted out of *Diversion,* he wasn't feeling too sanguine himself at the moment. Hal had never indicated that the trips back and forth to Oregon had been a problem, so to hear about it from Whitey pissed him off royally.

Jon hadn't taken any time off since Christmas, plus he'd been working his ass off. He'd managed all his assigned pieces, as usual. Better than usual, even. He'd been on a roll lately, on track for a raise, a promotion.

Maybe Whitey Irving wanted to cut back on expenses. He could hire two cub reporters for what they were paying him. Maybe he'd been looking for a way to fire Jon for months and the piece on Richard Arondi was simply a convenient excuse.

Power dynamics.

This wasn't a power struggle. Jon hadn't been insubordinate.

He'd been enterprising.

Journalists needed to be self-starters, go-getters with an eye for what others didn't see. That's what they'd valued in Jon. At the start, at least.

He got back into the car, gripped the steering wheel, and dropped his forehead over it. Now that the shock was wearing off, he felt overcome with fatigue. Every mile closer to Sunset Bay had increased his concern for his father.

Concern. More like a gut-clenching sense of being proven right. He'd known some kind of health crisis was coming. He'd told Roman it was too dangerous to live alone, off in the wilds, as he did.

Naturally, his father gave Jon the brush-off. He didn't take advice from anyone, let alone his son.

The anger at Whitey Irving was easy. There was a clear enemy, a bright white line between right and wrong.

There was nothing clear or easy about his anger toward Roman. Jon thumped the wheel with his fists. How was he going to convince his dad that he needed to be closer to civilization and the help and company of his only child?

How did you help someone who didn't want to be helped? How do you engage someone who's hurting, when they won't even talk to you?

Sometime during the last decade of Jon's thirty-two years, he'd been forced into the awareness that fear and pain and uncertainty don't disappear simply because a person is told to grow up, to buck up, to be a man. That river of emotion goes underground, morphing, gaining power, eventually erupting far from the source, unrecognizable and sometimes, uncontrollable.

He'd seen Roman erupt enough times to recognize the cycle. Only the knowledge of what lay beneath the rage allowed Jon to ignore it and keep pushing for an in.

He loved his father.

Couldn't stand to be with him for more than a few days at a time, but he still loved him.

The driver ahead of him was stomping back and forth in front of his car, peering through the line of vehicles and shaking his head. It looked like he was losing his own battle for control. Was he an entitled asshat, used to always getting his own way? Or was he already upset about something else and this accident was the last straw?

Jon understood that all too well. If Roman was any indication, self-awareness wasn't a skill prioritized by the older generation.

The man banged his cell phone against his hand and then threw it through the open window of his car. For a moment, he stood there, braced on the car door, hanging his head. He looked pitiful. And all too familiar.

Jon told himself there was no need to draw more lightning onto himself.

*Not your business.*

On the other hand, he could consider it a warm-up for dealing with his father.

Jon sighed, stepped out of his car, and walked over to the man.

"Excuse me, sir. If your phone is dead, you're welcome to borrow mine."

"What?" He drew back and stared at Jon. His face was florid and pulsating. Deep bags under his eyes suggested the man hadn't slept well lately, or maybe ever.

"My phone." Jon held it out. "If that will help."

The man looked at him suspiciously, as if unwilling to believe the gesture. An array of reactions passed over his features before it sagged like an overfilled balloon with a slow leak. He ran a hand over his scalp. "It's my wife's birthday. I've got dinner reservations. I promised that this year I'd be there." He stuck out a hand. "Don't know if she'll believe me, but a man can try."

He keyed in the number, spoke briefly, then handed the

device back. "Thanks," he said gruffly. "Hope I'm still married when I get home."

Maybe he was more aware than Jon gave him credit for.

"Good luck," Jon told him.

Twenty minutes later, the flag person returned, calling for drivers to return to their vehicles.

Finally.

As the line of drivers began starting their engines, the young worker walked toward him. He glanced at the car ahead and lowered his voice. "I thought he was going to rip me a new one. Thanks for calming him down."

"No problem. He's got a lot on his mind."

It was so much easier to be courteous to a stranger, no baggage, no strings between them. And the stranger's backstory was plausible, if weak; could be he was simply one of those people who took delight in creating misery for those around him.

Jon knew Roman's backstory. He understood why his father clung so hard to his independence and privacy, the pain that made him lash out at times, the betrayals that had destroyed his trust. But this last winter, his father's attitude had deteriorated to the point where Jon dreaded every phone conversation. When all you got was grief for not coming sooner, it didn't engender excitement for a return trip.

Once past the accident—a pickup truck with two sides smashed in, and a driver lucky to be alive—he quickly made his way onto the coast road toward the little town of Sunset Bay, his fingers tight on the wheel, the muscles in his arms like piano wires.

With nothing to distract him, dread at what lay ahead filled his mind. He drew in a deep breath and let himself feel what he'd been suppressing since he got Abby's call.

Fear, pain, uncertainty, and most definitely anger.

His dad was getting worse. It wasn't safe for him to be

living out there all alone. Jon knew something like this would happen; he'd predicted it, seen it coming a mile away, and had been forced to sit back and wait for the crash. They'd been lucky that Abby had found him when she did, but luck and neighborly kindness was hardly a long-term plan.

Not for Jon, at least. This was the last straw. If Roman wouldn't move back to Los Angeles with him, then Jon would have to find an assisted living facility in Sunset Bay for him.

Did a town of that size even have such a facility?

He hated the thought of his sharp-as-a-tack father living surrounded by dementia patients. Roman would never forgive him, but what choice did Jon have?

He loved his father.

But he had a life, too.

There had to be a better way.

He wished, not for the first time, that he had a sibling to share this responsibility with. But Roman had never remarried after the divorce, and the half sibs on his mom's side, schoolkids he barely knew, had nothing to do with this.

He turned the steering wheel into town, easing up on the gas and followed the signs to the hospital. The parking lot was empty and free of charge, one of the perks of small-town living.

He locked the car and jogged toward the emergency entrance. The last he'd heard from Abby was that his father was having diagnostic tests done but that it looked like he'd received only minor injuries. It was the longest conversation they'd ever had. Her voice had been husky with tears, which had surprised him.

He'd met her the previous summer when he was driving Roman and Chaos to the service dog training program at Sanctuary Ranch. Abby was friends with Jamie, the trainer who'd been working with the dog, but she usually disappeared whenever he showed up. She worked in the kitchen and gardens, he thought.

But apparently sometime during the winter, while Jon had been busy tanking his career, Abby and his father had become friends.

She'd warned him that Roman had banged himself up pretty good and had some spectacular bruises. Jon should prepare himself, she'd said.

Prepare himself? He'd been dreading a call like this for months. How much more broken could his father be? Another fall was about the last thing the man needed.

The glass door was locked after hours but a security guard got up from his post and greeted Jon through an intercom.

"My father was brought in earlier today," he said. "I got here as quickly as I could."

The guard checked his name against a log, then buzzed him in and directed him to the triage center. He glanced around. The room was lit up, but empty.

No, not empty.

"Hey, Jon." Abby's husky voice echoed against all the chrome, tile, and stainless steel.

He looked over to see her curled up in the corner waiting area. She unfolded her slender legs from the seat of an uncomfortable-looking chair and stood. Her hair was mussed and dark circles smudged the honeyed skin under her eyes.

Guilt over the fact that she'd been the one to find Roman, instead of him, the son, sharpened his tone. "What are you still doing here?"

She straightened, swiped a thick mass of hair over her shoulder. "I didn't want to leave him here alone."

Fatigue and hurt roughened her voice.

*Good job, Byers.*

He gritted his teeth and searched for his earlier calm.

"Sorry. Didn't mean to snap. It's been a long day. Traffic was a mess. I thought I'd never get here."

She gazed at him without blinking. Then one eyebrow lifted. "Sorry you had to come out."

The shot hit the mark and he took it, knowing he deserved it. A few hours ago, he was calming an asshat on the side of the road. Now he was that asshat.

He squeezed his eyes shut and pressed his index fingers against his temples. "Can I start over?"

The eyebrow arched higher. She crossed her arms and tossed her head, sending that strand of chestnut hair tumbling down her back. "I'm listening."

When she talked, which she didn't do a lot, her voice was like a hand-knit sweater, a little scratchy, warm, and comforting. But she listened with her whole body angled toward you, like she wasn't just waiting for her turn to speak, but really hearing what you had to say.

If this is how she always was, no wonder Roman liked her. Not a lot of people took time to listen to cranky old men.

"Of all people," he said, "you don't deserve my anger. Thank you for looking out for my dad. If you hadn't been there . . ."

He cleared his throat and looked away.

She reached for him, caught his hand, and led him to a chair. She smelled nice, like the outdoors and something blooming. Her touch was soft but firm. Something inside him lifted a sleepy head.

Hello, he thought. I wasn't expecting that.

Gently, Abby pushed him into the chair.

"You're exhausted," she said. "Can I buy you a cup of coffee? It's cheap and barely drinkable, but you look like you need it."

The color of her eyes made him think of hazelnut lattes. A smile tipped the edge of her lips. Her hand was still on his arm. "If you insist," he said.

When she walked away, he rubbed his arm, where the skin was already cooling.

# Chapter Four

From Abby's notebook:

*Prepare soil for spring planting. Incorporate
generous amounts of organic materials and other
amendments. Remember, well-rotted manure is your
friend. Death and decay is the bedrock of new life.*

Abby could feel his eyes on her as she walked away, feel the
weight of her secret and the guilt that came with it. Jon was
hurting and tired and her knowledge of what lay ahead for
him filled her with pain. She wished she could take off,
leave it all in the hands of the medical staff, but Roman's
wishes trumped everything, for now. Until Roman told Jon,
Abby was stuck in limbo. Aching to help, but without being
able to say why.

Roman was in good hands. Most of the staff knew him
and Aiden McCall, the physician on duty tonight, would
treat the man as if he was his own father.

He'd even become something of a favorite at Sunset
Bay Memorial, not for his personality, but for his service

dogs. Everyone had loved old Sadie and Chaos was quickly earning similar affection.

No matter how crabby Roman got, when people saw him stroking his dog's ears, or saw Chaos leaning against him, eyes soft with adoration, their hearts generally melted. No one who'd earned that kind of love from a dog could be wholly bad.

She hoped the reunion between father and son was going well.

She plugged money into the vending machine and watched as the thin dark stream trickled into the plastic cup. It had been a long day for everyone but now that Jon had arrived, her nerves sizzled with energy. The quietness of the hospital after hours and the urgency of the situation made it strangely intimate.

She wished she had come in her own vehicle so she could leave Jon to face this without having a stranger witness his reaction. But with Roman clinging to her hand, she'd automatically crawled into the ambulance and stayed at his side. The EMTs had allowed it, quickly seeing that she helped keep Roman calm.

She didn't know Jon well enough to say whether his discomfort at her presence would outweigh his appreciation for the support of someone else who cared about his father.

Jon would have questions for her, of course, since she'd been the one to find Roman. She'd have to be careful about what she could and couldn't say, without breaking Roman's confidence.

Abby had been in Jon's shoes, watching a loved one suffer, without being able to do a single thing to help, and now she ached for him. She knew all about the helplessness and rage, how being dependent on the wisdom and whims of others eroded your own power, made you want to hunker down and howl.

But it was more than empathy.

The truth was, there was something about Jon that pulled at her, awakened desires long dormant, dreams she'd never allowed herself. The memory of her first sight of him last summer was burned into her mind. Hair burnished gold by the sun, chiseled cheekbones and sunglasses that hid sparkling, smiling blue eyes. He looked like a man at peace with his life. Long, loose stride, firm handshake, and eye contact that said he really saw you when he looked at you.

Yes, there was a lot to like about Jonathan Byers. If a woman was in the market.

She could still feel the warmth of his skin beneath her fingertips and longed to sweep the hair off his forehead and ease the tired lines around his eyes.

But she was window-shopping only. Her future was as cloudy as the woods in winter, shrouded with uncertainty, no clear way through. She knew better than to let her heart further complicate matters.

When she returned with the cups of tepid liquid, Aiden was with Jon, sitting in the chair she'd just vacated. He leaned forward, speaking earnestly, and Jon nodded.

"Abby." He looked up at her, his eyes wide, his lips white. "Dr. Mac says Dad owes you his life."

Wild hope leaped inside her. Oh, thank God! Aiden had told him. The secret was out.

Wait. That didn't make sense. Jon would be in shock, not grateful.

Heat rushed into Abby's face. "I don't know what you mean." She rested one cup of coffee on the other and put a hand to her cheek.

"Lying in one position for so long made a clot form," Aiden said. "Thanks to you, we found it in time. It could have been bad." He turned back to Jon. "There are other issues, but he'd prefer to discuss those with you himself. You should talk to him about . . . his prognosis."

Aiden's voice was solemn. He'd been hobbled by Roman's wishes, too.

"Of course. More physio, more rest, more drugs. Dad's not going to be happy about this."

Poor Jon. He had no idea what was coming.

"He will be happy to see you, though." Abby stepped closer with the paper cup, wishing again that she could flee. "Here's your coffee."

"I've got to get back to work." Aiden squeezed Abby's shoulder gently. "Thanks again, Abby. See you later, Jon."

She bent to set the plastic cups onto the coffee table but her hand slipped and liquid splashed out from the top cup. She caught it in time to prevent a wholesale flood, but by the time she'd righted the flimsy container, the outdated magazines were all stained and her hand was dripping.

"I've got it." Jon grabbed a box of tissues, wiped the spill on the coffee table, and then took her hand in his.

"I'll wait here," Abby said. "Give you some privacy."

Give Roman time to do the right thing.

She tried to pull away but he'd put his other hand out too, capturing hers between them. She was achingly aware of the thin paper towel that was all that separated his skin from hers.

"Please stay," he asked her.

She couldn't say no.

Many years ago, Roman's film crew had been working on a project near Agua Dulce, northeast of Santa Clarita, when a chunk of sandstone collapsed beneath the set. Several actors had been badly hurt. One girl had died.

Roman had almost died, also.

Jon couldn't be in a hospital now, without remembering how his father had looked back then, his pelvis crushed, his ribs cracked, bleeding, bruised, and broken. But Roman's anguish over the death of that young actor had damaged him in ways that could not be seen on an X-ray or CT scan.

He'd learned to walk again, which the doctors said was a miracle. They said the pain would lessen, in time, with rehab and medication.

They were wrong about that, though Roman bulldozed his way through it. His legs were unreliable, his posture twisted, his skin scarred. Reminders of his biggest failure were etched into his very bones and, Jon believed, his spirit. Whatever contentment the driven man had once had was gone, withered away like the atrophied muscles in his hip.

The media referred to it as the Vasquez Rocks accident and lost no time turning the tragedy into a scandal. Rumors flared to life throughout Hollywood, like summer wildfires raging in the mountains. Had budgetary issues led to corners being cut, rules being bent, safety measures bypassed?

Had Roman Byers's negligence led to this catastrophe?

By the time Roman could defend himself it was too late. His reputation was destroyed, career over, everything crushed in the same pile of rubble that had buried him alive.

Jon knew all this about his father. Knew that the man had plenty of reasons to be bitter and angry. Knew that the safety of his cast and crew always, always came first. Knew he'd been screwed by scabrous lawyers playing both ends against the middle. Knew that grieving people needed someone to blame, whether there's fault to be found or not.

What better scapegoat than a rich, powerful man in a private hospital, with no one to speak for him?

Jon still itched to tell the truth of that story, but Roman had sworn all manner of violence against his son if he dredged it up again.

The psychology major in him knew that Roman's experience was part of what drove Jon to dig so hard on the story for *Diversion*. There'd been no defense for Roman, who'd taken responsibility and paid over and over for a disaster in which he'd been unjustly tarred a villain.

Richard Arondi was a true villain whose victims would never get justice unless someone found a way to expose him.

A nurse intercepted him outside Roman's door. "The trip to X-ray exhausted him. Keep it brief, okay? He needs his rest."

He thanked her and then turned to Abby. "Here goes."

She touched his arm. "You sure you don't want to greet him alone?"

"Absolutely."

It was always easier to be around his father when a third person was with them. Conversation flowed more easily, allowing them to bypass the speed bumps and land mines that littered the history of their interactions. Not that things were bad between them. Just . . . complicated.

Perhaps there was no such thing as an uncomplicated father-son relationship.

He knew, from their phone conversations, that Roman saw Abby frequently, that he enjoyed her company, that she'd helped him out a time or two. Roman, who hated people seeing his weaknesses, didn't feel threatened by Abby.

Then he walked through the door.

Immediately, he reached for Abby's hand. She gripped it, as if recognizing his reaction.

Seeing his father lying pale and somehow diminished against the stark white hospital sheets made him feel as if the intervening years hadn't happened, that they were caught in a scene loop, destined to relive this worst moment over and over again, the only change being the increasing fragility of the man in the bed until finally, Roman would be nothing more than an indentation on the pillow.

They tiptoed into the room. When he hesitated at the foot of the bed, Abby nodded her chin toward the thin metal-framed visitor's chair.

"He's sleeping," Jon whispered, his feet leaden. "I should come back in the morning."

The lights in the ward were dimmed for night. Outside the room, the staff went about their duties quietly, their soft-soled shoes barely a whisper on the polished tile, their voices low.

Abby stepped closer and nudged him with her shoulder, a gesture that, in the small room, felt like a caress.

"Stay for a little while," she whispered back. "He knows you're here."

Jon felt the hairs on his arms quiver at her nearness. She smelled of coffee and mint.

"You sure you want me here?" She glanced toward the door.

"Positive." Seeing Roman in this condition was uncomfortable. But seeing him in this condition, alone, would be worse. He indicated the seat on the opposite side of the bed. "Please. He'll be on better behavior if you're here."

She bit her lip, then smiled crookedly. "Okay. If you say so."

The lightness in her tone was forced and even in the soft light, he could see the color rising in her cheeks. She smoothed her sleeves, adjusted her purse, then interlaced her fingers and squeezed them, as if they might fly away if she didn't restrain them.

He waited for her to perch on the end of her chair, then made himself comfortable. He reached through the metal safety railing and laid his hand over Roman's.

His father's flesh was cool and dry, the bones beneath like dried twigs.

His throat tightened. No matter how old you got, you always wanted your father to be strong and wise, big and brave. A hero.

He lifted his gaze. Abby was looking at him, her eyes shining, holding her elbows, hugging herself, and Jon felt something flow between them. He imagined those arms around him and took comfort from the fantasy. For a long moment, they simply stared at one another and suddenly, his spirits lifted.

He wasn't alone.

Abby cared about Roman; he'd known that. Roman had friends on the ranch.

But this was something more. She also cared about Jon, enough to share the pain of watching a loved one suffer, as if she understood how desperately he needed someone to share this burden with him.

He'd seen her numerous times around the ranch, had spoken with her a few times, but he didn't really know her. He'd recognized her as an extremely attractive woman, of course. A man would have to be dead not to notice that. But he'd always been focused on his dad, and most of his dealings had been with other staff members.

Once, when he and Roman had been invited to dinner, Jon had sat next to Abby at the big harvest table. She'd been pleasant and courteous, but there'd been a distance, a barrier that gave off the subtle but unmistakable message that when it came to the usual male-female games, she was not playing.

He'd thought nothing of it. He was busy trying to keep his career going while keeping an eye on Roman. He didn't have time for games either.

But now he wondered.

All this was going through his head during that long moment while he was drowning in that warm dark gaze of hers.

Then, suddenly, Abby smiled. Her lips were still quivery at the edges, and moisture shone on her lashes. She reached out and lightly patted his hand, where it rested on Roman's.

The smile faded. "Go easy on him, Jon."

He felt his eyebrows rise. "Of course. It's not his fault. Well, not exactly."

She exhaled audibly. "This is what I mean. Don't fight with him. Just listen. Promise me."

What was she talking about? Was his frustration that obvious? He opened his mouth to protest, then let the words die away. He sighed. "Sure. Whatever."

She squeezed his hand lightly, then sat back in her chair and laced her fingers together again. "I'm glad you're here. You might not believe this, but he needs you now more than ever."

The hand beneath his twitched and Jon jumped. "Dad?" He leaned closer. "Are you awake?"

Something that sounded like "harrumph" came from Roman. One rheumy eye peeled open, then the other.

"You scared the hell out of me." He patted his father's bony shoulder, feeling the weight of Abby's eyes on him as he did so. "How are you feeling?"

"Like shit." Roman paused to clear his rusty throat. "Nice of you to drop in."

He bristled, then forced himself not to react. "I got here as fast as I could, Dad."

If his father hadn't insisted on moving out to the back of beyond, they wouldn't be having this problem. Jon always feared it would come to this.

"Where's Chaos?" Roman peered around the room, squinting.

"I left him at your house," Abby said. "Don't worry, I'll bring him back to the ranch with me. We'll take care of him until you're home again."

"That dog is a pain in the ass," Roman muttered, "but I've gotten used to having him around. Never thought I'd say that."

Jon bit back a smile. "I'll find you a place that allows dogs."

Roman blinked.

Abby shot Jon a tight-lipped glance.

He ignored it and pulled his chair closer. "I'm just being realistic. What if something like this happens again? It's not safe for you to live out there anymore."

"I'm doing fine on my own."

"You're peeing into a bag." Jon rubbed his gritty eyes. "It's time to face reality. A fall like this was inevitable. I'm just glad it wasn't worse."

"My hip hurts." Roman clicked the button that administered his painkiller, waited a moment, then clicked it again. "Is this damn thing even working?"

Abby took it out of his hands. "It's preloaded so you can't accidentally overdose. Jon, you're tired and worried. You can talk about future plans later, after the two of you have had a chance to catch up properly. The main thing is, you're together now. I'm sure you can both agree on that, can't you?"

Roman gave a laugh that turned into a cough. "Bossier than she looks, isn't she, Jon?"

"I'll say." He'd always thought Abby seemed a bit shy. Maybe he'd been wrong.

"If I were thirty years younger," Roman said.

Abby slapped her thighs and got to her feet. "Roman. You promised."

Jon looked between the two of them. "Promised what? What's going on?"

"Promised I'd behave myself." Roman shifted in the bed and winced.

Jon snorted and gently punched the pillow next to his father's shoulder. "I'll believe that when I see it."

Abby shook her head at them, her expression troubled. It looked like she wanted to say something, then thought better of it and left the room.

# Chapter Five

From Abby's notebook:

### MORNING GLORY MUFFINS

Bursting with nutrition, this recipe is also chock-full of flavor. It's flexible, as well. Mixing the bran and old-fashioned oats in with the wet ingredients, instead of the dry, helps soften it before baking. Unlike similar traditional recipes, which use white flour only and *five times* the amount of sugar, these high-fiber, nutrient-dense muffins will quickly become a family favorite.

¾ cup all-purpose flour
1¼ cup whole wheat flour
¼ cup brown sugar
3 teaspoons ground cinnamon
2 teaspoons baking soda
½ teaspoon salt

3 eggs
½ cup vegetable oil
1 teaspoon vanilla extract

½ cup unsweetened applesauce
¾ cup mashed ripe bananas (2 medium, or substitute
    with additional applesauce)
¼ cup bran
¼ cup old-fashioned oatmeal

2 cups grated carrots (can substitute zucchini, or use
    a combination)
2 small apples, grated
⅔ cup crushed unsweetened pineapple, drained
½ cup sweetened, shredded coconut
½ cup golden raisins
¾ cup chopped walnuts

Preheat oven to 350 degrees F.

Mix the first six ingredients in a large bowl.

In a second bowl, combine the eggs, oil, vanilla, apple-sauce, and bananas. Then add the bran and oatmeal.

Stir in carrots, zucchini, apples, pineapple, coconut, raisins, and walnuts.

Fill greased or paper-lined muffin cups two-thirds full. Bake at 350 degrees for 20–24 minutes or until a toothpick inserted into the center comes out clean.

Cool for five minutes before removing from pans to wire racks.

Makes two dozen muffins.


As soon as Abby sat down in the waiting area outside the emergency room, fatigue overwhelmed her. It was the worst time of day, that last hour before dawn, when the birds weren't singing yet and shift workers dozed off and drivers crossed the midline and insomniacs cried and prayed and made outrageous online purchases.

She dropped her head into her hands, letting her hair flop around her like a curtain. The nocturnal world was full of whispered secrets, shadows, and shapes she could neither escape in sleep nor pretend away in daylight.

"He's sleeping the sleep of the drugged again," Jon said as he entered the waiting room, his keys jingling in his hands. "Sorry about how he was talking. He gets that way sometimes."

Abby made herself smile. "I know. He's always worse when he's insecure. Did he . . . say anything more?"

She already knew he hadn't. Jon wouldn't take that news casually.

Jon nodded. "Told me to remind you to bring him something to eat tomorrow. Says hospital food is worse than cancer."

Abby twitched. She was going to kill the old man herself if he didn't tell Jon soon.

Jon looked toward the exit. "I'm going to head back to his place. Thanks for staying with me. I appreciate the moral support."

"No problem." Abby stood up and her knees made an audible crack. "Um. Actually, I rode in the ambulance with Roman, so . . ."

"Ah," he said. "I get it. You were stuck."

"I'd have stayed anyway," she protested. "I didn't want to leave him alone."

He cocked an eyebrow. "So it was all about him. Not at all about me."

She could see he'd inherited his father's sense of humor.

"I barely remember you," she said. "What's your name again?"

He laughed. "Come on." He gestured for her to precede him down the hallway. "You can help keep me awake on the drive."

"Don't know how good I'll be at that," Abby admitted.

"But at least I haven't spent my day in transit. You must be wiped."

As they walked through the exit doors into the darkness, he touched the small of her back. It was a simple, old-fashioned gesture of courtesy, nothing more, but it sent warmth flooding through her body, along with a quivering, distracting, unexpected awareness. In the confines of the vehicle, they were close enough that she could feel his body heat and smell the leather of his jacket and something mildly woodsy and crisp. His soap? Cologne? It was clean and subtle and she breathed it in.

They didn't speak much during the drive, but instead of being awkward, the silence was easy. Comfortable.

When they arrived at Roman's place, Abby went to her truck, then paused and looked upward. Stars dotted the black velvet sky, a crescent moon hung like a sickle, and dew scented the chilly air. In the shelter of the trees, with the soft rustling sounds of small creatures going about their business in the underbrush, the night no longer seemed full of menace. Instead, it enveloped them, like they were the only two people in the wide universe and it was good.

She'd stayed for Roman, of course. But she *had* been thinking of Jon, possibly more than was good for her. She'd forgotten how nice he was.

It didn't mean anything, though. He was Roman's son, he was a good guy, and she'd done what any good neighbor would do under the circumstances.

"Do you want to come in?" Jon hesitated, glancing toward the house. "You probably know the state of the pantry better than I do, but could I offer you something before you go?"

The tentative way he said it tugged at her heart. She had a lot of work left to get the garden ready for visitors. She ought to go home and try for an hour or two of sleep, but he looked so forlorn.

Then she heard Chaos, throwing himself at the gate. She'd opened the doggy door for him while the EMTs had been loading Roman into the ambulance, so he'd have access to the yard, but the poor dog was desperate for company.

"All right," she said. "Chaos needs some attention and I just remembered there's a big mess in the bathroom. What kind of friend would I be to leave you alone with all that?"

Jon threw her a relieved smile.

The smile made something bloom inside her, something that whispered she wouldn't be able to sleep now, anyway, that she had a civic responsibility to be a good neighbor, that he was nice and she was nice and spending a bit more time together might be . . . very nice.

"I'm really glad you're here," she said. Then she ducked her head, embarrassed. "I mean, Roman pretends he doesn't need you, or anyone, but he does. He feels bad about you coming all the way here, though. Missing work to be with him."

"I'll bet he does. Probably reminds me of the times he took off work to stay with me, when I was a kid. Oh, wait. That never happened." Jon smiled, to take the sting out of his words. "My mom took care of me. Dad worked. It's what fathers did in that generation. Caretaking wasn't their strong suit. Unfortunately, it makes them difficult to care for, too. They've kept themselves apart from sickness, from neediness. Makes them uncomfortable. They're supposed to be strong. Superhuman. Bugs the hell out of them when they find out they're not."

"Sounds like you've thought this through." Abby didn't want to say too much.

"I've had a lot of time to think about it. He's been more or less disabled for years. He's a terrible patient; you know that. But as bad as he is now, you should have seen him when he was first hurt." He shuddered. "I honestly didn't know if he'd make it, then. I'm not sure he wanted to. But he did. I always told myself, if he could get through that, he could get through anything."

*How about brain cancer?* she wanted to ask. *Can he get through that?*

"He's happy you're here," she said, instead. "He's awfully proud of you, you know."

Jon's eyebrows lifted. "He says entertainment journalism is an oxymoron. Emphasis on the moron. I'm starting to think he's got a point." He gave a little laugh, as if embarrassed, and turned his attention to unlocking the gate.

The second he got it open, Chaos darted through and began dancing around them, whining and woofing with joy.

Abby crouched down and stroked his ears. "Sorry, buddy, it's just us. Your master can't come home yet. But we'll look after you."

They walked through the gate, their footsteps crunching lightly on the path. She always marvelled at Roman's ability to work with, instead of against, the natural environment. All around them in his wild, woodland paradise, dew-laden leaves sparkled with reflected moonlight, like millions of tiny diamonds.

"It's so beautiful here," she said. "I can see why he doesn't want to leave."

Jon exhaled. "This place is too much for him, now. The yard work alone."

"It's low maintenance, mostly. He loves it so much."

"I know." Jon's voice was soft. "But he has to face facts."

"Does he have to face them right now, though? His bruises will heal and then he'll be just like he was last fall."

Except for the brain tumor.

"Maybe you're right," he conceded. "But it's just a matter of time. A crisis has been coming for years. I never expected him to stay this long out here and he never would have without the dogs. He needs a place that will look after him."

Roman would throw himself off a cliff before accepting

that. She was beginning to understand why he wanted to keep the truth about his illness quiet for as long as possible.

They went inside and set about putting things to rights. Water from the overflowing bathtub had leaked through to the basement, as well as down the hallway, and they went through all of Roman's towels cleaning it up. By mutual, unspoken agreement, they both continued cleaning, working their way through the kitchen and great room as well until, finally, as she threw the final load of laundry into the washing machine, they stopped and looked at each other.

"I think that's it," Jon said, wiping sweat off his cheek. "Man, I thought the yard was bad but this is way too much house for him, too. I need to find him something more suitable."

"Give him another chance, Jon. He's too young for a nursing home."

"I've looked into this, Abby. He's got options. And yes, I'm assuming he'll be mobile and independent again. He won't need someone to help him with things like bathing and dressing, but he still needs someone there, in case of an emergency. In an independent living community he could have his own private suite, maintain his independence, come and go as he pleases. He could keep the dog. But the place would have round-the-clock staffing and building security. Sure, it wouldn't be as secluded as this, but he also wouldn't lie in his own piss for half a day if something happened."

It was definitely a safer option. She squeezed her eyes shut against the memory of how fragile, how vulnerable Roman had looked curled up on the floor.

"He'll never go for it. He's so proud."

"Yeah, that he is. But I can't live like this anymore. Maybe it would be different if we got along better, or if I lived closer. But he was in his forties when I was born, at the height of his career. We didn't spend a lot of time together."

"Your mother is . . . ?" She hoped she wasn't touching a nerve.

"Off the hook," he said. "They've been divorced for a long time. She's remarried, to someone her own age, and had a couple more kids. She'd probably talk to Roman if I asked her but I won't. She went through a lot with him. She doesn't deserve to be drawn back into it. We were her starter family. She's got her real life now."

He rubbed his face, the palms of his hands making a rough sound against the stubble of his chin. Abby's fingers itched to feel that stubble for herself.

"What about you?" he asked suddenly, surprising her. "Are you close with your family?"

Abby turned away and let her hair fall in front of her face but the words came out before she could stop them. "What family?"

He paused and leaned on the mop. Silence loomed between them. She could practically hear the questions building in his mind.

She didn't talk about her family. It was easier that way. Besides, what was there to say? There was no family, just two sisters against the world. But he'd shared so much with her that he deserved something in return.

"It's just me and Quinn."

She allowed a quick side glance at Jon. He'd set the mop aside and was leaning against the wall, his arms crossed, looking at her. This is why she tried to keep from getting close to anyone. When she started to trust someone, she wanted to confide in them, to unburden herself, just a little. And it always ended up with them looking at her the way Jon was now.

With pity.

She forced herself to smile. "Quinn and I are fine. With all the crap I hear from people about their families, sometimes I think we're the lucky ones." She got to her feet and exhaled loudly. "I'm guessing this is the cleanest this house has been in a long time. Roman won't recognize it."

Abby had snapped shut like a clam. One minute, they'd been talking. She'd been listening with what seemed like genuine interest to his frustrations about Roman. They were really connecting. Then, after giving him the barest hint of her own background, just enough to intrigue him, she dropped the subject and backpedaled as if he'd tricked her into revealing state secrets.

So she and Quinn had no one, no parents, no uncles or aunts, no siblings. Is that what she meant? There was definitely a story there, yet she brushed it off as if it was nothing, certainly not something to dwell on.

Jon tucked the information away. He smelled a mystery, and if it involved Abby, it would be worth solving.

Outside the east window, dawn was touching the stand of cedars, turning them a soft gray.

"I could make you some coffee, but I owe you more than that." Jon swiped the back of his hand over his damp forehead. "Can I buy you breakfast in town?"

Abby had bound her hair in a thick tail at the back of her neck. She reached up and lifted it, then, shuddering, plucked at her T-shirt. "Absolutely not. I smell like sweat and bleach and wet dog. I need a shower in the worst way. But I've got a counteroffer."

Her cell phone rang. She pulled it out of her pocket and walked to the other room.

"Quinn?" he heard her say. "Everything's fine. I'm with Jon at Roman's. . . . Yes, he's in the hospital . . . I think so . . . Tell Daphne I'll be back soon. . . . Yes, I figured . . . I'll tell him . . . Love you."

The easy affection between the sisters touched him. If

they'd had to stick together from an early age, no wonder they were close.

"Let me guess," he said, once Abby had ended the call. "You're supposed to bring me to the ranch for breakfast."

Abby made a gun with her thumb and index finger and pointed it at him. "Got it in one. You'll pay Daphne for breakfast by sharing all the latest details on your father, Hollywood, and the world at large. In that order."

After a quick shower, shave, and change of clothes, he felt ready to join the people at Sanctuary Ranch. He followed Abby's truck in his rental car. As promised, she brought the dog with her, rather than leave him in Roman's house. Jon planned to head back to the hospital after he'd eaten, so this was definitely a better place for the poor mutt. Chaos had spent enough time alone.

His stomach growled as they bumped onto the ranch driveway. He'd eaten at Daphne's table enough times to know that no matter what was on the menu, it would be delicious, it would stick to his ribs, and there would be lots of it.

The cook met them on the porch, wiping her hands on the chef's apron she wore over her blue jeans. She was a strong-looking, comfortably built woman with nondescript short bullet-gray hair that curled around her ears. She wore glasses this morning, low on her nose, and surveyed them over the tops of the lenses.

"You've had an exciting night," she said, waving them up the steps to the porch. "I told Roman he was going to crack his skull in that bathroom of his one of these days. Too proud for a grab bar, so this is what he gets."

She surprised Jon with a quick, hard hug.

"He's lucky that's all he did," Jon said. "Those bones can't take much more."

Daphne held Abby out at arm's length, clucking. "Look at you, honey. Like a cat that got caught in the rain barrel and been swimming in circles for three days."

"Gee, thanks," Abby said, with a laugh.

"Never mind," Daphne said. "Tarred and feathered, you'd still be the prettiest thing this side of sunrise. You go fix yourself up while I put on a fresh pot of coffee."

Jon was relieved to see that aside from her two assistants, Daphne's kitchen was empty. A couple of guests staying at the resort lingered over coffee in the great room beyond, but most of the staff had already left to begin their work.

"Hey, Jon." Jamie waved a paring knife at him from the workstation where she was chopping carrots. Another young woman worked next to her, flattening a ball of dough with a heavy wooden rolling pin while keeping her eye on the room beyond, where sounds of baby chatter could be heard. Sage and . . . what was the baby's name? Sal. That was it.

"Hey, Jamie." He stooped to pat the large dog that snoozed in the morning sun. "How you doing, Jewel?"

The dog lifted her gray muzzle, slapped her tail on the floorboards once, and went back to her nap.

"How's Roman handling hospital life?" Daphne set a steaming cup of coffee in front of him and perched on a stool at the island.

Industry and community. Not your typical workplace. Nothing at all like the backbiting environment at *Diversion*.

Jon sipped the hot brew, which was every bit as tasty as it smelled. "Miserable as ever. I don't know how they put up with him. He's lucky Abby found him when she did."

A light hand landed on his shoulder as Olivia Hansen entered the room. "Good morning, Jon. Nice to see you again." The ranch founder wore her silver-blond hair in a loose braid and had the weathered skin, lithe limbs, and ropy muscles of someone who'd spent long years working hard in the fresh air.

"Abby told me you'd been asking after Dad," Jon said,

smiling at her and the cook together. "I appreciate it and I know he does too, whether or not he expressed it."

"We care about Roman," Olivia said. "How soon will he be home again? I'd ask Haylee, but I haven't heard from her yet today. The baby's teething and I don't want to risk waking them."

Olivia's niece Haylee was married to Aiden McCall—the same Dr. Mac who'd looked after Roman last night—but Jon was surprised at Olivia's expectation that Aiden would break doctor-patient confidentiality.

Then he chided himself. Roman had become a de facto family member, so naturally, information would be shared around.

He should be grateful. He was grateful.

Still, guilt etched the inside of his stomach. He was Roman's family.

"He's got some new soft tissue damage," he told them. "Not much they can do for him except physio and rest."

He heard Abby's voice, speaking with someone in the other room.

Daphne leaped to her feet. "There she is. I'll fix a couple of plates. After the night you've had, you both need a true Daffy special."

Abby entered the kitchen, pulled up the stool next to him, and accepted the mug Olivia passed her.

"Sounds perfect." Abby took her first sip, closed her eyes, and moaned. "Oh my, this is ambrosia from heaven."

The gravelly sound she made in the back of her throat traveled through the countertop, up into Jon's elbows, and then down to the base of his body, resonating like a tuning fork in his groin. He almost groaned, himself, in response.

The woman sounded like sex, personified. How could someone who looked so innocent have such a smokey, enticing voice?

She gripped the mug with both hands, her fingers long

and graceful, her skin smooth. Her nails were unpainted, clipped short and square. A small tattoo graced the inside of her left wrist, a symbol, a stylized semicolon set inside a heart.

His pulse jumped. He knew what that meant.

The writer in him loved her use of the symbol, the simple elegant pause indicating that there was more to come in a sentence, a story.

A life.

Yes, there was definitely more to Abigail Warren than met the eye. Something he couldn't quite put his finger on.

She wasn't wearing a lick of makeup, she'd dressed in a plain white T-shirt and clean denims that hugged her thighs nicely when she sat but were meant more for work than as a fashion statement. She smelled of soap and fresh water, no artificial scents or perfume.

There was nothing about her that indicated awareness of how attractive she was and certainly nothing to make him think she had any inklings of the sexual sizzle he'd felt arcing between them last night.

But it was there. And it was real.

Wasn't it?

Lost in worry and fatigue as he'd been, he might have misinterpreted her kindness as something more. She'd been there for him at a moment of emotional vulnerability and that had spawned a sense of intimacy.

Now, in the light of day, he reminded himself that she was doing a good deed for Roman, her friend and neighbor. It wasn't personal, it certainly wasn't directed at Jon. If there was a sizzle, he was the only one feeling it.

"Spinach and goat cheese omelet, bacon, buckwheat pancakes with maple syrup, and fruit salad," Daphne announced. "But you can get started with these."

She set a plate of steaming muffins in front of them. They smelled amazing, rich with spices and fruit and toasted nuts.

Jon's stomach made an audible growl.

Abby looked at him and laughed. "Someone's hungry."

The nerves in his belly rippled at the sound, as if she'd run her finger along the notches of his spine, the way a child would drag a stick along a picket fence. That throaty chuckle made the most innocent comments sound like foreplay. Surely she knew that. Surely someone had told her the effect it had on a man. Maybe it was time someone reminded her.

Jon angled his head toward Abby and lowered his voice. "You have no idea."

# Chapter Six

It had been a long time since anyone had flirted with Abby, especially someone like Jon. Stellar good looks were one thing. She'd seen a lot of good-looking men. But honorable, hardworking, and kind, too?

Those were not thick on the ground, in her experience.

The ripped body she'd glimpsed beneath the sweaty T-shirt while they were mopping up the bathroom didn't hurt either.

To cover her confusion, she broke open a muffin and took a bite. "These are great, Daphne."

She tasted banana, apples, carrots, and nuts. She tried not to smile. This was her recipe, the one Daphne said she'd never try.

*Don't gloat.*

She focused on the flavors but triumph—and Jon beside her—kept tugging her lips upward.

Delicious food.

Delicious man.

"I see your face." Daphne trained her eagle eye on the two of them, searching.

Abby felt the hair on her arm quiver, as if the space

between her and Jon was electrified. It took all her energy not to look at him and she was unable to squelch that smile.

Fortunately, Daphne was preoccupied with something else.

"Yes, Abby," she said with a huff. "It's your recipe and yes, they are delicious, despite the reduced sugar. I wouldn't have guessed it but it's not too late to teach this old dog a few new tricks."

A few weeks ago, someone in her book group had contributed a plate of muffins that had offended Daphne's foodie sensibilities. She couldn't get over it.

"'No sugar!'" Daphne said, mimicking the excited voice of an acquaintance. "'No shit,' said I. Who brings flavorless bran bricks to a book club meeting? The discussion was supposed to be about celebrating our woman power under the magical Mediterranean sun, not how we can improve our—"

"Daphne." Olivia glanced meaningfully toward the great room, where a few guests lingered over their coffee before the trail ride planned for the morning. "I hope you didn't say it out loud."

Abby tucked her chin and sipped her coffee, hoping to hide the amusement that the cook's outrage often evoked.

"Me, I'm the soul of discretion." She gave a little sniff. "And I'm happy to report that my individual salted caramel cheesecakes were a huge hit. Good thing I made a double batch."

"I love those," Abby said. "They are definitely decadent and worthy of a social event."

Daphne gave an emphatic nod. "Right? I've taught you well, my child. And now I can show them that good flavor and good nutrition are not mutually exclusive. You've also taught me, young grasshopper."

Abby tossed a wadded-up paper towel at her, aware that Jon was watching their interaction.

"Will you be okay today, Abby?" Olivia's lined face was full of concern. "You've been burning the candle at both ends. Perhaps you should take a nap."

Olivia's concern warmed Abby's heart but she shook her head. "Weeds wait for no woman. The sun is finally shining and the tulips are about to open. I want to make sure everything is perfect for the festival."

"Festival?" Jon asked. He'd finished his pancakes and was working on the omelet now.

"Every year Sunset Bay runs a festival to raise funds for the community center," Olivia explained. "The festival includes a garden hop, and this year, thanks to Abby and Quinn, Sanctuary Ranch is participating. It's basically an open house that starts when the tulips open and ends when they're done flowering. Usually about three weeks, maybe more if the weather cooperates. Gayle, my partner, is on the town council now and suggested we join in."

"Suggesting is the easy part, isn't it?" Daphne said, arching one eyebrow severely. "But will Gayle be here when people are trampling all over hell's half acre, littering and scaring the horses?"

"The garden hop will be great, Daphne," Olivia replied evenly. "Gayle will help if she can. She's got a lot on her mind right now. I'm glad that she thought of us."

There was a strange undertone to her voice. Abby hadn't seen Gayle's car outside Olivia's cabin for some time, nor had Gayle been around for meals lately. If she and Olivia were going through something, Abby hoped it wasn't serious. Their relationship had weathered many storms. They'd even been talking about marriage at one point.

"How does the garden hop work?" Jon asked.

"I think Daphne explained it quite well," Jamie said. "It's basically an invasion." She pushed the bowl of carrots aside and began shredding glossy green kale leaves. Another win for the covered winter garden, Abby thought. Still, she looked forward to the fresh, baby veggies they'd be enjoying in a month or two.

"Come on, you guys. Where's your team spirit?" Olivia pursed her lips, then addressed Jon again. "People buy tickets, which allow them admission to participating gardens. All proceeds go to funding the new library, so it's an excellent cause. Abby has such a green thumb that our property has never looked better. Now I'm afraid it's asking too much."

"Not at all, Liv." She glanced at Jon. She didn't want him feeling bad that she'd spent the previous day with Roman. "I've had tons of help. Plus, I enjoy it."

She'd done the bulk of the garden design and planting the previous fall. Huck and Ezra had helped place the flagstones for the lookouts, and Tyler and Duke had dumped wheelbarrows full of soil, manure, and mulch where she directed. Everyone had pitched in, hauling bags and boxes of bulbs and tubers and roots and dormant perennials.

She was excited, if a little nervous, that it was almost showtime.

"The ranch is already such a busy place," Jon said. "Won't having strangers touring through disrupt your usual routine?"

"My question exactly." Daphne scraped the last morsel of omelet onto a plate and set it in front of Jewel, but the dog only gave it a sniff, before turning her head away. "Everyone's a critic," Daphne muttered.

"We'll all have to pitch in," Olivia said. "It will be good for the ranch, and much as I hate to bring this up, we can use the exposure."

"Ah. The truth comes out." Jamie popped a chunk of carrot into her mouth, crunched loudly, then spoke around it. "It's advertising."

Olivia didn't bat an eye at Jamie's comment. "This winter was slow. We have a little ground to make up."

Abby knew that the ranch was financially secure. Funding

for the original land purchase had come from a combination of the buy-out package Olivia had received from her previous job in San Francisco, and the life insurance amount paid to Haylee following the death of her father, Olivia's brother. The tourist trade kept the day-to-day cash flowing.

"Most of our guests have discovered us through personal references," Olivia continued, "and we've been fortunate to have an extraordinarily loyal following. With a few exceptions."

"Remind me, what's the metric?" Daphne said, looking up from the skillet she was scouring in the sink. "You need ten good reviews for every bad one?"

Olivia sighed. "At least."

"Ah," Jon said. "I'm beginning to see. A couple of unhappy campers causing trouble?"

"We had"—Olivia paused and looked down at her coffee cup—"a bit of a public relations issue last summer."

"She means me." Jamie said the words matter-of-factly. "I wasn't always the image of sweetness and light that you see before you now."

Abby knew that her friend still struggled with guilt over the events that had occurred the previous year, even though she'd been vindicated and had in fact, been hailed a hero.

"I can't recall if you were here then or not. The local paper chose to print a biased version of an event Jamie was involved in," Olivia explained.

Daphne slammed a cupboard door closed. "They lied."

"They printed a retraction, Daphne," Olivia said.

Jamie snorted. "You're a reporter, right, Jon? You know how it goes."

"I certainly do. Stories headline front page, above the fold, twenty point Times New Roman. Retractions land on page eight, below the grocery ads, barely big enough to read." Jon shifted in his seat and Abby saw a dull flush rise above the collar of his shirt. "I remember and I'm sorry that happened. I didn't realize it had caused ongoing problems."

"Oh, it hasn't and it wasn't the paper's fault." Olivia reached out and touched his arm, as if recognizing his discomfort. "But it made me realize that we don't have enough brand recognition in town. If more people knew who we are, what we do, what we stand for, that complaint would never have gotten off the ground. So, we're joining the festival in hopes that it will take away some of the mystery, let the people in the Sunset Bay area know that Sanctuary Ranch is something to be proud of."

Abby pushed a forkful of eggs around on her plate, her appetite suddenly gone. She hoped that the bulb garden and surrounding landscaping would live up to Liv's expectations.

"Maybe I can help." Jon leaned back in his chair. "Is the local paper covering the festival?"

"They've listed all the garden hop participants on the local community activities page."

His eyes glinted a deep hyacinth blue. "How about I write a short piece about the ranch? Small publications are always looking for material. I'm a decent enough photographer, too, so I could provide them with art. They'd jump at it, I'm sure."

"But surely you've got more important things to do." Olivia frowned. "Don't you usually have magazine assignments to work on while you're here with Roman?"

A shadow drifted across his face, so quickly Abby wondered if she'd imagined it.

"I'm, uh, on something of a sabbatical." Jon glanced around the room. "You all have done so much for my dad. If this would help you, please let me. As a thank-you. From both of us."

"What kind of piece?" Daphne's voice held deep skepticism. "I don't want my private life out there for anyone to pick through."

Abby tightened her grip on her mug. She felt the same way.

"The content is entirely up to you." He stood up and started walking around the kitchen, tapping his index finger against his bottom lip.

Abby closed her eyes briefly and forced her shoulders to relax. Jon meant this as a favor. Of course he would respect their privacy.

"A local interest story, featuring a hospitality business with unusual charitable endeavors. Everyone loves dogs. I'd love to include how Jamie helped Dad with Chaos."

Jamie's face lit up. "Really? That would be awesome."

"And the therapy horses," Jon went on, "especially the ones you rescued from slaughter, Olivia."

"Nothing about Duke," Olivia said, nibbling on the corner of her lip. "He's still in the system. What about you, Sage?"

"I'll talk if Haylee talks." She looked down at the play-pen. "Sal and I have nothing to hide anymore."

"I suspect your mother would happily participate." Olivia smiled at Jon. "We've got enough stories for a book. I won't speak for anyone else, or ask anyone to be interviewed unless they're comfortable with it. But I think it's a great idea, Jon. Thank you for suggesting it."

"No, Olivia, thank you." His warm smile encompassed them all. Then his gaze settled on Abby and she forgot to breathe. "I know exactly where I'll start."


Jon followed his nose into the kitchen where Daphne was just taking a baking tray out of the oven. His brief e-mail pitch to Ambrose Elliott, the managing editor of *Sunset Bay Chronicle*, had yielded an almost immediate positive response, provided Jon could deliver the piece promptly. The *Washington Post,* it wasn't. It wasn't *Rolling Stone,* it wasn't the *Tribune,* or the *Herald* or *Economist* or *Vogue* or *Elle* or any other publication that might take pride of place on a curriculum vitae. It was a regional magazine and as such, well . . . it could be worse.

Jon suspected that it was his offer to write the piece pro bono that had cinched the deal.

He was starting with the cook because she loved to talk, she loved Abby and she was interesting in her own right. Like most of the ranch staff, she had a rocky past, had even done a stint in prison. But she was cagey. Would she share anything worth writing about?

"That smells heavenly," he said. "What is it?"

She set the metal pan onto a large wooden board. "Blueberry buttermilk coffee cake. Some people say that eating baked goods will kill you. I say, move your ass and you'll be fine. It's sitting in front of a computer all day that'll kill you."

Jon pulled out his tablet. "Speaking of which, can I quote you on that?"

"For your article? Sure thing. I'm a font of wisdom. More people should listen to me." She cut a slice of the steaming cake, set it onto a plate, and pushed it toward him. "I've got fresh coffee, too. Want some?"

Jon smiled inwardly. It wasn't the first time he'd been bribed by someone who wanted to come out looking good in an article. "You bet. I don't know how much will end up in the finished piece, but any background you'd like to share is welcome. Let's start with what you do, who you work with. A day in your life."

He lifted a forkful to his mouth. Beneath the crumbly topping, the cake was buttery soft and light, bursting with warm juicy berries.

"Let's see." Daphne peeked inside the pot on the stove. "I'm Chief Cook and Bottlewasher here at Sanctuary Ranch. I like my job, I'm good at it and I dare you to find better people anywhere on the planet. I also like old movies, long walks on the beach, and singing in the rain. I use my power for good, not evil, and believe everything goes better with a nice merlot. How's that?"

Great, if this was a personal ad but not exactly what he was looking for.

"It's a little generic," he said. "Let's back up. Tell me about the ranch itself. What made Olivia Hansen, a successful software executive, cash in early and start a ranch with her orphaned niece?"

He'd already been told bits and pieces about the ranch's history from Jamie and Haylee, while they worked with Roman and his dog. But different perspectives were always valuable and the quicker Daphne relaxed, the quicker he could bring the conversation around to Abby.

"First off," Daphne said, "Olivia and Haylee share ownership equally. Second, are you looking for dirt on my people, Mr. Byers?"

He pulled back and blinked at her. "No, of course not."

"Then don't use me for a shovel. Ask me anything you want about old Daffy and I'll tell you. Unless I don't want to." She gave a wicked wink. "Boundaries are important. Good fences make good neighbors, as we say."

Jon took a sip of coffee. "You don't trust journalists, huh?"

She gave him an innocent look. "What makes you think that, Mr. Byers? Am I not cooperating?"

He exhaled. Whatever had happened in her past, he guessed the media hadn't been kind to her. But he was writing a puff piece, one step away from advertising, as Jamie'd said. Daphne had no reason to think he was looking for "dirt." And this was barely a conversation, let alone an interview.

Maybe that was the problem.

He consulted his notes and adjusted his posture.

"I hear you're a self-defense expert with a green belt in kickboxing. How'd you get into that?"

"Fitness," she replied, lifting a leg, stocky with muscle, onto a chair. "You don't get gams like these by accident."

"You're someone who can take care of herself. I admire that."

"Thank you," she said. "I learned the hard way. A lot more women my age should do martial arts. But our generation was trained for marital arts instead."

"Really." He raised his eyebrows. It sounded as if this wasn't the first time she'd said that, but it still made a great quote. "What classes were those?"

"We were trained to be nice, pretty, to smile, to be good and never make waves. Useless shit like that."

He took another bite of cake. A great quote, but not for a community paper. Time to change the subject.

"Tell me about your family."

"Was married once," she said. "He died."

"I'm sorry."

"I'm not. I killed him."

Jon dropped his fork. "Pardon me?"

He could imagine the feisty cook guilty of civil disobedience, not paying parking tickets, perhaps arguing with a traffic cop.

But murder? No.

"That's right. Tried, convicted, paid my debt, here I am." The lines on her face settled into an expression of such serenity that she'd either had a lot of time to make peace with the event or she was messing with his head.

"What, uh, what happened?"

"The man was talking when he should have been listening so I whacked him on the head with my rolling pin. Actually, I didn't so much swing, as I lifted it when he ran at me. The rolling pin killed him. It was not a helpful distinction in the trial."

A tendon in her neck twitched. Not so serene after all, then.

"I can't tell if you're serious or not."

"Life's too short to be serious all the time." Daphne grinned. "Now, quit wasting your time on an old woman like me. The piece is about the garden. You should be talking to Abby."

Perfect segue. He'd follow up on the dead husband later. Or not.

"Yeah." He cleared his throat, pulling his thoughts together. "She doesn't like to talk about herself. She's obviously very talented. Has she studied horticulture or garden design professionally?"

Daphne narrowed her eyes. "Newsflash, Peter Parker. If she doesn't want to talk, that's your problem, not mine. I'm sure she has her reasons."

"Fair enough. How about this? How long have they been here at the ranch? You can tell me that, right?"

She considered this. "Okay. They first came here a couple of years ago, seasonal workers, to help out in summer, general labor, cleaning rooms, gardening, helping me with meals. I don't know where they were before that or where they went after. But they were both good workers. So when they came back looking for permanent work, I voted to bring them on."

She clipped the last word short and snapped her lips shut tight. It was a tiny emphasis, a subtle but certain something that rubbed beneath her saddle blanket.

He could practically see the words leaping at the inside of her teeth as she fought to keep them corralled.

"Did someone vote against them?"

That was hard to imagine. From what he'd seen, Abby and Quinn were polite and quiet. They worked hard and didn't make waves. If anything, they weren't rough enough for this group.

The cook kept her back to him, stirring her soup, but Jon saw her back stiffen. A protective mama bear with split loyalty. She wasn't going to tell him anything more. He could almost see the sentences, the meat of his story, fading away before his eyes.

"Listen, handsome, you're sitting in a place of peace and harmony, looking for trouble, and I don't have time for that. You want to know more about Abby, talk to Abby, not me. But know this." She turned around then and her expression was like ice. "The Warren girls are like daughters to me and I protect my own."

The vehemence in her tone made him think she was entirely capable of bashing a man's skull with a rolling pin. Her fast, fierce reaction told him there was far more to Abby and Quinn's arrival than she wanted him to know about, but instead of putting him off the trail, it only increased his curiosity.

Her implication, however, hit a nerve.

"I'm not here to hurt anyone, least of all Abby." He got to his feet, scraping the feet of his chair against the floor. "I owe a huge debt of gratitude to her and all of you for your kindness to my father. I offered to write this piece in hopes that it would benefit the ranch and Olivia seems to think it will. If you feel otherwise, you ought to bring it up with her so I don't waste my time."


"We lived in Los Angeles when I was small but we moved around a lot. Schools weren't great in the neighborhoods we could afford." Quinn Warren glanced around Jon as if looking for someone. Her hair and skin were fairer than Abby's, and she was a bit thinner, but her high cheekbones, expressive eyes, and graceful movements identified them clearly as sisters.

Right now, her tight shoulders and fidgeting fingers indicated nervousness. Like Abby, she had a heart-shaped tattoo with a stylized semicolon on her left wrist. He knew better than to comment on that, at least for now.

He'd specifically chosen to interview her in front of the wide window in the main house great room. Comfortable, private but not alone. A few guests sat on the couches by the fire, reading. Beyond them came the muffled sounds of kitchen utensils, running water, laughter.

"Do you miss it?" Quinn was so reticent, he probably wouldn't do more than mention her in the article, but since she was Abby's sister, he wanted to make her part of the process.

And learn a little more about Abby.

"No." Quinn bit her lip. "We lived in Portland after that but I didn't like it there. As soon as I finished high school we went to Eugene."

"You and your family?"

"Me and Abby," Quinn said.

No parents? But before he had a chance to ask, she jumped back in, her words quick, her tone high and tight. The kind of voice people used when they were anxious not to seem anxious.

"Abby wanted me to go to college, become a teacher, maybe. Or get into graphic design. I like art, you know? Tuition was cheaper there than in the bigger cities." She smiled wistfully. "I didn't do very well, though."

"I'm sure that's not true."

"Then we went to Lincoln City for a while. She still wanted me to go to college and thought a different school might be better. It didn't work out, though. I kept telling her she's the one who should go to college, not me. She was always taking online courses through community college programs, or open source learning. Even YouTube videos. She said that was enough for her. Maybe, if we'd had more money . . ."

She trailed off, rubbing her left wrist with her thumb.

"Sounds like Abby wanted to make sure you had a solid future ahead of you. You two are close, I take it."

The girl gave him a startled glance. "Yes, of course."

"Was she always interested in gardening?"

"Gardening?" Quinn gave a little laugh. "Maybe. She always had a couple of houseplants we packed from place to place. She read a ton of books about it before we got here. She's good at it, and I know she loves it, but she's good at everything she does. She's worked at so many things, and not just housekeeping and waitressing. She's worked in a bakery, done bookkeeping, learned coding so she could build websites, helped out on movie sets." She stopped abruptly, and pressed her fingertips to her mouth. "Anyway, we needed a change and when she heard about the ranch, she figured, why not? I wasn't thrilled. But it turns out I like it here better than anywhere else we've lived. It's quiet, you know?"

She got to her feet and rubbed the sides of her jeans, as if unable to keep her hands still. "I should get back to work. Is that enough?"

"Of course. Thanks for your time, Quinn."

He watched her go, thinking not so much about what she'd said, but what she hadn't said. She'd casually skipped over everything that happened before high school. Nothing about her childhood. Nothing about her parents. Next to nothing about herself. Mostly, she looked like all she wanted to do was jump to her feet and flee.

Why?

Later that evening, Jon met Abby on the back porch, overlooking the distant ocean. The gold and crimson light danced on the water, painting her dark hair auburn, her cheeks pink. She'd pulled two wicker chairs up to the railing, and was curled up with a cup of tea, one bare foot tucked beneath her.

She gestured to the glass-topped matching wicker table. "I made you a cup. Lavender-and-lemon balm, with a bit of honey. It'll help you relax."

He smiled. "Do I look stressed?"

She lifted her eyebrows. "Your dad is in the hospital. You're away from home, trying to figure out what to do with him. Not to mention that 'uh, sabbatical.' I'd be surprised if you *weren't* stressed."

So, she'd picked up on that.

"About that." He sat down. "I'm not working for the magazine anymore. Freelancing is more flexible, which is what I need right now. Dad doesn't know though and I'd rather keep it to myself for the time being, if you don't mind."

"Of course," she said.

He lifted the mug and took a sip. The crazy newsroom pace had turned him into a die-hard coffee addict, but this was nice.

He met her inquiring gaze. "I feel better already."

"See? I knew what you needed."

The smile on her face bloomed slowly, starting with her eyes, spreading to her cheeks and then her mouth. It wasn't the tea that was sending warmth through him, but he'd let her think that it was.

"I talked to Quinn earlier today," he said.

For a moment her expression stayed the same. Then, the corners of her mouth tightened almost imperceptibly and she turned back to the sunset. "I hope she was helpful."

"She's certainly a big fan of her older sister."

The pink in Abby's cheeks grew stronger. "No more than I am of her."

"She says that you're a self-taught gardener."

He let the statement hang, without adding a question. People usually jumped on any opportunity to talk about themselves, but Abby merely nodded, then let the silence drag.

He wondered what it would take to ruffle that calm exterior, to make her face light up with joy. Or outrage.

Or desire.

"Quinn implied that you were orphans but then she took off without explaining more. I know Olivia often hires former foster kids. Is that how you found your way here? Were you and Quinn raised in the system?"

Her shoulder jerked. "Absolutely not. I made sure of that."

So much for serenity. He leaned forward. "If you don't want me to include your family history in the article, I won't. But you're an interesting person, Abby. You've got more than a green thumb. You've got a gift and people love success stories, especially when they involve challenges."

Her cheek twitched in a half smile. "Challenges. Yeah, you could say we've had them." She set her mug down and gave a big sigh. "Okay. Our dad died when I was eight. I don't remember much about him but Mom never got over it. Quinn was just a baby when it happened and I liked looking after her. She was like my own living doll."

Her face softened at the memory.

"You must have been a great help to your mother. It explains your work ethic, too."

It would have been very tempting for an overwhelmed, grieving woman to allow a precocious eight-year-old to take on too much responsibility.

"Mom always struggled to make ends meet. I wanted to do my part. Life wasn't easy for her." Abby hesitated. "It wasn't easy for us, either, but Quinn and I did okay. I always worked. We always had enough to eat, clothes on our backs and a few African violets sitting in the windowsill. They're easy to grow and so cheerful. I guess that's where my green thumb began."

*Enough to eat?* Hardly a ringing endorsement of their childhood.

"What kind of work did you do?"

"Oh, the usual. Babysitting, waitressing, cleaning, retail. Once, I got an after-school stint in Hollywood walking dogs for a couple of actors, while they were on set shooting. That was fun."

She smiled at the memory, but then the smile faded.

"So you worked throughout high school?"

Abby nodded. "Except for when I was looking after Quinn. Mom wasn't around a lot, with work and stuff. It's hard, being a single mother. She really struggled. But she taught me to be self-reliant and that's a huge gift." She looked down. "She's gone now, too."

It was the second time she'd mentioned her mother's struggles.

Jon frowned. "How old were you when she passed away?"

She waved her hand and gave a little laugh. "Let's talk about happier things, instead. You need some quotes for your article, right? Let's see." She tapped a finger against her bottom lip. "I believe that when life tests you, it's an opportunity to learn, to change course, to start over, try something new. Gardening is all about change. It forces you to slow down, to really look, to breathe, to be patient. Our garden makes people happy and helps them heal. Working in our garden, being surrounded by all that beauty, makes me happy."

She was wary about giving details of her past, but this had the ring of truth. Her peace was hard won but she'd prevailed and in that, he envied her. His career had stopped bringing him happiness long before he'd been fired, he realized. He had no hobbies or personal life to speak of, his family was complicated, his connections with them weak.

As he drove back to Roman's that night, he wondered if he'd ever had the kind of purpose he sensed in Abby. Writing celebrity gossip was supposed to be a stepping stone to something more, not the stumbling block that ended his career. But maybe getting dumped by *Diversion* was the wake-up call he needed to sort out his true goals. Maybe this was his chance to start over, too.

On her way to the hospital the next day, Abby stopped in at the local bakery to pick up a few treats. She wished she could have brought Roman something she'd made herself, but in the mental turmoil following her conversation with Jon, she'd forgotten.

Chaos whined in the passenger seat as she closed the door, leaving the window open a generous crack.

"Stay here, boy," she told him. "I'll be right back."

There were so many other things she could have mentioned in the interview, benign responses that safely deflected anything truly personal. Yet when he'd asked about her childhood, her parents, she'd answered. His perceptive gaze had lowered her guard, made her want him to know things about her.

That wasn't good. He was a journalist, for heaven's sake. He was trained to make people feel comfortable confiding in him.

He was good at it.

She pushed open the door to the bakery, setting aside her thoughts and focusing instead on the fragrant pleasures of butter and yeast and spices.

Over the winter she'd gotten to do a lot more of the baking at the ranch and had grown to enjoy the process, often getting up early, when she couldn't sleep, to get a jump on the breakfast favorites. But now, with the rush to get the garden ready for the festival, her kitchen time had been curtailed, and she missed it.

"Hi, Goldie," she said, as the proprietor came to the counter.

"Hi, Abby! Hi, Chaos, you sweet boy." Goldie leaned over the counter and waved at Abby's truck, where Chaos's muzzle was poking out the window. His whole back end was wagging. He couldn't hear Goldie, but his sense of smell told him exactly where they were.

"He's a little excited at the moment, so I thought I'd spare you the destruction."

The dog also knew they were going to see Roman. How he knew, Abby wasn't sure. But there was no doubt. He also loved Goldie's, though. He'd been there enough times with Roman, and the kind baker always had a dog biscuit waiting for him.

"When are you going to take over for me, Abby? It's too much work for an old woman, but someone like you could bring it back to its heyday."

Sunset Bay's old-town charm depended upon businesses like Goldie's. Developers waited in the wings, with outrageous offers out for waterfront properties, but so far, the town had stayed united. Rows of condos above expensive, franchise shops might bring more profit to the town, but it would destroy the character.

"My kids tell me to take the deal from FrontCo," Goldie said, "but once one of us sells, the whole street will go, like dominoes. I love this place too much for that."

"If only I could be in two places at one time." Abby peered through the display glass. "Alas, I've more than enough keeping me busy these days."

She adored Goldie's shop. It was on the main street for

maximum tourist visibility and had a view of the ocean on the back. No wonder FrontCo wanted it. It had a covered deck on the side, so that on nice days, customers could watch the waves and listen to the gulls, while they enjoyed their baked treat.

Before Abby had gone full-time at the ranch, she'd helped out at Goldie's and had recognized within a few weeks what loving mismanagement was costing the place. Untapped income streams. Unchecked expenses. Minimal brand recognition. Zero online presence.

If Goldie expanded the menu and updated the decor, she could increase her walk-up trade immediately. She'd never pursued the catering side, or made contact with businesses who might want regular deliveries to sweeten meetings. A simple Web site could facilitate orders and they had plenty of access to local couriers.

But the baker made no secret of the fact that, at sixty-seven, she had no interest in starting over. She was ready to hang up her apron and go off in search of warm beaches and cold margaritas. And Abby was in no position to take on a struggling business, no matter how much potential it had.

"I heard about Roman." Goldie's round, apple-cheeked face grew solemn. "How's he doing?"

Roman's true condition was still under wraps. But news about ambulance trips traveled fast through Sunset Bay.

"He's restless and grumpy, which means pretty much normal." Abby smiled. "I'm on my way to see him now and thought I'd bring him something to sweeten him up a bit."

Goldie sold a variety of muffins, turnovers, danish, scones, butter horns, croissants, and cinnamon buns. But looking them over, Abby realized that the outstanding fare at Sanctuary Ranch had spoiled her. Goldie's muffins, while delicious, were made from a single base recipe. Whether blueberry, chocolate chip, or cranberry, they all tasted more or less the same.

Same thing with the scones and turnovers. There was something to be said for consistency, certainly, and Goldie had her regulars who appreciated knowing exactly what they'd get each day.

But her yeast breads and rolls were excellent, wonderfully textured with golden brown crusts, fine crumbs, and well-flavored fillings.

"I'll take a half dozen cinnamon buns," Abby said.

Goldie packaged up the treats, throwing in a couple of items Abby hadn't seen before.

"For Chaos," she said. "I've been working on a new recipe. Let me know how he likes them."

Abby offered the treats to Chaos in the truck, so Goldie could enjoy his reaction. In ten seconds, all that was left were crumbs. She gave two thumbs up to Goldie, who beamed with pleasure through the window.

Unfortunately, Roman's reaction in the hospital was less enthusiastic. As soon as he'd patted Chaos and allowed the dog to give him a good sniff-over, he took the bag from Abby.

"These aren't from the ranch," he said, looking at the package.

"Good eye," Abby said. "The box with the name Goldie on it is a dead giveaway but I guess for a man with a brain tumor, every cogent thought is worth celebrating."

"Don't toy with me, girlie."

"Girlie?" She shook her head. "Look, my friend. I've got a high-powered ace up my sleeve. If you want me to keep hiding it, you'd best give me the respect I deserve."

Bantering with him always brightened his spirits.

He took a large bite, chewed, swallowed. "Nothing against Goldie, but these are crap."

Abby took one herself. The texture was good, soft with just enough chew, but the frosting was a little sweet for her taste.

"That's the tumor talking," she said, speaking around the mouthful. "These are delicious."

He ate a few more bites. "Okay, not crap."

"What a concession."

"But not as good as yours."

"You mean Daphne's."

"You bake them, too. I've seen you."

She did, but she used Daphne's recipes. Okay, she added a bit of her own flair, but she knew how lucky she was to learn at the knee of a master.

"Next time, bring me something you baked yourself."

"You'll be home before you know it, enjoying the life-style to which you've become accustomed, which already includes more goodies from Daphne's kitchen than you know what to do with," she promised. "As for me, I'm busy in the garden right now. I'm not inclined to do you any more favors until you talk to your son. This keeping secrets is going to eat a hole in my stomach."

Roman pushed aside the remains of his treat. "I told you, I'll tell him when I'm ready. Maybe when I'm home."

"Promise?"

"No, I don't promise. I said maybe for a reason."

"What are you so scared of?"

His expression darkened. With a flip of his hand, he sent the rest of Goldie's baking sailing onto the floor. "He already wanted to ship me off to a home somewhere, before. When he finds out . . ." He trailed off, then cleared his throat, and went on. "You know that things are going to get worse. He'll be relentless, pushing me around, deciding what's best for me. I told you, I want to die at home."

"You're selling him short, Roman. Everything he does is because he loves you."

He twitched. "I could do with a little less love, then."

From the towel on the floor, the big dog whined, as if hurt by his master's comment.

To hide her emotions, Abby reached over and patted his head. "It's okay, boy. He's only joking."

Only the abject fear deep in Roman's eyes mitigated Abby's desire to strangle him where he sat. How could he say something like that? How did he not see how truly rich he was to have a son who cared for him the way Jon did? She'd watched Jon's face when he talked about Roman. His handsome features and expressive, deep blue eyes spoke of a parent-child bond Abby could only wish for.

How could she make him see this?

She sat on the edge of the bed and scooted closer to him. "Roman, you and Jon are so lucky to have each other. Don't waste the time you have left on a fight he might not even want to have with you. Tell him the truth so he can help you enjoy the rest of your life. Give him that gift."

"Gift." Roman sniffed. "No one wants a gift like that, Abby-girl."

"It's either that, or he lives with the pain of knowing that when you needed him the most, you didn't trust he'd be there for you. That you didn't believe he cared."

He was quiet for a time. Abby watched the sheet over his chest move up and down. She sensed he was fighting a battle inside himself, and she was lucky he wasn't yelling. She knew it was a huge sign of how helpless he was feeling that he'd unburdened himself to this extent with her.

"I know he cares," he said eventually. "But I won't let him put his life on hold indefinitely. Maybe when I'm closer to . . . you know. But now, when it could be six weeks or six months, I can't ask that of him." He cleared his throat roughly. "He's a good man. He'll drop everything, as soon as he knows, which is why I can't tell him now. Not yet. He's got a future. I don't. I'm protecting that. He'll thank me for it." He gave a bark of laughter. "Well, probably not because I'll be dead. But he'll come to appreciate it."

She shook her head, out of arguments. "I don't know what to do with you. You're so stubborn. You think the world is one big pissing contest and the first one to admit to any kind of human failing or weakness, loses. You have no idea that everyone else is feeling the exact same way."

"It's not just that." Roman's customarily gruff voice was barely audible. "We've had our issues, my boy and I. I don't want his last memories of me to be . . . like that. Like that look on your face. Sad. Pitiful. I won't have it."

His voice broke.

She reached for his arm, squeezed it, unable to respond.

After a few moments, he found his voice again. "I want us to get along, to have fun, to sit in the garden and drink beer. That's all."

"He'll understand that. He'll realize that your wishes are what's important."

Roman shook his head. "He's not ready. I'll know when he is, and then I'll tell him."

A nurse came in then with papers in her hand. "Congratulations, Mr. Byers. We're kicking you out. Here are your walking papers. We need your signature here, here, and here."

She stooped to greet Chaos, who was wagging and grinning at her. "We're going to miss you around here, you big sweetheart."

"Going home." Abby turned and gave Roman her biggest, brightest smile. "What great news. I'm so happy for you. I can't wait until you're settled in again, with Jon. You two have so much to talk about."

"We just called him," the nurse continued, while Roman

took care of the paperwork, ignoring Abby. "He'll be here in a few minutes to take you home."

She gathered the pages together, smiled, and left the room.

"I didn't promise," Roman said, giving Abby a stern look. "I did not promise."

"We'll see," she said.

# Chapter Seven

From Abby's notebook:

## SANCTUARY RANCH CINNAMON BUNS

Dough:
   1 teaspoon sugar
   ½ cup lukewarm water
   2 tablespoons traditional dry yeast

   3 cups milk
   ⅓ cup butter
   ⅓ cup sugar
   1 tablespoon salt
   2 large eggs
   9 cups all-purpose flour, approximately

Filling:
   ¾ cup melted butter
   1½ cups brown sugar
   2 tablespoons cinnamon
   1 cup raisins (optional)

To make dough:

Proof the yeast: Dissolve one teaspoon sugar in lukewarm water. Stir in yeast and let stand in warm place for 10 minutes.

While yeast is proofing, heat milk in microwave or saucepan until very warm but not boiling. Stir in butter, sugar, and salt. Cool to lukewarm.

In large bowl, combine milk mixture, eggs, and dissolved yeast. Stir in five cups of flour and beat well for 10 minutes. Gradually add only as much flour necessary to make a soft dough.

Turn onto lightly floured work surface and knead until smooth and elastic, adding additional flour only as necessary. (Too much will make the buns tough and dry.)

Place in well-greased bowl and flip once to grease entire surface of dough. Cover with parchment paper and a damp cloth and let rise in warm place for about one hour, or until doubled in size.

Punch down dough and return to floured work surface. Divide in half and roll each piece into a 9 x 13 inch rectangle. Brush generously with melted butter, sprinkle with brown sugar, cinnamon, and raisins, if desired. Roll up from the long side, until you have two 13-inch logs. Pinch edges to seal. Using a sharp knife, cut each log into nine 2-inch slices and place on large, well-buttered pan. Cover loosely with parchment paper and let rise until doubled in size, about 45 minutes.

Bake at 350 degrees F on middle rack of oven for 30–35 minutes. Invert onto wire cooling rack while still hot.

Makes 18 large buns.

By the time Jon had loaded his father into the vehicle, they were both hot and irritated. Chaos was so excited to have

Roman back, he could barely control himself. Jon finally put him on sit-stay on the grass beside the parking lot, while he figured out how to adjust the passenger seat so Roman would be comfortable.

"It's a half-hour drive, Dad," he said. "I don't want you to be in misery the whole way."

Roman had to wear compression stockings now, because of the clot, which made traveling in the seat of a car even more uncomfortable.

"I'm in more misery standing out here watching you. Let me sit down and I'll figure it out myself."

"Fine," he heard himself say, and smiled.

With a grunt, Roman lowered himself into the seat, leaned back. He squinted and tugged down the visor, then rested his head and closed his eyes. "Seat's fine. Just get me home to my own chair."

Abby had gone ahead to open the gates and put on the kettle. She wanted him and Roman to be able to relax and talk, she said. She'd brought cookies.

But when they got there, straightaway, Roman insisted on taking a nap. With Chaos at his side, he limped into the bedroom and banged shut his door.

Abby looked between the door and the kettle. "I've got tea and everything. He makes me so mad."

"No big deal, Abby. There's lots of time to visit."

"Yes, but . . ." She looked away. "I made him cookies. It's a new recipe. Coconut pecan. I wanted to see if he liked them."

"I can taste test them for you." Jon took one from the plate and bit into it. His eyes widened as he chewed.

"Well?"

"Delicious." He swallowed. "Crunchy, chewy, nutty. You invented these?"

"Hardly. But I didn't follow a recipe, if that's what you mean. You should tell your dad about your job. He's worried that being here is causing trouble for you. He'd rest easier if he knew that you'd gone back to freelancing."

Jon flinched at the sudden change in subject and glanced at Roman's door. "Shh. I'll tell him when he wakes up."

Abby raised her eyebrows.

"I will. Sheesh." Though he wasn't looking forward to it. Roman had definite opinions about everyone at *Diversion* and Jon wasn't interested in hearing the inevitable I-told-you-so's.

He thought of a follow-up question he'd been meaning to ask Abby.

"You mentioned working as a dog-walker," he said.

"Yeah. Why?" Her voice was guarded.

"Did you do any other work in Hollywood?"

She turned away. "I helped out with craft service a few times. Why do you ask?"

"I'm a curious guy, remember? Did you enjoy it?"

Thanks to his work on the Arondi story, he sometimes forgot that not everyone connected to the film industry was dirty. He wanted to reassure himself that Abby had been untouched by the ugliness.

"Not as much as dog walking, but it paid better." She took a sip of tea, and hesitated as if editing her thoughts. "Quinn and I got asked to be extras a few times, too. It was exciting at first. All those big stars, the lights and cameras, the makeup, the beautiful people. I never got to be more than Crowd Person Number 8. But Quinn's hair was very on-trend, so the back of her head actually made it into a few scenes." She gave a little laugh. "It felt very glamorous—until it got boring. We had to be there at six in the morning and hang around all day and sometimes they didn't even end up using us. Still, the money was good and it beat waiting tables or cleaning toilets. Best gig I'd had at the time, actually."

"Why did you quit?" Jon asked.

Her expression changed, went casually blank in the manner of people who were about to diverge from the truth. A chill rippled up the back of his neck.

"Quinn was too young," she said, brushing a cookie crumb off her sleeve. "It took too much time away from school. She was letting her grades drop. I was very glad to get her out of there."

"Is that when you left L.A.?"

She nodded. "Quinn needed a change. I needed to lower our expenses. Seemed like the right move."

It was a plausible reason, but he had a feeling they were dancing around something more. At the very least, she must have heard the rumors.

At the worst . . . He didn't want to think about the worst.

"Abby," he said, "you look like you are remembering something unpleasant."

He waited for her to reply, but she didn't bite.

"Did you ever meet a producer named Richard Arondi?" he asked, finally.

She gave him the same calculated stare but this time, behind that bland expression, he saw something ignite.

"No," she said. "And I hope I never do."

### THE SPRING FESTIVAL GARDEN HOP
### CONTINUES WITH A VISIT
### TO SANCTUARY RANCH

By Jonathan Byers—
exclusive to the *Sunset Bay Chronicle*

Set against the rolling foothills and within walking distance to the ocean, Sanctuary Ranch may be the best-kept secret of the area.

Established by aunt-and-niece team Olivia

Hansen and Haylee Hansen-McCall, this little-known gem of the Sunset Bay area is a rustic resort offering guests a boots-deep opportunity to experience life on an organic, cruelty-free, sustainable working cattle ranch. Or they can go beachcombing, ride horses, eat great food, and simply unplug and unwind in the wild coastal beauty.

This is more than a dude ranch, though. Its raison d'être, as hinted at in the name, is the sanctuary they provide for dogs, horses, and even sometimes, people.

"We're all strays here one way or another," Hansen-McCall says. "In rescuing others, we rescue ourselves."

Hansen-McCall runs a boarding and training kennel called Companions with Purpose on the property, through which she trains assistance dogs. Her pet therapy program is in demand in nursing homes and schools as well as Sunset Bay Memorial Hospital.

Olivia Hansen, whose passion is horses, says riders are amazed to find out that their mounts were once untrained, unwanted, or abused animals. Some guests return year after year specifically to catch up with horses they've bonded with.

This month, the quiet ranch is opening its gates so the public can share in their beautiful five-acre oasis filled with crocuses, daffodils, hyacinths, and irises, and especially, the dozens of tulip varieties that are now bursting into color.

Interested visitors can also watch dog agility and training demonstrations, and enjoy pony rides for the little ones, but the blooms are the main attraction and they are spectacular.

When Abby Warren offered to redesign the flower gardens, the owners had no idea that she had something like this in mind. "Abby has the soul of an artist," says Olivia Hansen.

Warren, however, credits to teamwork and Mother Nature. "We have the perfect soil and microclimate. Everyone pitched in to prepare the beds. After that, it's easy."

In truth, nothing's easy on a ranch except the sleep afforded by fresh air and exercise, and even then, for those accustomed to city lights and noise, it's an adjustment.

Warren admits it took time for her and her sister, Quinn, to adjust to the quiet. Like everyone at the ranch, they came to escape something else but instead, found a home and even a family, something the Warren sisters have never known.

"Every day here is a joy," Warren adds. "I never want to leave."

Freshly picked tulips and flower arrangements created by Warren will be available for purchase, as well as baking and preserves from the ranch kitchen. Pack a blanket for a picnic in the apple orchard if you like and be sure to bring your camera. You'll never find a more beautiful backdrop for family photos than the riotous display of red, orange, yellow, white, pink, and purple blooms set against the rolling foothills of Sanctuary Ranch.

# Chapter Eight

From Abby's notebook:

## HONEY ALMOND CHOCOLATE BISCOTTI

These delicious twice-baked cookies are perfect for dunking in a cup of afternoon coffee. Though hard and crunchy when fresh, after a day or two the honey and nuts give them a slightly softer, chewier texture and more pronounced flavor.

   1 cup all-purpose flour
   1 cup whole wheat flour
   ¾ cup brown sugar
   ¾ cup unblanched almonds, chopped fine
   ¾ cup whole unblanched almonds
   ½ teaspoon baking powder
   ½ teaspoon baking soda
   ¼ teaspoon salt
   ½ teaspoon cinnamon
   1 teaspoon instant coffee
   ½ cup chocolate chips

   ⅓ cup warm water (may need slightly more)
   ⅓ cup liquid honey

1 egg, beaten
1 tablespoon raw turbinado sugar

Preheat oven to 350 degrees F. In large bowl, stir flours, sugar, chopped almonds, baking powder, baking soda, salt, cinnamon, and coffee until well mixed. Add chocolate chips and whole almonds and mix well.

Stir liquid honey into warm water until blended. Stir liquid mixture into dry mixture. If it doesn't hold together, add extra water, one teaspoon at a time until it forms a stiff dough.

Divide in half. Roll each half into a log about eight inches long. Place on parchment paper–covered baking sheet and flatten into a rectangle approximately ¾ inch thick. Brush with beaten egg for a nice sheen. Sprinkle with raw turbinado sugar.

Bake at 350 degrees F for 30 minutes or until firm and golden. Leave logs on baking sheet to cool for at least one hour.

When cool, remove logs from baking sheet and place on cutting board. With large serrated knife, cut each log into about 18 slices, approximately ½ inch thick. Place slices back on baking sheet, cut side down, and bake again at 350 degrees F for ten minutes.

Cool completely and store in tightly covered container.

Makes approximately three dozen.

Quinn stood at the gateway to the garden holding a tray of snacks from Daphne's kitchen. It was her job to offer everyone a little bite on their way in, and to remind them to stop by the sales booth on their way out.

Talking to strangers was not her strong suit, and the day stretched long before her.

"Oh, is that a salted caramel brownie?" asked a teenage

girl. Her stylish boots and perfectly ripped jeans made Quinn all too aware of her sneakers and hoodie.

"Best you'll ever taste." Quinn used the metal tongs to lift the paper cup containing the morsel and put it into the girl's hand. "Enjoy the garden."

The girl's phone buzzed then and she left without replying to Quinn.

A group of middle-age women followed, all appreciative of the food, but more excited about the flowers.

They should be, Quinn thought. She and Abby had busted their butts getting it to look this nice. She actually didn't know how Abby was still standing. Worked all day in the dirt, then up to Roman's place to do whatever she did there, then back to the ranch where she spent half her nights in the kitchen, baking up a storm.

Abby said baking relaxed her. Quinn didn't buy it but then, her sister had always been a little tightly wound and it's not like she had a lot of other outlets.

She needed a hobby, instead of work, work, and more work.

A young couple was next, pushing a stroller containing a squirming, red-faced toddler.

Quinn liked kids. Kids didn't judge. And parents were usually so frazzled, they were just happy to have someone to talk to.

She bent over and addressed the kid. "Would you like a cookie, honey?"

The little girl stopped fussing and blinked huge, black eyes.

Quinn looked up at the mother. "Our baker makes a version with almond meal, no whole nuts, no choking hazard."

The mother's face softened with relief. The child grabbed for the treat and immediately stuffed it into her mouth. "She's teething," said the woman. "These are perfect, thank you."

Quinn stood up and turned the tray around. "Can I tempt you with the grown-up version? It's chocolate-almond-espresso and it's delicious."

"Does it come with coffee?" asked the father. His dark

complexion clearly showed where the baby's coloring had come from.

Quinn grinned and pointed him to the snack station. "Of course."

She watched as they walked to get their drinks. The woman looked to be about Abby's age, resembled her too, with that red tinge to her hair and that creamy skin. If Abby had a baby, she'd get to be cool Auntie Quinn.

But that wasn't likely to happen, not while they stayed out here in the back of beyond.

"Are we allowed in, too?" came a familiar, crabby voice.

She looked up, and started. It was their neighbor, Roman Byers, leaning heavily on his cane, his friendly dog, Chaos, at his side. He always seemed mad about something, though he was nice to his dog, which made her feel better about him. Today, though, he sported a big black eye, which didn't exactly warm him up.

"Hi, Mr. Byers," she said. "Of course you can come in."

"Ignore the shiner. The other guy looks worse."

"Dad. Next you'll be telling people that I beat you."

Mr. Byers's son was with him. He had the kind of movie-star hotness that made her even more nervous.

She wasn't sure what to say, so she held her tray out of reach and bent to pat the dog. Most service dogs were trained not to interact with people but ranch dogs were different. Part of their job was to help their people in social situations. She liked that. Some days she wished she had a dog to help her in social situations.

"Hi, Quinn," said Jonathan. "You've met my dad, right?"

She stood up and rested the tray awkwardly on her arm to give them a little wave.

"Yeah," she said, turning to Roman. "Do you, um, want a snack?"

"Later. I want to see those flowers Abby's been going on about." Roman scowled and pushed past her.

Jon gave her an apologetic smile. "He's a little ticked, I

think. He's gotten used to her visiting him. Doesn't quite get it that people have jobs."

"This place is crazy right now. Everyone in town must have read your article."

He felt a little burst of pride. It was a small favor that cost him nothing and was having exactly the effect he'd hoped for here at the ranch.

He selected a tiny chocolate tart and popped it in his mouth. "Oh, man," he said, wiping a crumb from his lip. "That's the best thing I've ever tasted. Who makes those?"

"Abby."

He glanced over to where Abby's red jacket was visible among the blooms. "When does she have the time?"

"She doesn't sleep a lot. Enjoy the flowers."

"I will. Thanks." She let him take a second tart before he left and watched him walk toward her sister. His head didn't turn once to the flowers, but stayed trained on Abby.

Interesting, thought Quinn.

Maybe what her workaholic sister needed wasn't a hobby. Maybe she needed a boyfriend.

Roman was quiet after their trip to Sanctuary Ranch to view the flowers.

"You tired, Dad?" He slowed the car over the bumpy driveway leading home. Roman tried not to let Jon see when he was in pain, but the old man had a white-knuckle trip on the oh-shit bar above the door. Riding in a car was one of the worst positions for his hip.

"Tired of people," Roman said. "All those tourists, kids running through, making a mess. After all the effort Abby put into it."

The bruising from the cut on Roman's head had settled out underneath one eye. The doctors said it would take longer than usual to resolve because of the blood thinners they'd needed for the clot in his leg.

Some people would have wanted to hide while it healed. Roman said it gave him a rakish mystique and if people didn't like it, they could look elsewhere. In fact, since coming home from the hospital, he acted like his energy had been renewed, as if all the new bumps and bruises were badges of honor.

"You want to take a nap before supper?"

Jon planned to make an old favorite, angel hair pasta and marinara sauce. Roman claimed hospital food had destroyed his taste buds so Jon was pulling out all the stops. So far, only the baking Abby brought by seemed to tempt him.

Chaos leaped out of the backseat, then planted himself in front of the passenger seat, so Roman could use his harness for leverage.

"Nah." He grunted as Chaos pulled him upright, then exhaled. "I'll sleep when I'm dead. I'm going out to the blind. There's a northern spotted owl in the area."

"Really?" The blind wasn't far from the backyard but the path was rough. Roman had fallen there before.

"Yup," Roman said. "Read about it on one of my birding sites."

"I meant—"

"I know what you meant." Roman limped away from the car, leaving Jon to close the door. "This is a threatened species. I'll probably never get another chance to see it. So I'm going."

"Or you could rest now and see it later."

"I could die in my sleep and never see it."

"Don't be morbid."

"Don't follow me. I've got the dog. We'll be back for supper."

He stopped to grab his binoculars from the patio table, and the walking stick that stood next to the door. Chaos,

knowing where they were going, galloped toward the gate at
the back fence, his tail fanning the air wildly.

Jon watched them go, unsure if he should follow behind or
let them be. Roman wasn't his usual self but Jon couldn't say
if this was a good thing or a bad thing. He was certainly taking
interest in the world, which was a heck of a lot better than the
depression he'd fallen into after his original injury. Then, Jon
had worried that Roman was simply waiting to die.

Now, Roman acted like he wanted to wring every bit of
life from each day.

It was good, he told himself. Yet he kept a close eye on
the back gate while he puttered about the kitchen.

As first one hour passed, then another, he grew annoyed.
His father insisted he was able to judge his own ability, but
Jon didn't have to look back far for evidence that Roman's
judgment wasn't what it used to be.

What if Abby hadn't come around that morning? How
long would Roman have lain in the bathroom, bleeding and
unable to move? What if Jamie and Gideon hadn't been
riding in the forest the day his father had slipped while walking with Sadie and Chaos?

And what about the events Jon didn't know about? There
were scorch marks on the kettle that made him think it had
burned dry at some point. The lint trap in the dryer was so
thick it could have been used as a carpet. Roman never remembered to turn off his heating pad. The mayonnaise in the
fridge had been best before January 2016.

Scores of little things showed that Roman wasn't safe on
his own anymore.

At least Chaos was working out. Roman had been furious
when Jon first brought the puppy home, unwilling to allow
another dog into his heart, unwilling to accept that Sadie was
dying, unwilling to believe that another creature could attain
her skill level.

They'd almost given up, too. Chaos was a young energetic

dog and Roman was older and frailer than he'd been when he'd trained Sadie. It wasn't until after Sadie's death that Roman had finally begun bonding with the pup. The training they received at the ranch had helped them become a team.

Jon looked out the window again. It was a beautiful day. Roman was probably fine. Chaos would come back alone if Roman fell.

Probably he was dozing under the big tree where he watched for owls, too stubborn to take a nap, because it had been Jon's suggestion.

While the olive oil heated in the pan, Jon opened three tins of Italian plum tomatoes and crushed a handful of garlic cloves. They'd both have garlic coming out of their pores after this, but it would be worth it.

He wouldn't have chosen this dish if Abby was planning to stop in. But until the garden hop was finished, she had little time to spare.

And it wasn't as if they'd be kissing.

Though he wouldn't mind it if they were.

She intrigued him like no woman had in years. He marveled now that he'd barely noticed her last summer. Her burnt chestnut hair and flawless skin, her long, lean limbs, strong from outdoor work, the way her legs moved beneath those loose jeans, the soft swell beneath the endless supply of white T-shirts she had . . . He must have been brain dead not to see it then.

But he'd been distracted by Roman, and always pressed for time, flying back and forth for work.

Now, with no reason to rush back to Los Angeles, and seeing her as often as he did, he knew there was something special there, and not just the body hiding beneath her work clothes. He had the sense she was someone truly rare, worth taking the time to get to know, even though she didn't like to talk about herself.

But there was the challenge. She flirted back with him,

but somehow still held herself aloof, as if she'd already decided that there would be nothing more between them.

It bugged the hell out of him.

And made him more determined than ever to figure her out. He could stay a bit longer, maybe do some more free-lance stuff, work on the book proposal noodling in the back of his mind. He still needed to convince his dad to consider moving, and who knows how long that would take?

He'd have to land another job soon, but for now, maybe it was okay to set that aside, hang out. Be a tourist.

Maybe Abby would show him around.

The tomato sauce bubbled merrily in the pan, sending its rich, garlicky aroma throughout the house.

He glanced out the window again. "Come on, Dad," he muttered. "You've been gone long enough."

# Chapter Nine

From Abby's notebook:

*Once blossoms fade, use gentle cuts to shape and
thin overly exuberant spring-blooming shrubs
and trees.*

The peonies were poking pink and green fingers up
through the black soil and Abby could already see that the
spread of the blooms would be wider this year than last.
She'd carefully worked around the roots in fall, making sure
not to disturb them as peonies were sulky flowers that did
not appreciate interference. That's okay. She was good at
waiting. Gardening was nothing if not an exercise in delayed
gratification.

Delayed gratification. Story of her life.

"I've been hauling compost for two hours," Quinn announced, swiping a gloved hand across her forehead. "Isn't
it time for a break?"

Quinn seemed her usual self, Abby noted with relief,
which meant that Jon hadn't brought up the subject of
Richard Arondi in their interview. Abby had no desire to

stir all that up again. Quinn was doing so well now. She was becoming friends with Sage, breaking out of her shell in a normal way, as opposed to the frenetic, desperate, dangerous ways she'd sought company in the past.

"You've been participating with Mother Nature in the creation of new life," Abby replied. "Come on. Channel your inner goddess."

"My inner goddess currently requires more of the lilac-and-lily side of nature and a little less of the shoveling shit side. Also, I'm hungry. I'm going to see if there's any coffee cake left. Want me to bring you a piece?"

"No, I'm good." She wouldn't mind working alone for a while. Quinn was in a talkative mood, which was good, but Abby found that she got more done when she could get into the zone. The tulips were holding up and bringing with them a torrent of visitors. The garden had to stay perfect for another week or two.

High above them, a hawk rode the thermals, screaming its thin, piercing cry. The damp breeze was scented with rotting pine and cedar chips, composted mushroom manure, and the salty spray of the Pacific, far below.

There was something healing about working in a spring garden. It was a lot of work, certainly. But it was so full of potential. That's what excited her. Potential, with a little mystery. Which perennials would return, in what condition? What, if any, volunteers would appear? Last summer, several new stands of lavender shoots had appeared in an area where nothing else had taken.

New growth meant established plants were always a little different from year to year, and—

"Abby!" Quinn's voice broke into her musings. "Come look what I found."

Abby propped the rake against the wheelbarrow and walked to the edge of the vegetable garden, to where Quinn was bent among the shrubbery.

"It's a baby bunny," she said softly, as Abby knelt beside her.

The creature fit into Quinn's palm, a tan-colored scrap of fur with bright shining eyes that didn't blink and a tiny pink nose that twitched continuously.

"She's so small." Quinn stroked the little back, which made the animal quiver.

"How do you know it's a girl?" Abby asked.

Quinn shrugged. "I don't. Isn't she cute? She shouldn't be out here all alone."

Abby's heart sank. "She's probably from a nest nearby. The mother might be watching right now, waiting for you to leave her baby and go away."

"Or," Quinn said, "she could be moments away from being eaten. My inner goddess is telling me that I'm the heroine of Calliope's story right now, Abby."

"Calliope?"

"Everyone needs a name."

A stubborn note had entered her voice and Abby knew there'd be no arguing with her. She celebrated the strength Quinn had gained in the past few years but with strength came battles.

"You know you can't keep it, right?"

Tuxedo, the black and white kitten they'd adopted last summer, had grown into a sweet, playful cat. But he was still a hunter at heart.

Quinn stood up, cradling the bunny against her chest. "I can't just leave her here."

"Oh dear." Abby pointed to the back of her sister's hand. "Is that blood?"

After a quick consultation with Haylee, they were in the truck, on the way to town. Dr. Janice Corbin looked after all the animals at Sanctuary Ranch and Quinn insisted that they bring the injured rabbit to her veterinary clinic immediately.

Haylee had warned them that wild bunnies rarely survived

even minor injuries. Over the years, she'd worked with people who rehabilitated wildlife, and had learned that the usual cause of injuries like these were from cats. Coyotes and hawks rarely failed and the damage they inflicted, even if the target did escape, was usually too severe for survival.

A seemingly inconsequential cat scratch, however, usually resulted in overwhelming infection and death.

"Hang in there, Calliope," murmured Quinn into the downy fur. "You're stronger than you think."

She kept her head bent over the rabbit during the drive and Abby saw tears slipping down her thin cheeks.

*Oh, Quinn. Please, don't do this. Not again.*

One of Dr. Corbin's technicians took the little rabbit from Quinn and asked them to take a seat in the waiting room.

"But," Quinn protested, "I want to go with her."

"Wild rabbits are actually very stressed by human handling," the young woman explained. "We're going to put her in a warm, dark, quiet box while Dr. J finishes her last appointment. It won't be long. She'll call you as soon as she's ready."

Quinn sat in one of the metal chairs in the waiting room and put her face in her hands.

Abby sat next to her and rubbed her back. "It's okay," she said. "They're used to this kind of thing. They know what to do."

"I know." Quinn sniffed and nodded. "I know you think I'm getting carried away but, Abby, when I saw that little rabbit hiding in the brush, I felt something. Like I knew exactly how she felt. Yeah, I'm overidentifying, letting my emotions get the best of me. I know. But I've been thinking about . . . stuff lately."

"What stuff?" Abby didn't want to know, but had to ask.

"You know." Quinn swallowed. It took her a long time to continue. Finally, she said, "I was talking to Jon about that article and I couldn't help but remember."

"What did you tell him?" She could hardly get the words out. Maybe she'd been wrong. Jon was clever. He knew they were hiding something.

"Nothing." Quinn's shoulders slumped. "Same thing I've always said."

Abby knitted her fingers together in her lap and took a deep breath. "Good. That's good."

"No. It's not. I don't care what Carly said."

"Please, Quinn, don't start with that again." Abby forced herself to slow down, but the panic that started whenever Quinn got on the topic of Carly wouldn't be denied. "She didn't want that. It's over. She's moved past it. We've moved past it."

"I haven't."

It was almost three years since they'd left Los Angeles and still memories of that time hovered in the wings, ready to tarnish even the most unexpected moments.

"You've been doing so well," Abby said, feeling her own throat tighten. "I wish I'd never let Jon talk to you for that interview."

"I'm not sorry." Quinn lifted her tearstained face. "It was wrong to keep quiet then and it's still wrong now. I don't care what Carly said. She didn't mean it. She was trying to protect me."

"And herself. She's a smart girl."

"See? You get so angry, we can't talk about it. It's like you want to pretend that our life before Oregon didn't happen. Carly." She hesitated. "Mom."

Exactly, Abby wanted to say. Rebecca Warren had done enough damage. A fresh slate, starting over, no baggage. Clean as the tide-washed beaches; that's the history she wanted for them. Why couldn't Quinn see this?

"But it's my life, too. You don't get to decide my memories. Or what I do with them."

"Really?" Abby forced herself to stay calm. "You want

more memories of Mom? How about all the times I forged
her signature so you could go on field trips? How about the
time she threw up all over the lasagna you made for her?
How about when we had to move in the middle of the night
because she'd forgotten to pay the rent? I was always the one
left behind to pick up the pieces after she showed up like a
hurricane in our lives. Do you remember that, Quinn?"

Quinn hunched her shoulders and pulled away. "That's
not all she was."

"That's right. There was also the crying, the staying in
bed all day, the online shopping, the canceled credit cards."

"I remember *The Velveteen Rabbit.*"

Abby's chest constricted. If she hadn't been sitting down,
her legs would likely have collapsed.

"The Skin Horse," she whispered.

"'Once you are Real,'" Quinn quoted, "'you can't be
ugly, except to people who don't understand.' That's what
Mom always told us. Remember?"

What Abby recalled wanting, with all her heart, to believe
that Rebecca could change, could overcome the demons that
haunted her. Could pull herself out of the sucking quicksand
of her life, for the sake of her daughters.

But instead, she'd been someone with sharp edges, who
had to be carefully kept, someone who fractured easily and
often.

"She wanted to be real, Quinn," she said. "But she was
broken."

The receptionist called them then, thankfully. Quinn
jumped to her feet and Abby followed.

But Dr. Corbin's face was grave.

"I'm sorry, Quinn," she said. "The baby rabbit died while
I was examining it."

"What?" Quinn's voice was faint. "I don't understand.
She seemed fine."

"Wild animals are like that." Dr. Corbin spoke kindly, but

with a firmness Abby appreciated. "They have the ability to mask the extent of their injuries, so that predators don't know that they're hurt. This one had a chest puncture. I'm guessing a hawk attack. The rabbit couldn't have survived, Quinn. That's why you were able to pick it up. Healthy rabbits are hard to catch. I'm sorry."

Quinn was quiet on the way home and back to work in the garden, digging and spreading bark mulch with ferocious energy.

Housekeeping wasn't exactly the career Quinn had imagined for herself when she was in high school, cramming for algebra and organic chemistry and physics, which she loathed.

She pulled the wheeled supply cart over the bark-mulch path between cabins. Cabin 3 contained a couple of horse enthusiasts, who'd gone out with Gideon and Huck for an early trail ride, so they were first on her list.

She'd wanted to be a veterinarian, at one time. She loved animals, even though she'd never had a pet of her own. Just as well that hadn't worked out. She couldn't handle seeing animals in pain.

She made up the bed, wiped down the bathroom, put out fresh towels, and swept the floor. Tomorrow, she'd change the sheets, she thought as she pulled the door shut behind her and moved to the next cabin.

Abby had always pushed her, telling her that education was the only way to dig themselves out of the hole that a bad genetic legacy had plopped them into. But without money for college, high school education only got you so far.

Their dad couldn't help dying when he had. Quinn was too young to remember, and Abby didn't like to talk about it, so for many years, all Quinn had known was that he'd been in a car accident, that it was a tragedy, and that their mother had never recovered from her grief.

Her curiosity grew as she got older though and eventually she came to understand that their mother's grief had been complicated by the mountain of medical bills their dad had racked up before dying.

Dad couldn't have foreseen being T-boned by a one-ton truck, but a little insurance would have been thoughtful.

Quinn let herself into Cabin 5, a larger unit with two bedrooms and a pull-out sofa. A family of four was staying in this one, nice people although their small son hadn't mastered the art of standing up to pee.

She got down on her knees to wipe the base of the toilet, unable to be irritated with the boy. He was about kindergarten age, she guessed, with a gap-toothed grin and enthusiasm for every single thing about the ranch. Feeding the horses, walking the dogs, gathering eggs in the henhouse, digging for winter carrots in the kitchen garden.

If she had her way, she'd spend her days showing him things like how the apple cider press worked or where milk actually comes from.

She liked kids. They had a wide-eyed wonder about things that made Quinn feel happy, hopeful. There hadn't been a lot of time for wide-eyed wonder in her own childhood.

She searched her memory for times when she and Abby and Mom had been happy, but all she found were cloudy mental snapshots. Mom, wraithlike and insubstantial, smiling desperately beside a tiny Christmas tree, or next to a store-bought cupcake with a numbered candle on it, sometimes standing round-shouldered at the stove, stirring boxed macaroni and cheese. As the images progressed, Mom occurred in fewer and fewer, until she disappeared completely and it was Abby standing at the stove. Abby, walking Quinn to school, nagging her about homework.

It was always Abby who came home with grocery bags in her arms, Abby who took out the trash and made sure the rent was paid.

She picked up the sodden towels and then polished the mirror, looking at her reflection. Did she look like Mom? Abby always said so but aside from blond hair and blue eyes, Quinn couldn't see any genetic similarities.

There were other similarities, though. She knew Abby worried about her, watched for signs that she was like Mom in other, hidden ways.

When the police officers had arrived at their apartment door, solemnly asking for Rebecca Warren's next of kin, Abby immediately stepped in front of Quinn, as if to shield her, then sent her to her room.

Quinn could still hear the muffled conversation.

*We're sorry to inform you that the body of a woman we believe to be Rebecca Warren has been discovered. We need someone to confirm her identity. Who should we contact?*

Where had she been found? Abby wanted to know.

*In a Zipcar. Downtown. Behind the Regent Theater.*

How did she die?

The pause before the answer. *A suspected overdose. No sign of foul play.*

Abby had calmly gone with them and calmly returned a couple of hours later, to calmly report that Mom wouldn't be coming home but that everything would be okay because Abby had a good job and all Quinn had to worry about was finishing high school.

Quinn realized now that although her older sister had already been long adjusted to their mother's absence and had probably been expecting news like that for some time, the preternatural calm she'd projected must have cost her dearly.

It was different for Quinn. Sure, Mom had been gone a lot. But waiting for her to come home had become Quinn's natural state. Mom always came home, eventually.

Quinn tidied the kids' room quickly, noticing that one bed was only slightly rumpled. But the master bedroom sheets were a tangled mess. As she straightened them, she found the little boy's teddy bear balled up in the comforter.

She picked it up and held it to her chest. She imagined the child awakening in the night, in a strange, dark place. Afraid but knowing, without hesitation, that he'd find reassurance and safety between the warm, sleepy bodies of his parents.

That's how it should be, she thought. That's how it would be for her, if she ever had kids.

She'd never lost the sensation that something was missing from her life, that she was still waiting, watching, as if Rebecca was simply running late, caught up in a job, missing her daughters as much as they missed her and planning to make things better for them, one day. One day.

Quinn lifted the mat at the door and shook it onto the path. Bits of grit and evergreen needles flew out. A piece of dust must have landed in her eye because as she pulled the door shut and started down the trail to the next cabin, her vision was blurred with tears.

# Chapter Ten

From Abby's notebook:

*Not all bugs are bad. Learn to identify beneficial insects and add plants such as coriander, candytuft, sunflower, yarrow, and dill to attract them to your garden.*

Abby thought she'd been prepared for the garden hop, but she hadn't realized how difficult it would be to complete her usual duties with strangers constantly around her. The compliments were gratifying and the blooms had been fantastic. But it would take her all day to move a single wheelbarrow full of yard waste to the compost heap. She'd move ten feet, stop to talk with someone, get three rows farther, stop again. Another row and someone had a question for her; it never ended. All day long.

It made it tough to keep in touch with Roman, as well, though she'd managed to drop in most evenings. Three days ago, Daphne was called away for a family emergency, leaving Jamie and Abby to handle the meals, on top of their usual tasks.

Rain had killed the last week of the hop and by then, Abby'd been more than ready to have it over with. It was a relief to be out of the public eye, and she enjoyed a chance to bake again, but she was anxious to see Roman again. Today, however, they'd gotten the lunch and supper prep done early. She was taking a few minutes between rain showers to take out the compost and pull a few weeds, then she was heading out to check in on them in person.

Jon called and texted regularly, assuring her that they were doing fine. That was both good and bad news, since it meant Roman still hadn't told Jon about the tumor. She'd pleaded ignorance when Jon inquired about some of his father's medication, but urged him to ask Roman about it.

He'd asked again about her and Quinn's experience with the production company.

Sure, she'd heard rumors, she'd told him. But it was so long ago. They'd only been there a short time. So sorry she couldn't help.

She could tell it had only piqued his interest further when she asked him not to talk about it with Quinn.

Roman and Chaos miss you, he'd said.

What about you? She'd wanted to ask. Of course, she didn't.

"Need a hand?"

Abby dropped the handle of the wheelbarrow, sending a small pile of weeds onto her freshly raked path.

Jamie stood at the entrance to the bulb garden. She had a brown and white dog with her, jumping at the end of the leash.

Abby looked at the mess she'd just created. "I'm not turning down any offers."

Thinking about Jon and Roman wasn't productive. Sooner or later, Roman would deteriorate. Jon would find out about the cancer and he'd be furious that Abby hadn't told him. Whatever crush or flirtation they had going on right now would end. She'd be lucky if he spoke to her at all. Conversation with Jamie was just what she needed.

"Is it okay if I let Cookie off her leash?" Jamie asked. "I want to work on her recall."

"Of course."

The dog raced up to Abby. She squatted to greet the squirming bundle of energy. "Hello, sweetheart."

Cookie was the most recent dog to begin training with Jamie and Haylee as part of the pet therapy program. She was part beagle and part Shetland sheepdog, with maybe some terrier thrown in there. She had a short coat, a long muzzle, and beautiful black-lined eyes that gave her a mischievous appearance.

"How's she doing?" Abby asked.

Jamie grabbed a rake that was lying near the path and evened out a patch of bark mulch made lumpy by footsteps. The dog, finished with affection for the moment, headed down the path, her nose to the ground, on the trail of who knew what.

Jamie held up a finger. "You'll see in a second."

She waited until the dog was at the far end of the path, then called her.

"Cookie!"

The dog lifted her head and whipped it around to look at Jamie. Instantly, Jamie depressed the device in her hand, and a sharp *click* sounded.

"Come, Cookie!" Tufts of bark mulch kicked into the air behind the little dog as she pelted toward the source of the noise.

"Good girl." Jamie patted the panting animal and gave her a treat from the pouch attached to her belt. "Good Cookie."

The dog crunched the treat, licked Jamie's hand, then went out to explore again.

"Impressive," Abby said. "Is any of that Quinn's doing?"

Since the episode with the rabbit, Quinn had been spending more time with the dogs. She barely talked to Abby, but seemed otherwise okay.

"Um, hello? Who's the master clicker trainer? Me. That's who."

Abby laughed. Jamie had worked her butt off to learn her dog handling skills and wasn't about to let anyone forget it.

"But your sister's pretty good, too," she conceded.

"She seems to enjoy it. Probably more interesting than cleaning rooms or babysitting."

"Cleaning rooms, for sure. She seems to enjoy the rug rats though. Cookie, come!"

Once again, the dog peeled out of the shrubbery and raced back to Jamie for a treat.

Abby laughed. "She's making a mess, James!"

"I'll clean it up. Question for you. Do you think Quinn would be interested in doing more with the dogs? They really respond to her. She recognizes when they're scared and knows how to calm them down. She's good at interpreting body language."

The legacy of an insecure childhood, Abby thought. No matter how hard she tried, she could never make up for the lack of parents in Quinn's life.

"I think she'd jump at the chance. Why?"

"Haylee and I were thinking that if we had another person on board, we could expand the pet therapy program. We've got a waiting list of places that want us to visit."

Abby felt hope spring to life within her. It was exactly the sort of thing Quinn needed. Perhaps if she had something positive to focus on, she'd forget about Carly and Los Angeles. And Mom.

"I've already talked to Olivia," Jamie continued. "She said she can hire someone new to take over Quinn's housekeeping duties. Bookings are up, thanks to the exposure from Jon's article and all the foot traffic."

"So why are you asking me?" Abby said.

Jamie rolled her eyes. "Come on, Abs. Everyone knows you're a total Mama Bear when it comes to your little sister. No point getting Quinn excited about something if you're just going to put the kibosh on it." She turned her attention to the sun, drifting toward the horizon. "Plus, you never talk about your plans. No one knows if you're here for good, or what."

The familiar tension ratcheted up inside Abby again. They'd been at Sanctuary Ranch longer than any place she could remember. She didn't want to leave. But you never knew. Keeping your options open was the safest bet.

"I have no plans," she said. Which was the truth.

A grin broke across Jamie's face and she exhaled loudly. "Glad to hear it, girlfriend. You're hard to peg sometimes, you know that? But I've gotten used to having you around. And not just me. If you took off, Daphne would hunt you down and make you pay. No one wants that."

Abby laughed. "True, that." She gave her a one-armed side hug.

Jamie was a good friend, though she was cautious with her affection. Falling in love, or rather, having her love returned, had transformed her. No, Abby amended. Not transformed. Jamie was still the same funny, opinionated, passionate woman she'd always been. But since she and Gideon had become a couple, the sharp edges of insecurity had softened.

They made their way to the far end, where more weeds were popping through the mulch.

"So I can ask Quinn if she's interested?" Jamie asked.

"Go ahead. She'll be thrilled. She looks up to you. I think she identifies with you."

"Poor soul," Jamie replied with a laugh. "But hey, I live

to inspire others. If nothing else, I'm a cautionary tale. Never use shoe polish on your hair. It takes forever to grow out."

She patted the stubby brunette ponytail high on her head. Jamie's appearance had changed subtly over the winter as well. Her hair was longer, she didn't paint her nails black anymore and she'd let a few of her facial piercings grow closed. Instead of hiding behind a shell of Goth and sarcasm, she was now just . . . herself. Comfortable in her own skin.

Funny, thought Abby with a pang. Jamie had used her rough exterior to hide a tender heart while the softness that everyone saw in Abby was only skin-deep, a mask for her shriveled soul.

"You're quiet." Jamie tossed a handful of weeds into a bucket. "Have you and Jon had a spat?"

Abby froze. "There's no me and Jon. I mean, we're friends. I'm helping him with Roman so we've gotten close . . . but there's no . . . nothing . . ." Abby sputtered to a stop.

Jamie burst out laughing. "You love him."

"Stop it."

"You . . . love . . . him." Jamie turned each one-syllable word into at least three.

Abby tossed a chunk of crabgrass at her.

Jamie snatched it out of the air and dropped it in the bucket. "Okay, you like him. Is that better?"

Abby groaned and dropped her chin to her chest. "No. It's worse. Do you think he likes me? Oh, God. I just heard myself. It's like high school all over again."

"Everyone likes you." She waggled her eyebrows. "But he *likes* you, likes you. It's pretty obvious."

"To who?"

"Me, of course. Which means Gideon knows." Jamie held out her fingers, one by one. "Haylee. Aiden knew before any of us, according to her. He saw you in the hospital together. Daphne, naturally. Probably Olivia."

"Stop. Do you think Quinn knows?"

Jamie cocked her head. "Why wouldn't she? Do you two not talk?"

"Not about this. Even if there was something to tell, which there isn't," she emphasized. Maybe that had been a mistake. "Our mom didn't have a good track record with boyfriends. I don't want to perpetuate that."

"So," Jamie said, "you don't talk about it, or you don't date?"

"Both, I guess."

Jamie's eyebrows went up. "So Jon is a big deal, then."

"Yes. No!" She exhaled. "I don't know what he is. And I don't want her to have to worry about losing me. Not that there's any reason to think that would happen. I mean, Jon and I are just hanging out. To think it's anything more is completely presumptuous."

"Where is it going?"

"What is this, an interrogation? I don't know. Nowhere, probably. I mean, he's got a life in L.A. I live here." She gestured helplessly. "There's nowhere it can go."

"So, a relationship is impossible because you're staying in Oregon. Is that it?" Jamie blew her a raspberry. "Your optimism is positively inspiring. Look, Gideon and I shouldn't have worked. His ex made him choose between me and Blake. He almost lost his son, because of me. *That* strains the viability of a relationship. Your only problem is geography."

Jamie made it sound so simple. But that was because she didn't know the whole story. Uprooting Quinn wasn't an option. And certainly not to go back to California.

That was assuming Jon was still willing to talk to her, once he knew the truth about Roman.

She knew better than to count on that.

# Chapter Eleven

Jon's afternoon with his father went as well as could be expected. Roman downplayed his pain—as usual—declared he was just fine—also as usual—and went into his bedroom to take a nap.

He knew better than to revisit the idea of Roman moving to a more suitable residence, but that didn't stop him from researching the options, when he got back to the house.

Thing was, the best place depended entirely on where Jon found a job. Something he'd spent the last two days working on, with zero results.

Whitey Irving hadn't been kidding when he said Jon was done. Every entertainment magazine between Mexico and British Columbia had been expecting Jon's call. And without exception, they'd all sent form rejections.

Via e-mail.

Well, he wasn't desperate. It wouldn't be the worst thing to spend some time here cooling his jets, thinking about what he really wanted.

Exploring his options, as they said.

He shut his laptop, got up from the table, and stretched his arms overhead. At least the bed in his dad's spare room was comfortable, a king with a supportive mattress and nice linens.

Roman still enjoyed his creature comforts, Jon was glad to see. He didn't know how long he and his father could live under the same roof but so far, so good.

It was quiet in the house. He opened the refrigerator. Not a lot of inspiration there. He ought to go grocery shopping. He rinsed out his coffee mug, watered a wilted plant on the windowsill, straightened the shoes by the back door, and then stood there, looking over the backyard.

Dad must have had help with the yard. The graceful lines and carefully placed shrubs suggested that Abby had been involved.

As soon as the thought came into his head, he was grabbing his jacket. He was going crazy here. He'd head over to the ranch and see if she was available for a coffee, maybe pick her brain on how best to warm Roman up to the idea of moving.


Daphne told him to look for her in the garden.

Abby, however, was nowhere to be seen. He followed the path down to the little bench overlooking the ocean. Her wheelbarrow stood next to a tidy row of hilled soil, with a rake and a spade leaned up against it. Her leather gloves lay inside.

But no Abby.

He sat down on the bench, wondering where else he should look for her. They needed to talk. She had more than enough to do here with her own work, without looking after Roman, too. He appreciated all she'd done, without a doubt. But he wanted her to know that he'd look after things from here on out.

Something else had been bothering him. Not only had she refused to talk about her time working as a movie extra, but she'd specifically asked him not to discuss it with Quinn. She'd implied that the subject brought up memories of when their mother had died, but Jon had a feeling there was more to it.

Far down the long, wooded slope, he could see white-capped waves drifting into shore. From this distance, he could only hear the sound if he really focused his ears, and even then, he expected it was his imagination. But he could definitely hear the cries of the gulls as they swooped above the shore, angled toward the ridge, eyeing him as if wondering what he was doing.

The peace of the place drifted over him like autumn leaves riding a breeze, and for the first time since his mad rush out of the *Diversion* headquarters, he allowed himself to examine his feelings about the event.

He wasn't screaming. That was a good sign.

It still seemed unreal. He was no longer an entertainment journalist. The shining climb of his career was over. No more interviews with stars and celebrities. No more invitations to red carpet events. No more having his finger on the pulse of Hollywood.

He was done.

He knew it. The dozens of rejected e-mails made that clear. But he hadn't allowed the truth of it, the scope of the event, to soak in.

He was done.

Jonathan Byers, *Diversion* magazine, was no more.

Memories of his office, his colleagues, the place he went for coffee every morning, washed over him. The inside of his chest felt raw, hot, ragged, like it had when he'd been down with pneumonia. He hadn't wanted anyone to see him then, and he sure as hell didn't want anyone to see him now.

You were vulnerable when you were down.

Whitey Irving had done this. And all because he was protecting Richard Arondi. It was so unfair.

He breathed, in and out, letting the anger roll through him until it wore itself out, turned to something else. A loss like this was a kind of death, he supposed. Not as deep as the loss of a loved one, of course. But if Jon was no longer the man he'd worked so hard to become, if that man was gone, how else could he make sense of it, on a gut level, but to react as if that part of him had died?

Then it struck him that this must be exactly how his father had felt, when Hollywood had turned on him. As soon as Roman had been released from the rehabilitation center, having recovered as much as he ever would, he'd sold the house, packed what little he wanted, and left L.A. Jon had been in college then, immersed in his own life and future plans. He'd done what he could to help, of course. But the gravity of Roman's experience hadn't come home to him the way it did now.

Sadness settled heavily on him. He and Roman both, screwed over by the same industry, in different ways.

Something caught his eye, a flash of red.

He peered closer, shading his eyes against the bright light of the sun behind the clouds.

It was Abby, down the ridge, doing something in a little sheltered area. He quickly found the rough deer trail she must have used. Carefully, he followed, picking his way through brambles and ferns and moss-covered branches, all damp with mist.

The forest enveloped him, green-smelling, fresh and full of life. Once full summer hit, this place would be almost in-accessible and rampant with birdcalls and insect life. But for now, it was full of dripping silence, swollen and waiting. The hush felt almost worshipful, the tall cedars around him creating a cathedral-like grove, welcoming and warning at the same time.

He found her sitting on a boulder. She'd been watching his approach for some time.

"Hey, Jon," she said. "You found my secret lair."

"Am I intruding?"

She considered, then pressed her full lips together and tilted her head, indicating a second boulder next to hers. "Sit, if you want."

As he stepped over a mossy nurse log, something grabbed his sleeve. He pulled away from the thorny vine, only to find another one tugging at him.

"Hold still," Abby said. "Those blackberry canes will cut you to ribbons if you're not careful."

"Blackberries? As in the fruit?"

Abby pulled a small pair of pruning shears from the pocket on her thigh. "As in the fruit. We pick gallons of these every fall."

"Without bloodshed?"

She smiled. "Oh, there's always bloodshed, especially with newbies. Eventually you learn to work around the thorns. And you learn to wear boots, jeans, and long sleeves. No shorts and flip-flops, no matter how warm it is. It's so worth it."

She was close enough that he could smell her hair. One warm hand held his arm, while the other snipped.

"There's nothing like the taste of blackberry pie, baked fresh from berries picked yourself, that very day. There." She patted the sleeve. Was it his imagination or did she linger a half second too long?

"You've got a little tear in your shirt. Sorry about that."

"It's just a shirt." He took a seat on the rock. An opening in the vegetation provided a windowed view to the ocean and from here, the sound of the surf was soft, but clear. It would have been, if he hadn't been busy listening to the beat of his heart, thrumming from her touch.

"So," she said. "What brings you out here?"

She gazed at the distant horizon and spoke as if she was tired.

"First," he said, "I want to thank you for everything you've done for my dad."

"Stop." She kept looking at the horizon. "He's my friend. I'm happy to do what I can. What's the second?"

He leaned forward on his elbows. She was about six inches away from him but he could smell her unique scent, her skin warm from working, touched with earth.

"You've done enough. I'll look after things from here on out."

She laughed. "Okay. We'll see what Roman says about that."

"What do you mean?"

"He's like the lion with a thorn in his paw. I pulled it out, so I'm stuck with him now." She made a face. "That didn't come out right. I don't resent helping him. But I greatly appreciate you being here. You have no idea."

An unexpected warmth ran through him at her words.

"It's always nice to be appreciated."

They sat in companionable silence for a moment.

"Was there a third thing?" she asked. "I should probably get back to work, although I could sit here like this all day."

Jon hesitated. "You never said anything about the piece I wrote about the ranch."

She raised her eyebrows, then looked out to the ocean again. "Olivia was pleased. It was fine."

"Fine." He nodded. "Yeah. I'm a word-man. You know what *fine* means, in today's popular vernacular? Especially from women? It means, 'Go ahead, I've got a high pain threshold.' Or, 'I don't like it but you're going to do what you're going to do no matter what so there's no point arguing.' Or, 'You bore me and I want you to go away.' Which is it this time?"

Amusement brightened Abby's eyes. "I actually do have a high pain threshold. But sometimes fine is just fine."

"Whew." He mimed wiping sweat off his brow. "I don't bore you. That's a relief."

"Hey. That's subject to change at any moment."

He watched as her smile faded, then probed further. "Why didn't you want me to write the piece?"

She dropped her head slightly, nibbled the corner of her mouth. "It was good for the ranch, so I'm glad you did it. I'm a very private person, that's all."

"But you're the one who created the garden, Abby. That was my hook." He frowned. "You should be proud to take credit for it. Everyone can see you're an amazing gardener."

"I'm not an amazing anything. I'm a hard worker. I've read a lot of books on gardening, but I'm hardly an expert." She hesitated. "I just like to keep a low profile. Same with Quinn. That's all."

Was it false modesty? Or was she truly uncomfortable with praise?

In Jon's experience, most people were more than happy to talk about themselves and their achievements, usually at far more length than he needed.

"I couldn't write about the garden without mentioning you. But I didn't betray any confidences. How could I? You didn't give me any." He paused. "It was a little disappointing, to be honest. Nothing a reporter loves more than a story."

She gave a little sniff of amusement. "No story here. Sorry."

"Why not let me be the judge? You fascinate me, Abby Warren. How about this? You tell me something and I'll tell you something."

Her eyebrows lifted. A breeze rustled the blackberry bushes behind them, sending a strand of hair over her cheek. She brushed it away, then sighed.

"Fine." She gave him a bland look. "What do you want to know?"

"There's that word again." Quick, he thought. Ask her something non-threatening. "What made you come out here today?"

"I came out here today for the same reason I always do," Abby said. "To think. FYI, you ruined that."

"Sorry. What do you think about when you're out here?"

"This and that. Past and present. Good and evil. The usual." She looked off to the horizon, as if searching for something miles away.

He followed her gaze. It was easy to believe in infinity, out here. That there was no beginning, no end, that none of the petty, everyday burdens mattered. That life followed the rising sun and the sea and the little blades of grass beneath their feet.

"You didn't mention the future. Most people worry about the future, but you didn't say that."

"Good try. Okay, my future. I'm teaching a pie baking class tonight. You should come. Bring your dad. Now it's your turn. Tell me something about you."

The more she danced away from him, the more curious he became. He wanted to know what was behind the serene face of Abby Warren. What made her more interested in listening to others, than talking about herself? What made those big brown eyes go distant, why did she duck away from praise or attention, how had she and Quinn ended up alone in the world?

She plucked a piece of dried grass and twirled it between her fingers. The sun broke through the clouds to cast a ray of light over them. She lifted her face to the warmth, her expression beatific, like a cat who'd just found the best chair in the house.

Her lack of interest irritated him, made him want to say something, anything, to get a reaction. "I'm not actually on sabbatical. I got fired from my job."

That did it.

She sucked in a quick breath, turned. "What?"

He swallowed. "First time I've said that out loud. I think this place bewitched me. Or maybe it was you."

He hadn't planned to tell her. It was like a reflex. Long stretches of silence were useful in getting people to open up. He'd used that technique often but rarely got caught by it himself.

"When?" The full force of her attention was on him and it hit his bloodstream like a drug. She was genuinely interested, genuinely concerned. Can't unring that bell, he thought. Might as well make the most of it.

"Last month. Same day Dad fell. In fact, I got your message as I was being escorted off the premises."

"That explains why you've been so laid back about being here. What did you do?" She cringed. "Sorry, I mean, what happened?"

He waved a hand. "You were right the first time. I did something I shouldn't have. I thought I was someone I'm not. Attempted a story I was not ready for. Tried to be David to the Goliath of the magazine industry."

"David took down Goliath."

"Yeah, well it's in the Bible because it was a hard news item. It shouldn't have happened. Most Davids of the world fail."

She reached out and touched his arm, patted it lightly. Before she could withdraw, he caught it, held her hand between his.

"What will you do now?" she asked.

Her eyes were so warm, he could melt into their depths. "I have no idea."

"This could be an opportunity, you know."

"Oh yeah?" He'd moved slightly closer to her. Their eyes held. "That sounds like a typical silver-lining kind of response. When God closes a door, he opens a window, everything happens for a reason, yada-yada, ad nauseam. Not really feeling that."

"No platitudes from me. I just meant . . . you don't have to worry about getting back to L.A. Roman must be happy you're free to stay with him longer."

"I haven't told him."

"What? Why not?"

"My father's favorite words are *I told you so*. He warned me that Whitey Irving was a snake. I didn't think it mattered, as long as I did my job. Turns out Dad was right." Humiliation washed over him again at the memory. "I'll tell him once I've found something else. I'll spin it that I was looking for a change. He doesn't need to know the details."

"I'm so sorry, Jon. Are you okay?" Her voice was like taffy, smooth and sweet. He wasn't sure if he wanted to listen to it, or taste it.

He forced his thoughts back to her question. Was he okay?

"Sure," he told her with a wry smile. "I'm *fine*."

"Ah, now you're bored with me."

He reached out and captured her hand. "Never."

She looked steadily at him, without withdrawing her hand. "Do you want to tell me what happened?"

And he found himself doing that. He hadn't unloaded a problem onto someone else in ages and he found it incredibly cathartic.

"They fired me over a story, Abby. It's a good one, one that needs to be told. It's got it all, scandal, injustice, a powerful man preying on vulnerable young women. But turns out he's more powerful than I realized. He's got my magazine—my former magazine—on his payroll. He's untouchable. And now, since I took a poke, I'm untouchable, too. I might never work again. You might say that's an opportunity, but it doesn't feel like it from where I'm sitting."

Stillness had come over Abby. "I know what that world's

like. You asked me earlier about Richard Arondi. That's who you were writing about, isn't it? He's your Goliath?"

Jon's breath caught in his throat. "Yes."

Abby looked out toward the horizon. Her voice was steady but there was a vein of ice running through it. "I wasn't entirely honest with you earlier. We were on one of his sets. He's not a nice man."

"Oh, Abby," Jon said.

"It's okay. Neither of us worked directly for him, thank goodness." She shuddered lightly. "We saw what he was like, though. That's why we left. You should write that story anyway, Jon."

"For who? No one will print it. I'm persona non grata, thanks to Irving."

Her encouragement warmed him, or maybe it was just the overwhelming relief that she and her sister hadn't fallen prey to Arondi's appetite.

He wondered if she could point him to more sources but before he could ask, she laid a hand on his arm. She wasn't looking at him any longer. Slowly, she raised her index finger to her lips. Her eyes darted sideways, and he followed.

A dark-eyed doe stood in the shadows beyond the blackberry bushes, a spotted fawn at her side. They could have been statues, yet there was a tension about them, an awareness that sizzled over the air. They were wild animals, trusting no one. Yet they'd stopped to look at the two humans.

Curious enough to risk exposure.

A crow cawed its harsh, raucous cry overhead and the deer bolted, leaving nothing but quivering shrubbery to give evidence that they'd ever been there.

"She had two fawns, last time I saw her." Abby spoke with a hushed sadness.

Then she blinked and seemed to come back to herself. "It sucks that you got fired, but looking at it another way, you're no longer tied to the rigid demands of an editor who, by the sound of it, was not an ideal employer. You're free to do what you want now."

He sighed. "Couldn't resist the silver lining, could you?"

"Hey, I see what I see. I don't mean to minimize this though, Jon. I know it hurts."

Her gentle empathy flowed over him like balm. "I'll stay a bit longer, figure out what to do with Dad. Maybe work up a book proposal. I'll figure something out."

She swallowed. "What if you took more than that? What if you stayed for a month or two? Or even the summer?"

"What, with Roman?"

She nodded. "You've got the time. I know he'd appreciate it."

Jon tried to imagine spending a whole summer with his father. Roman had been getting progressively more irritable lately. He forgot to take his medication now and then and snarled when reminded. Jon had to pretend not to see his father drop things or stumble into furniture, mopping up spills and straightening chairs when Roman wasn't looking.

"He's tired of having me around. He wants his privacy back."

"I'm sure you're wrong about that."

He eyed her. "Did he tell you he wants me to stick around?"

She inhaled, started to speak, then closed her mouth.

"Abby? What is it?"

"He's too proud to admit it, but he missed you a lot this past winter. I'm not saying that to make you feel guilty, just that you being here has made him really happy."

"My father? Really happy? You've met him, right?"

Abby punched him lightly on the arm. "Come on. Tell him you'll stay longer. It would make his day."

He suspected most of Roman's bad temper stemmed from embarrassment. Jon felt the same way. He hated witnessing his father's weakness, but at the same time, he couldn't imagine leaving him on his own. But trying to get Roman to consider an assisted living facility was like banging his head against concrete.

"Now that the garden hop is finished," Abby added, "I can get back to looking in on him every day. Help you make sure he eats and takes his medication, does his exercises. In case that part stresses you out."

Jon thought of his condo, sitting empty in L.A. He could easily sublet it. He could go month to month, see how things went. With Abby to help diffuse the tension, maybe it wouldn't be so bad to stay longer.

He felt a slow smile break over his face. "I think," he said, "that you just made me an offer I can't refuse."

# Chapter Twelve

From Abby's notebook:

*Rhubarb is a good source of magnesium, dietary fiber, vitamin C, vitamin K, calcium, potassium, and manganese. It's very easy to grow and this pie is a delicious way to use it. One pound of raw rhubarb yields about four cups of slices, which cooks down to about ¾ cup rhubarb mash.*

### RHU-BERRY PIE

Food Processor Pastry:
2½ cups pastry flour
1 teaspoon salt
2 tablespoons wheat germ
⅔ cup cold, unsalted butter, cut in pieces
2 egg yolks
4 tablespoons ice water

Put flour, salt, and wheat germ into processor bowl. Using steel blade, pulse to blend. Add butter and pulse until it resembles coarse meal. While pulsing, add egg yolks and water. Process only until dough has formed a ball on top of the blade. Remove dough, divide into two balls, wrap and chill for at least a half hour or overnight. Can be made ahead and frozen.

Makes enough for one 10-inch double-crust pie.

Filling:
3 cups rhubarb, sliced ½ inch wide
2½ cups sliced strawberries
⅓ cup packed light brown sugar
⅓ cup granulated sugar
¼ cup cornstarch
¼ teaspoon salt
1 tablespoon orange juice
1 teaspoon orange zest
½ teaspoon pure vanilla extract
2 tablespoons unsalted butter, cut into small pieces
1 large egg, lightly beaten with 1 tablespoon milk
1 tablespoon raw turbinado sugar

Preheat oven to 400 degrees F.

Mix rhubarb, berries, sugars, cornstarch, salt, orange juice, zest, and vanilla extract together in a large bowl. Set aside.

On a floured work surface, roll out one ball of chilled dough (leave the other one in the refrigerator). Carefully place dough into pie dish, leaving slight overhang. Using a slotted spoon, place the filling into the crust. (Discard excess liquid in the bowl.) Dot the pieces of butter on top of filling.

Remove the other ball of chilled pie dough from the refrigerator and roll into a 12 inch circle. Cover the filling with top crust and cut slits in the top to form steam vents. Trim and crimp edges.

Lightly brush the top of the pie crust with the egg/milk mixture. Sprinkle the top with raw turbinado sugar.

Place the pie onto a large baking sheet and bake for 20 minutes. Turn the temperature down to 350 degrees F and bake for an additional 25–30 minutes. Cover with tin foil if top is browning too quickly.

Allow the pie to cool for 3 full hours at room temperature to allow filling to thicken, before serving.

From Abby's notebook:

> *In the Pacific Northwest, rhubarb can be harvested about every four to five weeks beginning in spring, once the stalks have reached 10–15 inches in height.*
>
> *To harvest rhubarb without damaging the rhizome beneath, stalks should be pulled out, not cut. Grip stalk firmly with index finger inside, at the base. Pull slowly but firmly while twisting as close to base as possible.*
>
> *Cut off the leaf, leaving a two to three inch "crowfoot" at the end to help retain moisture during storage.*

Abby's teaching station was all set up in the kitchen and she was awaiting the arrival of one guest, a woman named Lydia. She found the woman in the great room, standing at the window, looking out over the view to the ocean. The far-off breakers lent the water an image that, from this distance, undulated gently, like old lace, yellowed with age.

Lydia was thin, with silver hair and sad eyes. It wasn't her first visit, but they knew little of her, other than that she was from California, and that early retirement had given her the freedom to come and go as she pleased.

She had first stayed with them for a week over Christmas and spent most of her time either in the kennels or the stables. She spoke little, smiled less, and answered questions in such a way as to make clear that hers was a story not yet ready for the telling. Group activities were not her thing, and when she wasn't with the animals, she could be seen walking the lonely ridges and valleys surrounding Sanctuary Ranch, her head down, her shoulders hunched against the damp, her steps determined as if she had to either keep on or give up entirely and disappear.

Abby understood. They all understood, as a matter of fact. Everyone had secrets and the ranch was a place of safety, where one could start over and be something other than the person they'd been in whatever life they were escaping from.

This visit, Lydia had surprised them all by signing up for Abby's pie-making lesson. She'd ignored yoga, trail rides, vegetarian cooking, horsemanship 101, canine behavior, and Daphne's lesson in knife skills, but on her registration form checked off pie baking, with a note that read "as long as Abby's teaching it."

Daphne, who'd taught Abby everything she knew about pastry, was affronted. Abby was flattered, if slightly alarmed. It was a lot of pressure.

"I'm ready to start, Lydia." Abby spoke softly, not wanting to startle the woman. "There's an apron at the work-station and you can wash up at the sink first."

Lydia turned her gaze and stared at Abby, as if dragging her thoughts from someplace far, far away. Then she smiled. "Of course. Thank you."

Abby led Lydia to the lesson area just off the main kitchen. The others had already gathered and nearby, Daphne wielded a large utility knife on a hapless pile of carrots.

As Abby brushed past Daphne, the cook cut her eyes at them. "Have fun." She punctuated the comment with a vicious chop.

Abby elbowed her. "We will. This way, Lydia."

Lydia walked past Daphne without a word, and picked up the apron set out for her.

Abby stood in the center of the U-shaped island off the main kitchen and surveyed her students. Besides Lydia, there was a mother, forty-something, and her twenty-something daughter, here to bond over horses and good food. A fit, handsome older gentleman named George, rejoining life after a massive coronary. He appeared to have a crush on Bea, who was here for the third time. She had snow-white hair, perfect makeup, and could ride the toughest of their horses. Abby guessed she'd opened a bottle of wine before class.

Roman and Jon were at her left, sharing a spot. Abby looked at each of her students in turn as she spoke. But she couldn't tell if she was looking at Jon too much, or not enough. It was distracting, having him here.

But she'd asked for it, hadn't she?

"'Can she bake a cherry pie, Billy Boy, Billy Boy?'" sang Bea. "When I was a girl, cooking and baking and sewing and cleaning were all prerequisites to getting a husband. So I broke the iron, burned the bread, and spent every minute I could in the barn."

"And did you get a husband?" asked George, sitting next to her.

"Two," Bea answered, arching an eyebrow at him. "Plus an education, a career, and a couple of kids. Now that I'm finally going to be a grandma, I'm ready to get domestic. Plus, I love pie."

"What's not to love?" Abby said.

"The calories?" said Elena, the mother at the far end.

"Nope," said her daughter, nudging her in the ribs. "We'll work it all off in the saddle."

"Exactly," Abby confirmed. "We work hard in the fresh air, with nature and animals, and when we're done, we nourish our bodies with healthy, flavorful meals and a few indulgences for our souls."

She felt Jon's eyes on her and pulled her thoughts back to the lesson with difficulty. She hadn't expected to be so distracted by his presence.

"Fat is essential in making pastry," she said, holding up the container of shortening. "Pie dough is different from bread dough in that when you make bread, you want to develop the gluten into long strands, which you do by kneading. But flaky pie crust requires as little handling as possible. You want the bits of fat to be layered in the flour mixture, so that when it melts, it creates the crispy flaky layers we all love."

She dusted flour off her hands. "Too much handling breaks down the fat and makes the dough tough. The more you practice, the sooner you'll get a feel for the right balance."

"Balance is important," Roman said. "But if this is what you do for fun, you need to get out more."

A chuckle rippled through the group and Abby smiled. "I enjoy baking, Roman. It relaxes me."

Roman nudged Jon. "She needs help, son."

"Roman!" Abby's felt her face go crimson. She couldn't look at Jon and felt the rest of the class perk up with curiosity. "Let's get back to the lesson, shall we?"

"You two would make a cute couple," Bea said. "I vote with Roman."

"Definitely," George said, nodding at Roman. "You're clearly a man of great wisdom."

Roman laughed, a sound Abby wasn't sure she'd ever heard before. It rumbled up from his chest in deep, contagious bursts. She was losing control of the group and could feel Daphne watching behind her.

Desperately, she pulled up a series of photographs on her tablet. "We're going to use a species of apple known as Jonagold," she said, passing it to Lydia, who sat in the station nearest her. "It's a cross between a Jonathan and a Golden Delicious and we grow them in our orchard here on the ranch. Jonathans have a honeyed aroma and a sweet-sharp flavor profile that makes them wonderful for pies."

"Don't you mean Jona*golds*?" George corrected.

"Right." Abby gave her head a shake. "Jonagolds."

Bea leaned over the table sniffing in Jon's direction. "Do Jonathans smell like honey? I'd believe it."

"If we could get back on track—"

"Sweet-sharp, too," Bea said. "Nice."

"What about cake?" Roman asked. "Would they work in cake?"

"Um, I suppose so. Let's begin—"

"I like cake better than pie." Roman's voice had gone from bantering to vague. "Cakes flutter by. Fake butterflies."

Abby's bemusement evaporated. Something was wrong with Roman. He was altered, subtly, but certainly.

She poured a glass of water and brought it to him.

"Here, Roman, drink this."

He took it, drank it all down, and handed her the glass back. "Thank you, my dear."

"Is he all right?" Bea asked.

"He's fine." Jon squeezed Roman's shoulder. "Aren't you, Dad?"

Roman nodded, blinking. He was back, Abby saw, but confused and embarrassed.

She reached behind her for a plastic tote and plunked it on the counter. "We'll be using frozen presliced apples. Each bag contains the exact amount needed for this recipe. While they thaw, we'll make the pastry for our double-crust pie. It's a processor recipe, the easiest and most reliable recipe I've used."

She was speaking too quickly but she had to do something to get the attention off Roman. While the students gathered their bowls and spoons, Abby took a moment to catch her breath.

"You're very kind," Lydia said softly. "He's lucky to have you."

Abby plucked at her sleeve. "Not at all. Jon was looking after him."

Lydia's eyes softened. She touched Abby's hand. "I meant, Jon is lucky."


"Way to embarrass her, Dad."

He and Roman had brought the world's ugliest pie back home with them. But, as Abby promised, it tasted good, especially with vanilla ice cream.

"You needed a kick in the right direction. I don't know why you haven't asked her out yet."

"She was working nonstop on the festival when I got here, Dad. Spring is the start of the busy season on the ranch."

"What's the matter? Aren't you interested? You're not seeing someone else, are you?"

"Dad. Stop. Finish your pie. You're tired and I have work to do."

"Work, work, work. Life's wasted on the young," grumbled Roman. He snapped his fingers for Chaos to bring him his cane, then limped off to bed.

He'd barely eaten half of his dessert, Jon noticed. He wrapped the remainder of their hideous creation and put it in the fridge for tomorrow. Maybe he'd offer some to Abby, if she came by.

He smiled to himself. She'd find that amusing.

Jon hoped she hadn't really been embarrassed about Roman's teasing. In fact, he was planning to ask her out. But the timing had to be right.

He turned back to his laptop and his draft of the Arondi

story. He had several police reports, all eerily similar, but without witnesses, they all boiled down to he-said, she-said. One complainant, a Ms. Cassidy, had a witness whose identity was protected by the court and was known only as Person X. Without more, he was stuck.

Learning that Abby and Quinn had worked for the producer sent chills prickling the back of his neck. She'd assured Jon that neither she nor her sister had been a victim of Arondi's alleged bad behavior but something about the way she said it gnawed at his gut. She'd looked him in the eye when she'd said it, too. Without blinking.

The Warrens were perfect targets. Two sisters, alone in the world. Cash poor, hungry for experience, desperate for opportunities.

Jon couldn't imagine Abby letting her little sister be in any danger. Nor could he imagine her letting Arondi off the hook, if he'd hurt Quinn.

She was more likely to find him in a dark alley and slowly and carefully relieve him of his gonads.

She was hiding something.

He tapped his pencil against his chin, looking at the material he'd collected on the story.

Roman returned to the kitchen to get a glass of water. "What are you working on that's so important?"

Chaos stood by his side, watching with his ears cocked, as if he was expecting something.

"A story." Jon tossed the pencil down. "Don't know why I'm torturing myself about it. No one wants it."

"Whitey Irving hassling you about editorial?"

There was no love lost between Roman and Irving. After the Valdez Rocks accident, when Roman had most needed friends at his back, Irving had been one of the first people to cut all ties, dropping him like a rotten apple.

"You were right about him. He is an asshole." Jon dropped

his head into his hands, figuring he might as well get it over with. "He fired me."

He didn't have the guts to look at his father. Surely he'd have plenty to say and Roman wasn't one to reject an opportunity to crow.

But he was wrong.

A slow clap made him lift his head.

Roman was nodding while he applauded. "Good job, son."

"What do you mean?"

"You must have done something to piss him off," Roman said, "and if it pissed Whitey Irving off, then it was the right thing. You stood your ground. Am I wrong?"

Jon felt the skin around his temples loosen. A chuckle lit up his chest. He sat back in his chair, laughing. "You never fail to surprise me, Dad. You sure you're feeling okay?"

"What? I can't support my only son?"

"Oh," Jon said. "You can. Absolutely. Bring it on."

Roman wrinkled his nose. "All right. So maybe I've been critical in the past. Maybe it's time I changed that."

"You can't afford the whiplash."

"Don't be smart with me."

They were smiling at each other in an easy way Jon hadn't felt in a long time. Years, maybe.

"I was working on a story, a good one. About Richard Arondi."

"Ah." Roman's expression darkened. His jaw slid sideways. "Untouchable Richard. It was only a matter of time."

"Yeah, well, it's not time yet. Whitey killed the story. Absolutely refused to touch it." Jon exhaled. "I've got solid leads, Dad. The rumors have been whispered about forever. *Watch out for Richard, he's a groper. Don't let Richard get you in a corner. Ignore Richard, that's just how he talks.* He's a sexual predator, Dad. Has been for years, and no one will call him on it."

"No one but you."

The pride in Roman's voice made Jon's heart soar, only to land in a heap a moment later.

"I took my shot and I lost. Without the magazine behind me, no one else will talk to me. I promised my sources that if they went on record, we'd expose him, make sure he wouldn't be able to do this to anyone else, ever again. But they're all scared now. Arondi's goons have threatened them, shut them up, even paid some of them to keep quiet. Without them, I've got nothing."

The quiet in the house was broken by a soft whine from Chaos.

Jon looked over.

"Dad?"

Roman's head bobbed. His hand twitched. The water glass near his hand tipped and crashed onto the floor.

Chaos barked.

"Dad?" He jumped to his feet and ran to Roman's side.

Roman's head lurched sideways. He muttered a curse. "I'm fine, Jon."

"What the hell was that? Are you okay?"

"It was nothing. I dropped my glass. I'm tired. Help me to my room. And bring my pills. The ones in the blue vial."

As Jon helped his father down the hallway, he wondered if he'd overreacted. Roman seemed annoyed. Embarrassed.

He wiped up the water and went to the side table in the front room, which held Roman's assortment of pills, ointments, and tissues.

He looked at the vials. Anti-inflammatories. Antacids to protect his stomach. Muscle relaxants. Tylenol with codeine. Topical pain reliever gel. All the accoutrements of chronic pain.

He picked up the blue container.

Valproic acid. He didn't recognize that one. According to the date, it was a new prescription.

He brought the pills to his father's room but the man was already snoring gently.

Jon went back to his laptop and looked up the drug.

Valproic acid was an anticonvulsant.

Why the hell was his father on an antiseizure medication?

# Chapter Thirteen

From Abby's notebook:

> *Manage weeds while they are small and actively growing. Once the weed has gone to bud, control will be much more difficult.*

Abby hadn't seen Quinn since sending her to gather vegetables for Daphne to make supper, thirty minutes ago.

Quinn was supposed to come back to finish weeding, but she didn't share Abby's joy in the garden.

She shut off the rototiller, straightened up, and surveyed the muddy strip of earth before her. On either side, and in parallel lines throughout the garden, tiny green shoots from seeds and cuttings and corms and tubers were bursting through the rich soil. Every year it was a miracle to her that such small, ugly, broken things once buried, would transform into beauty and nourishment and life itself.

As the engine rattled to a stop and silence descended, she lifted her chin, closed her eyes, and let the fecund fragrances of compost, manure, and leaf mold tickle her lungs, pushing past the tightness in her chest.

She stretched her arms above her head, tilting from side to side to work the kinks out of her spine. Shoveling shit wasn't for everyone but it sure beat some of the other jobs she'd had.

She'd enjoyed the garden hop more than expected, but still, it was a relief to be able to work in silence again.

She hauled the tiller over to the shed and went to the southwest-facing slope to check the greenhouse and cold frames. It was too early for new outdoor vegetables, but with the protection of glass and a little extra tender loving care, the ranch had fresh, home-grown produce almost year-round now.

As she feared, the basket sat near the door, filled with wilting beets and Swiss chard greens and crisp, crinkled kale. Her sister was nowhere in sight.

"Quinn?" Her sister had been quieter than usual lately. Even the prospect of her upcoming birthday party didn't seem to excite her. But it wasn't like her to forget her chores.

Quickly, she took the basket to the main house where Daphne stood at the door, her hands on her hips.

"I was about to send out a search party." The cook narrowed her eyes at Abby. "You okay? You look pale. I keep telling you to let Ezra do the heavy work."

"Sorry to keep you waiting." Abby handed the basket without making eye contact and busied herself brushing dirt from her jeans. Daphne's mothering instincts were strong and she had a knack for picking up when someone was troubled.

But Abby had long years of experience keeping her troubles to herself. Pretending was a survival skill and she'd honed it to a razor-sharp edge. She skipped off the porch, tossing a wave over her shoulder.

"Dinner's in an hour," the cook called. "Tell that skinny sister of yours I made her favorite for dessert, lemon meringue pie."

"I will," Abby promised.

She strode past the kennels, where the sound of voices and dogs barking told her a class was being held, angled around the corral, where Gideon was trotting a palomino stallion on a long line, and ducked into the first horse barn.

Sometimes Quinn liked to hide out with the rescue horses.

She blinked as her eyes adjusted to the dim lighting. Rustling and snorting sounded as curious horses poked their heads over stall doors.

"Quinn?" She kept her voice low. "It's almost suppertime. I brought the veggies in for you."

She walked from stall to stall, peering into the corners, stroking the velvety noses of the animals willing to accept human touch, keeping her distance from those that weren't.

She came to Quinn's favorite hideout, the stall where Apollo, an enormous and gentle draft horse, was housed when he wasn't outside. She lifted the latch, stepped inside, and yelped as she nearly ran into a broad chest that most definitely did not belong to her sister. She stumbled backward into the rough wooden planking behind her.

The horse snorted and tossed his dappled gray head.

"Whoa," said Jon, taking her elbow. "Didn't mean to startle you."

"Hey, Jon." She ducked sideways, pulling her arm away, her heart thumping inside her chest. "I wasn't expecting you."

Jon followed her out, closing the stall door behind them. "So I gathered. Do you want to try again? I suggest, 'Hey, Jon, nice to see you.' Or better yet, 'Just the man I was looking for.'"

His flirting was almost as disconcerting as the warmth she felt coming off his body, too near her for comfort.

"I'm looking for Quinn." She shivered, tugging her men's flannel work shirt tighter over her thin T-shirt. "Have you seen her?"

He shook his head. "Sorry. I'm looking for Dad. I brought

him to visit Apollo and now he's gone. Shall we search for them together? He needs to get home."

Abby's mouth opened to reject his offer, but no handy excuse came to her lips. Every time she was with Jon, she felt like more of a fraud. But he was a difficult man to resist.

She exhaled softly. "Okay."

They finished looking through the rest of the stalls without success. As they made their way back to the door, Jon stopped to give the big draft horse's broad Roman nose one last pat.

"So Quinn loves Apollo, too, does she? Dad adores that horse."

Abby knew that the animal had arrived at the ranch in a desperate state, his hip bones poking high above his rib-racked body, with horribly overgrown hooves, dull blank eyes, and a heartbreaking acceptance of his fate.

Love and care had returned him to vibrant health and brought out his sweet temperament. Now, Apollo earned his oats by letting people like Jon's father visit.

"Apollo's special," Abby said.

Jon touched her arm. "I have a question for you. It's about one of Dad's medications. Valproic acid. I've looked it up. It's an anticonvulsant. Do you know why he's on it?"

Abby put her head closer to the big horse's broad cheek, breathing in his clean, animal smell. "Have you asked him?" she said, buying time.

"He doesn't know. Or if he does, he won't tell me. He's on a lot of medications and I'm worried that some of his symptoms are due to drug interactions."

Dread filled her. "What kind of symptoms?"

"His hands tremble so badly sometimes that he can't hold a glass. He gets headaches. He doesn't think I know, but I see him massaging his temples. On sunny days, the light hurts his eyes. And"—he cleared his throat—"he's losing words."

All signs that the tumor was progressing.

"Have you looked up those signs?" she asked. Research was his thing, after all. Perhaps she could lead him to the answer he sought.

Jon made a frustrated sound. "Of course. It's used to treat mania in bipolar patients and to prevent migraines, but mostly, for seizure disorders. As far as I know, my dad isn't epileptic or bipolar, but when I asked him about his headaches, he said they were no big deal. I'm worried he's got dementia and doesn't want me to know."

"What do the doctors say?"

"Dad won't let me come into his appointments with him."

*Oh, Roman.*

She swallowed. She was going to have to betray Roman's confidence soon, if he didn't tell Jon the truth himself. "I'm coming over tonight. Do you want me to talk to him then?"

"Please," Jon said with relief. "He trusts you more than he does me. He's hiding something and it's starting to worry me."

As they left the barn, Chaos loped up to them, tongue hanging out, tail wagging. Jon looked over to his car, where Roman was sitting, waiting for him.

Jon rolled his eyes. "I guess I found my missing person. I should have known. There's a special on CNN he wanted to watch and his DVR doesn't work. We'd better hurry."

Abby waved at them and continued on to the kennels. Quinn wasn't there, but Jamie was.

"Yeah, she's in Haylee's old cabin, babysitting."

Sage used to live in the main house, but when Haylee moved into town with Aiden, she'd leaped on the chance to have more space for her growing child.

"Babysitting?"

Jamie shrugged. "Haylee's out with the therapy dogs and Sage had a class or something."

She found Quinn sitting cross-legged on the floor of the cabin, surrounded by a sea of multicolored toys of every description. Drooling on her lap was Haylee and Aiden's son, Matthew. Beside them, little Sal, Sage's daughter and Haylee's granddaughter, waded through the toys on plump little legs.

Jewel stretched out on the carpet in front of the window, snoring gently. Karma, Sage's dog, watched them from a safe distance.

"Hey," Abby said. "This looks like fun."

"Aren't they adorable?" Quinn bent down and bussed a raspberry into Matthew's golden curls. The little boy squealed with laughter. Sal pitched a green wooden block into the air and clapped when it landed with a clatter that made the old dog lift her grizzled head.

"Ju-Ju!" she chortled.

Karma's tail thumped the floor. Jewel blinked sleepily, then went back to her nap.

"What, um, is going on?" Quinn hadn't babysat so much as a goldfish in her life. "You forgot to bring the veggies to Daphne."

"Oh, geez." Quinn brought both hands to her mouth. "I'm so sorry. Sage sent me a nine-one-one text. She didn't realize that an exam of hers had been shifted so she had to run into town."

"It's okay. I brought the veggies in. Since when do you babysit?"

Sage and Haylee juggled childcare between them, but with Olivia and Daphne hovering in the wings and Aiden complaining that he needed an appointment to spend time with his son, babysitting was rarely a problem. Even Huck, the quiet wrangler, had formed a bond with Sal, though Abby guessed his crush on Sage had something to do with that.

"I like it. Kids are fun. I think it's so cool, Sage and Haylee raising babies together, even though they're mother and daughter. Mattie and Sal are so good together, too. Watch." She planted Matthew on his diapered bottom and handed a soft airplane-shaped toy to Sal. The family dynamics were complicated in the Hansen clan. But then again, what family wasn't complicated?

Sal lifted the toy above her head.

"Zoom, zoom," she said in her little piping voice.

She zoomed the toy past Matthew's head. The little boy giggled until he started hiccuping.

It was so sweet, Abby couldn't help but smile.

"Okay. Well, Daphne said to tell you she's making lemon meringue pie tonight. Don't be late."

Quinn checked her phone. "Sage is ten minutes out, so tell Daffy I'll be there soon to set the tables."

Abby walked back to the lodge, wondering how she'd missed this about her sister. Quinn looked like she enjoyed hanging with the babies a lot more than she did cleaning rooms or helping in the garden. Perhaps her worries were unfounded. Maybe Quinn wasn't restless. Maybe she wasn't revisiting things in the past and dredging up old memories that were better left alone.

Maybe she just needed to do something different for a change.

Jon lowered himself into the molded plastic chair in the editorial office of the *Sunset Bay Chronicle,* the publication that had printed his piece about the ranch, waiting for an interview.

The piece on Arondi still kept him awake at night, with Abby's cryptic comments fueling his fire, but without a break, he was stuck. In the meantime, he needed work. This would do as well as any.

He squirmed, feeling the rivets in his jeans digging into his butt. It was as if some designer had decided that the aesthetically repulsive chemical orange color wasn't enough, these ubiquitous chairs also had to provide crippling discomfort.

Ambrose Elliott, editorial director, managing editor, and chief reporter of the *Sunset Bay Chronicle,* lumbered back into his office, dropped into his swivel chair, and poked his finger onto the clipboard that sat among the clutter like a talisman against technological advancement, full of ink jottings that only he could read.

"So you want to string for me," he said, looking over the tops of his glasses at Jon.

"If you're interested." Jon scrunched his cheeks, hoping it looked like a smile. "Since I'm here, anyway."

The Sanctuary Ranch piece had come out before Elliott had heard the scuttlebutt about Jon. He now wore the expression of someone who'd just discovered that the used car his grandmother had given him was actually a vintage Mustang fastback.

And that she'd had it painted pink.

"I might be able to throw something your way," he said.

"Happy to contribute. It's a good paper."

Elliott wrote almost everything himself. This was his chance to get reliable content for a killer deal. Jon waited.

"As you know," the editor said finally, "we live and die by advertising. These days, since everyone reads on their phones, it's more die than live but we're still hanging in there. Advertisers rely on readers, and even if people don't read the way they used to, they still go out to eat."

Here it comes, thought Jon.

"Our annual restaurant round-up edition is coming up. I need a list of the best restaurants along the 101, your experience, comments from the owners, photos. I've collected a few dozen already but we need another twenty or so before the deadline. Fast food, slow food, food trucks, truck stops. Eateries, diners, coffee shops, everything from upscale trendy cuisine to local hole-in-the wall treasures. It's on the magazine's dime, so the more the better. Any questions?"

"Seems straightforward." Jon tried to look enthusiastic. "Restaurants along the coast highway. Got it."

"Think you can stick to that?"

Jon knew what he was asking. "No looking for a deeper story, no delving into anyone's secret past, no making this something it isn't. I got it."

This little publication, with its town council meetings and rezoning proposals and full-page ads for hardware store sales, was the best he could get now, thanks to Whitey Irving.

"It'll be fun." He gave Elliott his best, and most grateful, smile.

"That's the attitude I'm looking for." Elliott's expression softened. "I was idealistic once, too. But reality pays the mortgage, kid. Fact is, you blew it with *Diversion*. You had a sweet plum of a job and you had to go all Joseph Pulitzer on their asses before you had the chops to back it. Your heart was in the right place but you pissed off the wrong people. Actually you pissed off all the people. And for what?"

For the truth, Jon wanted to say.

For the kind of story that kept him thinking into the wee hours, digging, digging, asking the next question and the next, knowing that he was on the brink of something monumental, something that would create change, real change. Important change.

He'd gotten a glimpse behind the heavy dark curtain of the film industry, and the scared, broke, desperate actors willing to do anything for a break and learning too late that the price of a soul wasn't nearly enough for the fame they sought. Jon had names, dates, details, broken hearts, crushed dreams, and most of all, the man who thought he was untouchable.

But none of the people he'd talked to wanted to throw the first stone. If only he'd waited.

"I like you, kid. So just write the stuff I ask for, okay?"

Elliott leaned back, causing his chair to make an ominous creaking sound. "We're not making history, we're not winning any awards here, but it keeps us fed."

Jon had gotten into this business to make the world a better place, to tell the stories for those who could not speak for themselves. To seek the truth beneath all the dross and shine a spotlight on it, with words.

"Yes, sir," he said. "101 Eats. You got it."

"And there's your title." The desk phone rang and Elliott reached for it. "Bring a friend, and try not to look like a reporter, okay?"

Jon left the office. Restaurant reviews were hardly his thing. But they did provide him with a perfect opportunity.

The neon sign blinked like a lazy eye above the doorway of their lunch destination. The awning had streaks of rust and mold running through it. A sign in the window proclaimed their chili-cheese fries THE BEST IN THE WORLD.

"This is a contender?" Abby said. "I don't think I brought enough hand sanitizer."

"Do I know how to treat a lady or what?" Jon pulled the door open, making the bells above it jingle. "I've heard the chili fries actually are pretty good. After everything you've done for me and my dad, it's the least I can do."

A round-faced man in a stained white apron greeted them with open arms and a huge smile. "Welcome to Mario's Grill. I am Mario. Please, have a seat wherever you like. Julia will be by with menus for you right away. Julia!" he shouted over his shoulder.

They chose a booth next to the window. The dark wood table was clean and red leather upholstered seats surprisingly comfortable. Their server, a young woman with long dark hair, had a striking resemblance to the proprietor. Jon ordered the chili-cheese fries, a beer, and a share plate of the house special appetizers. Abby ordered a taco salad and a bottle of water.

"You don't owe me anything, Jon."

"You're doing me the favor." Jon leaned back and pulled out his notepad. "If this was a date, I'd pick a better spot."

"But it's not, so I can't complain. Is that it?"

He grinned. "Smart and pretty. It's a devastating combination."

She shouldn't be here like this, pretending everything was fine. But Roman had practically pushed her out the door. He'd lost weight in the past month, she thought. He still steadfastly refused to tell Jon anything more. Not while he still felt good, he insisted. This was their time to be together. Once Jon knew, everything would change.

Julia appeared with their drinks and the share plate. As soon as she left, Abby leaned forward, pointing to a half-dozen items on the platter. "Bacon-wrapped dill pickles?"

"Yup," he said, putting one on her plate. "You have to try them to believe them."

She stabbed it with her fork and moved it to his plate. "How about you try them and I'll take your word for it?"

"Why, Abby Warren," Jon said. "Where's your spirit of adventure?"

"I left it at the ranch. Where people eat normal food."

A calculating look entered his eye. "I dare you."

"Oh yeah?" She sat back and crossed her arms. "What's in it for me?"

Heat sizzled between them. When had she last enjoyed flirting with a man? She ought to know better, she ought to keep things simple, but she hadn't laughed like this in a long time. Life bubbled in her cells when she was with him and she didn't want it to end.

"You eat that dill pickle," Jon said slowly, keeping his gaze on hers, "and I'll . . . I'll let you in on a secret."

For a harrowing second she thought he'd figured out

about Roman. Then she realized that he wouldn't be teasing her with it, if that were the case.

He *was* teasing.

And she liked it.

The air thickened.

"Oh yeah? What secret?"

"If I told you now, you'd be robbed of the pleasure of culinary experimentation."

He held the pickle toward her on the end of his fork. She leaned forward, took a bite, then sat back, chewed, and swallowed.

"Huh," she said after a moment. "It's actually not bad."

She took his fork from him and ate the rest of the appetizer, the way she would a corn dog.

He watched, his eyes warm with amusement. "Not exactly the sound byte Ambrose Elliott is looking for, but I'm happy to be part of expanding your comfort zone."

"So what's this big secret?" She hoped she'd achieved the right casual tone.

He chose a stuffed mushroom, popped it into his mouth, chewed, and swallowed.

Julia brought the rest of their order right then and for a few minutes, they busied themselves with that.

Then, in a hushed tone, he said, "I'm still working on the Arondi story."

"What?" She hadn't expected that. "I thought you'd hit a dead end. And well . . . That no one wanted it."

Excitement gleamed in his eyes. "Yes, to both. But a contact of mine sent me a police report. It's the lead I've been looking for, Abby. There's an unidentified witness, a Person X. If I can find this person, she might be able to convince the victim to go public. Once I've got that, it's done. Arondi is toast. I'll be about to name my price."

Her appetite disappeared. She chased a cherry tomato

around her taco bowl, hoping Jon wouldn't notice her hand shaking.

He was too close for comfort.

She forced a smile. "That's great, Jon."

Jon looked at her salad. "You don't like your food?"

"It's fine."

The old Abby would have left it at that. She'd have kept her distance. But Jon triggered an unexpected desire to let him inside the barriers she'd built. She wanted to trust him. She wanted him to know that there were reasons she kept herself and her past private, reasons she and Quinn had arrived and stayed in this place as they had.

"I admire how you look after your dad," she told him, changing the subject. She couldn't talk about Arondi, but she couldn't shut Jon out completely.

He observed her for a few moments without responding. Then he sighed.

"Who else is going to do it? My mom remarried as soon as the divorce was finalized, has the life she always wanted— a new husband, a couple of kids, a life that doesn't include Hollywood scandals and lawsuits and medical bills."

"I'm not the only one with a past, then."

"Everyone has a past, Abby." His gaze softened. "How bad can it be?"

"Don't ask."

He reached across the table and touched her chin with the knuckle of his index finger, ever so lightly.

Wouldn't it be lovely if he really did want to know the real her? For a moment, she allowed herself to hope. He was a good guy, one of the few, rare, stand-up men she'd come across. He looked after his dad, a champion for the underdog, young, strong, handsome. Wouldn't it be lovely to share her burdens for once in her life? To have someone else by her side, someone she could trust?

She wanted to see the light of caring glow deeper in his eyes, instead of the hurt and betrayal she knew was coming.

She knew the risk. But the wanting, once begun, wouldn't stop.

"What did I say, Abby?" Jon asked. "Is it about the story? You said I should pursue it."

Yeah, but that was before she thought he could actually connect the dots.

"Sorry," she said. "I've got a lot on my mind."

Quinn's secret was safe. But each day that went on, Roman's secret weighed more heavily on her. She wanted to tell Jon, argued with herself that she owed it to him to reveal the truth.

"That sounds like an invitation." Jon put a twice-baked potato skin onto her plate. He arranged a few other items beside it, speaking without looking at her. "Do you want me to guess?"

The levity was gone from his voice.

"Not really," she said. "It's nothing. I'm not that interesting, Jon."

"That's where you're wrong." He ran his eyes over her face. "You've had a lot more to deal with, haven't you, Abby? You're a natural caregiver."

"I didn't have much choice." She wrinkled her nose. "That didn't sound right. I love my sister. I didn't resent having to look after her."

Jon lifted his glass. "Cheers to you, then. Most teenagers would have hated having a bratty kid sister cramping their style."

Okay, yeah, she felt that from time to time. She'd wanted to do things, join clubs, go out with friends.

"There was no time or money for me to do the usual teenage things. That was hardly Quinn's fault."

That was Rebecca's fault. She clamped her lips shut.

"Abby," Jon said. "How old were you when you lost your mother?"

She toyed with the food on her plate. Then she looked up and met his gaze straight on. "Almost eighteen. And before you start feeling sorry for me, we managed just fine. It took a little juggling, a little creative budgeting but I already knew how to get by on a shoestring. I put on my big girl panties and did what I had to."

Jon lifted an eyebrow. "But we have a system in place to help families like yours."

"We had a child advocate. She had so many cases worse than ours. She was happy to rubber-stamp us."

"And no one else stepped in? What about Quinn's teachers?"

The last move had meant she and Quinn had to start over in a new school district too, and not a better one. And it was senior year, the worst time to be the new kid. Unless you were in elementary school and crippled with anxiety, like Quinn.

But she shrugged the memories away. "We had good teachers, but if they got involved in every student's life, they'd never get through the curriculum. Drugs, gangs, weapons, teen pregnancy, suicides. They had enough to deal with already. Quinn and I weren't on their radar."

Jon shook his head. "That's just sad."

She saw wheels turning in his head, and it made her mad. "I'm not a victim, Jon. Neither of us are victims. We triumphed, okay? It could have been worse."

She turned away before revealing more. It was so easy to talk to him. It had been a long time since anyone other than Olivia and Haylee had peered into the murky past that had brought her and Quinn to Sanctuary Ranch. They'd done background checks to be certain that neither of them represented a risk to the well-being of the ranch or ranch guests. Abby had been honest about everything, how she'd kept body and soul together in those early years after Rebecca had disappeared. Quinn's drinking and especially her bouts with depression had been a concern but ultimately, they'd been welcomed, by everyone. No pity, no judgment, no censure. Just acceptance.

"You don't think being with foster parents would have been better?"

"I was almost eighteen. We'd probably have been put into a halfway house with kids who all had worse problems than us and fewer coping skills. They'd have taken one look at Quinn and seen a target. Foster kids learn early that the only way to survive is to be tougher than those around you. Ask Jamie. She knows. But that's not why I made sure no one knew about us." A tendon in her neck jumped and she tucked her chin, hoping Jon hadn't noticed. She never talked about this stuff but there was something about him that inspired confidence.

"You didn't want to be separated."

She looked up, startled, and felt a flush rise in her cheeks. "Maybe it was selfish. Maybe Quinn would have been better off with a good family. She didn't have much of a childhood. I've had so many jobs." She was exhausted, thinking about them. "I always told myself it was worth it because we stayed together. But Quinn spent a lot of time alone, watching TV with the door locked."

Second-guessing her choices now would only end in madness. Sure, she'd made mistakes. They'd been kids. But she'd done the best she could.

"The system failed you."

"The system works just fine in some cases. Maybe it would have worked for us. I'll never know. But on the whole, we were lucky, Jon. We didn't end up on the streets. We're not victims. Okay?"

"Hey, don't get me wrong. I admire you. You shouldered way more responsibility than you should have and you did a great job." He hesitated, as if knowing he was stepping through a minefield. "But what I'm most amazed with is your attitude. You could be jaded and hardened and bitter but you're not. Sure, you have worries. We all do. But underneath that, you're generous and kind with a deep sense of optimism and hope. Of faith in the future."

She couldn't look away. His words were like magic, weaving a tapestry around her, of what her life might be, rather than what it actually was.

"Beautiful fiction," she murmured.

He lifted a finger. "No. I write nonfiction, remember? I seek the truth. It's what I live for. Though I take beauty when I can get it. Right now, for instance."

She knew she should stop him, correct this rosy version he had of her, before he learned for himself how wrong it was. But she had no words. Jon had stolen them from her.

"I've seen you work in the garden. You take something small and shriveled, hide it in the dirt and wait, believing that out of the manure and mud will come something beautiful. What is that, if not optimism and hope? Same thing when you're baking. You take ingredients that are okay on their own, flour and buttermilk and whatnot, but then you add your magic, and this delicious miracle happens. Creativity is hope, Abby. I love that about you."

*I love that about you.*

"Stop." She sucked in a deep, shaky breath. "You're seeing things the way you want to see them, rather than how they are. I'm not a good person, Jon. I'm selfish and . . . dishonest."

He was a man who valued truth above all else.

"About what, Abby? About how you feel about me? There's something starting here. Am I wrong?" His eyes were solemn and in their depths, she thought she saw a glimpse of the little boy he'd once been.

"I don't know." She could hardly breathe. "I think so."

*I love that about you.*

Tell him about Roman, a voice whispered in her head. Tell him now.

But she couldn't do it. It wasn't her secret to tell.

"You take good care of everyone, Abby." His voice was like a caress, soft, sweet, irresistible. "But who takes care of you?"

She didn't need anyone. She'd never needed anyone.

But the thought of letting down her guard, letting someone else in, letting Jon in, was becoming a temptation she couldn't resist.

When they walked out of the restaurant at the end of their meals, their hands brushed against each other. When Abby curled her fingers around his, it felt completely natural.

It felt perfect.

# Chapter Fourteen

The next morning Roman was grouchy. He said he wanted a decent piece of toast and only Daphne's bread would do. He sent Jon to Sanctuary Ranch to beg a loaf and Jon couldn't get away fast enough.

He couldn't wait to see Abby again.

He found her in the lodge sunroom, clicking through screens on her laptop. Bright light streamed in the window but the temperature outside was chilly and the heat from the fireplace felt great on his back.

She directed him to the walk-in freezer, where Daphne in her prescience had already put aside a couple of loaves of her honey whole-wheat bread for Roman.

That task accomplished, he asked, "What's all this?"

In addition to her laptop, she had several recipe books strewn around her and a clipboard of notes, lists, and doodles.

Abby tucked the pen behind her ear. "Research. I told Daphne I'd find her more recipes for healthy baked goods. Olivia wants to accommodate people who want their treats to have more nutritional value."

"Don't tell me that means the end of Daphne's cinnamon buns?"

Abby laughed. "There'd be riots in the street if that

happened. No, we'll always have those." She shoved aside the books and moved over to make room for him. "How's your dad?"

The cushion was warm from her body and he stretched out so his leg touched hers. He wanted more than that, but for now it would have to do.

"Grumpy as a bear with a sore head. I told him he could come along and visit the horse but he said he'd enjoy the peace and quiet with me out of the house."

"You don't seem noisy to me," Abby said. "But I probably only see you on your best behavior."

"Definitely. Though maybe that should change." He shifted closer to her. "Maybe I ought to show you my bad behavior."

Abby wrinkled her nose. "Or maybe you should remember that there are people everywhere and that they could walk in on us at any moment. Do you want me to come visit Roman this afternoon? See if I can cheer him up? I'm more fun than you. You have to admit that."

"Fun and pretty. I'm no competition." He smiled. He was glad his father enjoyed Abby's company, and grateful that Abby was willing to spend time with him.

He nodded toward the material spread out around her. She had made notes about the effects of various nutrients on diabetes and heart disease and had drawn a complicated diagram using scientific notation. "What's that?"

"It's a schematic showing the biochemical process of sugar metabolism in the body." She rolled her eyes. "I kind of fell down an Internet rabbit hole. I always loved biology."

"Were you a science major?" The question was out before he remembered that she'd put Quinn's education before her own.

"College wasn't in the cards for me." Abby closed her laptop and ran her palms over the smooth surface as if to wipe it clean. "But with all the open source material out there these days, if you've got access to a computer, you can learn almost anything. I like learning. Solving mysteries, researching how things work."

"You and I have a lot in common, then."

That made her turn and look at him. "I dabble, for fun. That's all."

"Studying the Krebs cycle in your spare time is more than dabbling. Research is research."

"I don't sleep a lot." She shrugged off the compliment. "This makes the time pass productively."

She said it lightly, but he wondered if her insomnia was related to the perpetual air of watchfulness that surrounded her.

"Classic first-born overachiever stuff," Jon said. "I'm an only child so I get it."

"Did you always want to be a magazine writer?" she asked.

The question stopped him cold. Is that what he was? A magazine writer? There was nothing wrong with that, but is that what he'd envisioned for his career, back when he was starting out?

"A guidance counselor once told me," he said slowly, "that there are only two qualities necessary to become an investigative journalist. First of all, a need to ask, 'Why?' All the time. Which I had in spades."

Abby smiled. "A perpetual four-year-old. Your poor parents. What's the second quality?"

Jon hesitated, wishing now that he hadn't brought it up. "A burning desire to change what's wrong in society."

Had he ruined his one chance at fulfilling his life's purpose? Would he forever be writing about the best places to eat chili fries and which soccer team won the regional championship?

At *Diversion,* he'd been focused on making a name for himself, building his portfolio. The story about Richard

Arondi had ticked all his boxes, made him feel alive, like he was doing what he was put on this earth to do.

She didn't respond. A loop of silky hair slipped across her face, hiding her expression.

"Lofty goals," she said quietly. "I admire you."

"Abby." He captured her hand between his and patted it. "My copy ends up on the bottom of bird cages."

She didn't pull away. "Maybe it's not your time to change the world yet. That's a lot of pressure to live under every single day. Jesus and Gandhi and Mother Teresa probably had weeks on end where they were just putting one step in front of the other. You have talent and skill. And you never know when the thing you're writing will end up changing someone's life."

"Pretty sure my restaurant reviews aren't going to change anyone's life."

"You don't know that," she insisted, squeezing his hand. "What if there's a struggling diner owner out there, with four kids and a sick wife and he's so broke he has to choose between buying her medicine or shoes for the baby . . . ?"

"You listened to a lot of country music growing up, didn't you?"

Abby ignored him. "Business is going downhill and he doesn't have money for advertising. He's just a great short order cook who makes the best grilled cheese sandwich in the world, no, the universe, but nobody comes into his place because there's a brand-new fast food franchise down the block. Two dollar cheeseburgers are killing homemade sourdough bread and melted Gruyère and taking a man's soul with it."

She leaned forward, looking at him earnestly. Her eyes shone. "Then one day, a tall handsome journalist comes in. He sits down and orders that grilled cheese sandwich. He's kind of bored because he's supertalented—"

Jon couldn't help but laugh.

"—and this job is beneath him but he's a good soldier and this is his assignment, so he's going to do it to the best of his ability."

Abby lifted her palm through the air, as if painting the picture in her mind. "He sees the photos on the wall, asks the owner about his kids, the history of the place, why they chose this location, what's special about their town. The owner, or maybe his teenage daughter, who works with him because it's a family place, brings the meal out to the journalist. He takes a bite and oh my God. It's the best thing he's ever tasted."

Her expression was radiant with sensual delight.

"He compliments the man, thanks the daughter, takes a couple of pictures, goes home, and writes his piece. He puts in the details about the family, their love of the town, and the food they make. He describes the sandwich, the crispy grilled crust, texture and tang of the bread, the way the cheese oozes out the side. He adds how, every year, when she's well enough, the owner's wife puts up jars and jars of the cranberry marmalade they serve with the sandwich."

Jon couldn't help but smile. "You've put a lot of thought into this."

"Shh. I'm on a roll." She tapped their clasped hands against his thigh. "The paper comes out, with a photo of the man and his daughter standing at the front door, grinning and pointing up at their sign. A day or two later, business is up. People have read the piece and they're curious about this out-of-the-way diner they've driven past but never stopped at. Everyone wants to try this amazing grilled cheese sandwich they've heard so much about. He sells out that day. He stays up all night baking more sourdough so he's ready for the next day. He has to send the daughter out for more cheese. His wife gets her medicine. The baby gets his shoes.

The daughter who was waitressing gets a scholarship to medical school and, because they can afford to hire staff now, she becomes a doctor and finds the cure to her mother's disease. That, my friend"—she poked him in the chest with her index finger—"is changing the world. And it happened because a tall, handsome, extremely talented journalist did his job even though it didn't seem very important."

He'd never seen her like this. Her cheeks were flushed, her posture easy and eager. At this moment, there was nothing closed off or careful about her. He realized that for a few minutes, she'd been completely unselfconscious. But as he watched, she seemed to come back to reality. She pulled her hand out of his and shifted slightly away from him.

She gave a little laugh. "Oops. I kind of went off on you, didn't I?"

"You did," he said.

"Sorry. I do that sometimes." She started to get up but he recaptured her hand and pulled her toward him again.

"Don't apologize. That's the best story I've heard in, maybe ever. Abby, I've listened to career counselors and motivational speakers, I've read self-help trade journals on how to avoid burnout. But nobody has ever told me anything like that."

The power of her speech, her own belief in him, made him think that maybe he could still achieve the dreams that had once driven him.

"I never stopped asking why," he said softly. "But somewhere along the way, I stopped believing that I could change the world."

Her eyes shimmered. "Little things really do make a difference, Jon. You'll probably never know the many ways your words have impacted people. You're so lucky to be able to influence people like you do."

She was so close, looking up at him with those luminous

eyes that without thinking, he leaned over, let his eyes drift shut, and touched his lips to hers.

The kiss was electric, with every nerve of his body trained on the small, sensitive point of contact. He heard her quick intake of breath, but she didn't pull away. Her lips softened under his. So pliant, so warm. So delicious.

She twisted her fingers, twining them around his, first stroking his palm with her thumb, then threading them through his and holding tightly again.

He increased the pressure, touching his tongue to her bottom lip. She opened, tasting of fresh water and strawberries.

He found the back of her head and cupped it lightly, pulling her nearer. Her hair was like silk, spilling over his wrist.

He could have sat there for hours like that, holding her, kissing her, feeling the warmth of her body next to his, drinking in the delicacy of her scent.

But the sound of footsteps intruded into his consciousness. "Abby?"

Abby jerked away and put her hand to her mouth. "Quinn."

Jon blinked, unwilling to let the moment go.

"Where've you been?" Quinn frowned, looking between the two of them. "Jamie's waiting for us."

Abby leaped to her feet. "Sorry, I got carried away. With my work."

"Whatever."

"Hi, Quinn," Jon said.

"Hey." The younger woman slouched, one thin hip jutting forward, her hair falling over the blades of her cheekbones.

"I have to go." Abby gathered her books and notes together without making eye contact with Jon. "Quinn and I are joining Jamie on a school visit tomorrow. She wants to tell us what to do and say, in case we have to take over for her one day. She and Gideon have plans to . . . Oh, never mind."

Her discomfiture was more than embarrassment at being caught necking.

"You're coming to see Dad later, right?"

"Right, yes. Thanks for . . . um." She squeezed her eyes shut. "I'll see you later."

After that kiss, he thought, you better believe it.

# Chapter Fifteen

Since that first meal at the diner, Abby had begun to loosen up around him. The hand-holding had been like lighting a match to dry paper. Jon had to clench his fists to keep from pulling her into his arms every time she got within range. Every time he helped her off with her jacket, he let his fingers graze her shoulders. When she preceded him through a door, he put his palm on the small of her back, aching to feel those firm curves without the barrier of clothing, breathing in the light fragrance of outdoors that he now associated with her.

She'd unburdened herself to him in a way he hadn't expected and he sensed that he needed to back off, to give her lightness and fun.

And thanks to Ambrose Elliott and 101 Eats they were having that.

"Look!" She gripped his arm and pointed. She was standing close enough that he could feel the outline of her breasts against his arm. Did she have any idea what that was doing to him?

He forced his attention to follow hers. "Saltwater taffy?"

She gave him a cheeky grin that made the apples of her cheeks rise. "You could use a dose, couldn't you?"

Sweet and decadent.

Jon had a craving of his own but he was pretty sure he'd have to wait a while longer.

She poked him and tried to duck away but he caught the back of her jacket and pulled her close, trapping her arms behind her.

"You saying I'm not sweet enough?" Pressed against him, the length of her body felt so, so good. The fact that she wasn't pulling away felt even better.

She made a sound in the back of her throat, like a growl, or a purr. "I'd never say that." Her voice rasped down his nerves and traveled straight to his groin.

"What would you say?" he asked.

Her playful smile faded but the color in her cheeks had become more pronounced. Her eyes were wide and he could feel her breathing against him.

He could kiss her right now, right here in the street, he thought. She was close enough that he could see the green and gold flecks in her eyes. They were in a small city where no one knew them. He started to lower his head, but she blinked and pulled free.

"I'd say we better get there before they close." She grabbed his hand again and they jay-walked across the street.

Like all the stores on the main drag, it was cute in an off-beat, kitschy way. Wide, freshly painted pink and white boards in front with a rustic low-pitched shingle roof that extended to cover a narrow front porch where customers could sit with a cup of coffee while they enjoyed their goodies. A life-size wooden cutout of a man in a sailor suit stood next to the door, holding a welcome sign that also indicated the hours of business.

"See?" she said, tugging on his hand. "We've only got a few minutes."

The walls were lined with shelves containing clear glass jars filled with paper-wrapped pastel-colored candies. In the display case behind the counter were other treats. Saltwater taffy kisses, caramel corn, succulent-looking peanut brittle, and homemade fudge.

"Oh my!" Abby said. "I don't know where to begin."

"Hello, I'm Labron." A tall black man leaned over the counter, a pink-and-white-striped apron straining across his girth. His arms were like tree trunks. His head was shaved and glistening. His eyes twinkled like someone who was about to show off a new baby. "Welcome to memories of your childhood."

Abby introduced herself and Jon, then wrinkled her nose. "I've never had saltwater taffy."

"I'm speechless." Labron's jaw dropped and he put a hand to his chest.

Jon had a feeling the man had never been speechless in his life and smiled when Labron proved him right.

"This is a travesty," the man continued, "a crime against nature and culture. I knew there was a reason I decided to close up myself tonight. Abby and Jon, we were meant to meet today. Your saltwater education is about to begin, young lady."

With a flourish, he brought out a plate full of tiny pieces of candy, each in its own individual paper cup, and set it in front of them. "Try before you buy. That's my motto."

Then he turned to Jon. "And you, sir. Allow me to offer you a selection of our most popular products."

Labron was a little over-the-top, but he appeared to genuinely enjoy what he was doing. Many retail workers would be annoyed to see customers right at the end of the day. Not this man.

Jon picked a light brown piece of taffy.

"Excellent choice, sir." The man's smile got even wider. "Our buttercream saltwater taffy is a classic. We make everything on site and the cream for this flavor comes from a dairy down the road."

"Delicious," Jon said, as soon as he could speak. The

candy melted on his tongue but had a delightful chewiness as well.

"What's this one?" Abby pointed to a white candy flecked with blue and red.

"Ah, that's our cherry-vanilla." Labron nodded approvingly. "A sophisticated little candy perfect for someone with sophisticated taste."

Abby blushed. "I don't know about that."

Labron was a born salesman. He probably repeated that line a dozen times a day, every day. But Jon didn't care. Abby was enjoying herself immensely.

"Is there really saltwater in it?" Abby asked, sniffing the cherry-vanilla piece.

"I'm so glad you asked!" Labron rubbed his hands together. "Recipes vary from one candymaker to another, and are highly guarded, by the way. But they all contain sugar, corn syrup, cornstarch, water, butter, salt, color, and flavorings."

"Salt and water, but not saltwater, per se? So where did the name come from?" Abby persisted.

"The first soft taffy was made back East, in Atlantic City, New Jersey, in the 1880s. It caught on quickly and shopkeepers up and down the coast began to sell it. According to Jersey Shore legend, it got its name in 1883, when a storm hit Atlantic City. Have you ever been there?"

"New Jersey? No." Abby shook her head. "California and Oregon, that's where I've been."

Jon frowned. "Not even Las Vegas?"

She gave a little shudder. "Why would I want to go there?"

"Um, because it's fun?"

"If you say so." She turned her attention back to Labron. "What happened when the storm hit Atlantic City?"

"Well, the boardwalk at the time was smaller and lower than it is today. During the storm, waves washed right over and flooded several businesses with sea water, including a candy shop. A young girl came into the shop looking for taffy right after the storm, and the proprietor looked around his waterlogged store and jokingly told her all he had was 'saltwater taffy.' The girl didn't realize he was being sarcastic, so she bought some and went on her way. Someone recognized that the name was catchy and good for marketing so they kept it."

"Advertising," Jon said. "It really does run the world."

Abby elbowed him in the ribs. "Jon, don't be rude."

But Labron only laughed. "Your young man has a point. However it came about, I'm grateful that this candy made it to the West and that I get to come to this store every day and make it for good people like you."

"You really enjoy your work, don't you?" Jon said. No one at *Diversion* ever said they were grateful to come to work. Probably not *Sunset Bay Chronicle,* either. What did that say about his chosen profession?

"I really do." Labron reached behind the counter again and brought out another small tray. "Taffy is the specialty, of course, but my wife convinced me to start making fudge, too. Second best decision I ever made. Here. Mocha hazelnut."

Abby bit into a small piece of the dark confection and moaned. "This is amazing. Jon, you have to try this."

Labron looked at Jon with his head tilted to one side. "I believe the gentleman is more suited to the smooth peanut butter milk chocolate version."

Jon put the candy in his mouth. The slightly salty peanut butter mingled on his tongue with the sweet creamy chocolate just like something his mother used to make at Christmas when he was a boy. The flavor instantly transported him back to a time he'd all but forgotten, when his parents were happy together and they were a family.

"How do you know I'm a peanut butter fan?" he asked, once he could speak.

Labron's dark eyes were full of compassion, as if he knew what Jon had been thinking. "I've been doing this a long time, son. I have a feeling about things."

Abby selected a box of each fudge they'd tasted, plus a variety of different saltwater taffy flavors. Labron packaged them up prettily and handed them to her with a little bow.

"Thank you for stopping in. It's been delightful chatting with you. Please feel free to visit again."

At the doorway, Abby paused and turned back. "You said taking your wife's advice to make fudge was your second best decision. What was your first?"

Labron grinned, flashing a mouthful of straight, white teeth. "Not taking no for an answer. It took me three years to convince her to marry me. Everything good in my life followed that. The right things are worth waiting for. Worth fighting for too, if it comes to that."

Jon looked at Abby. She'd fought hard all her life. Maybe it was time someone fought for her.


Jon opened the back passenger side door and watched as Chaos leaped onto the seat, sliding on the quilted cover that protected the leather.

"Good boy," he said. Chaos wagged and grinned. A day that included a car ride was the best thing ever, to him.

It was a good day, period, Jon thought. Perfect for a road trip. Light cloud cover with breaks of sunshine, calm air perfumed with early summer. Roman was in a good mood. They had three stops planned, all of which would be right for the restaurant round-up.

"We'll hit the bakery first," Jon said. "Then we'll head north to Coos Bay, have lunch at a microbrewery I've been told we must try. How does that sound?"

After that, they'd check out the famous sand dunes. On the way back, there was a cheese factory and a lighthouse diner.

"I'm sick of Goldie's," Roman grumbled. "I'd rather stop at the ranch for snacks."

"Yeah, well, Daphne has paying customers to feed," Jon replied.

"Abby would get me something."

"This isn't Goldie's anyway. It's a new place outside of town. Come on, Dad. Let's have fun today, okay?"

There was a lot to see in Oregon but for someone who'd lived in the area for as long as Roman had, he'd experienced very little of it. But that was the lifestyle he'd chosen.

Would he have done more, if Jon had been around to go with him? Had his father been lonely, all those years?

He felt the guilt, then shifted it away. He couldn't change that. Roman had made his choice. Now, since his fall, they were doing things together, and getting along better than they had in years. For the first time, Jon allowed himself to consider that maybe it wasn't Roman who needed to move closer to Jon, but Jon who needed to move closer to Roman. He'd been here for several weeks already, he was getting enough work from Elliott to get by, with far less stress than he had in Los Angeles, and as they said, two can live as cheaply as one.

His father didn't want to leave his home and Jon could understand why, now. If Jon stayed around to help, who knows how many more years Roman could stay here?

And then, there was Abby.

"Don't forget my cane," Roman said. He eased himself into the passenger seat, already adjusted to his comfort.

"Got it." Jon tossed it into the back. Chaos thumped his tail approvingly. "Anything else? You've got your pills? Your jacket? Your hat?"

"When did you get to be such a mother hen?" Roman complained. "I've got what I need. Let's go."

The bakery was about an hour north of Sunset Bay and by the time they'd reached it, Roman was stretching and shifting uncomfortably.

"You feeling okay, Dad?" he asked, as he handed Roman his cane.

"I'm fine." Roman gripped the cane in one hand and Chaos's harness in the other. "Nothing a cinnamon bun won't cure."

The aroma inside was redolent with yeast and spices and sugar. And coffee.

They purchased their treats and took them to a nearby gazebo where they could see for miles and miles, all the way down to the water.

There was a young family picnicking on the grass between the shelter and the parking lot. Father, mother, and two boys. Chaos looked at them longingly.

"He likes kids, huh?" Jon said.

"Loves them." Roman grunted. "He ought to be a family dog, instead of being stuck with me."

"He adores you."

"He's a good boy."

Chaos looked at Roman and thumped his tail at the words.

"He's a young dog," Roman said. "He'll probably outlive me. If that happens, I want you to have him."

"Geez, Dad, way to take the shine out of a nice day. Of course, I'll look after your dog. But you'll be around for a long time yet. Only the good die young, remember?"

Roman reached down and patted Chaos. "You never know."

He was not a man given to sentiment and the exchange troubled Jon. Roman had been quieter than usual the past few days, not snapping as much, not complaining about

Jon's cooking, or the times when Jon and Abby had gone out, leaving him behind.

In fact, he'd encouraged them to go, practically pushing Abby out the door, promising her he'd do nothing more strenuous than watch television while he was alone. Her concern was touching, if a little over-the-top. But Roman tolerated it from her. In fact, they seemed to understand each other in a way that made Jon feel like an outsider.

He took half of the cinnamon bun they'd ordered and put it in front of Roman. "Here," he said. "Tell me what you think. Something I can use in the story."

Roman took a bite, then gave an indifferent shrug. "Bigger isn't always butter. I mean, better."

"Awesome." Jon burst out laughing. "But either way, I can't use it. Say something good."

"I taste cinnamon? They're not burned?"

"Let me get my notepad so I can write all that down. Come on, Dad." He looked down at his half of the pastry. "Are they that bad?"

"Probably not," Roman allowed. "But once you've tasted the baking at Sanctuary Ranch, nothing comes close."

Jon took a bite. Dad was right. "I guess Daphne's spoiled us."

"And Abby."

Jon nodded.

Roman napped on the way to the microbrewery, where he ordered a large meal that he claimed he couldn't eat because of the earlier pastry.

Instead of walking the dunes, they sat at an overlook. Chaos stuck close to Roman's side, nudging him frequently, and one time, Jon had to repeat himself twice before his father responded.

At the cheese factory, he nibbled on samples, feeding most of them to the dog, while Jon chose from the menu and purchased a few items for Daphne.

Roman was asleep again when they hit the lighthouse, so Jon ordered a couple of meals to go and went straight home.

But when they got there, his father was too stiff to get out of the car. He seemed dazed, in pain, and angry, batting away Jon's helping hand.

Jon called Abby. "Do you mind coming out? Dad's being difficult."

With Abby's cajoling and help lifting, they got Roman upright, after which he made his way into the house unaided.

But his mood remained surly, and given the lateness of the hour, Abby left almost immediately. Their previous closeness was gone, as if it had never been there.

Not exactly the successful outing Jon had envisioned.

# Chapter Sixteen

From Abby's notebook:

## HEAVENLY COCONUT PECAN COOKIES

There's nothing like these delectable goodies to round out a cookie platter. The cracked caramel tops and chewy, nutty interior are a textural delight and the flavor is simply heavenly.

1 cup unsalted butter, softened
⅔ cup lightly packed brown sugar
⅔ cup white granulated sugar
2½ teaspoons vanilla extract
¼ teaspoon almond extract
1 egg
1 cup all-purpose flour
1 cup whole wheat flour
1 teaspoon baking soda
½ teaspoon salt
1 cup toasted pecans, chopped
3 cups fancy shredded coconut

Cream butter and sugars until light and fluffy. Add vanilla, almond extract, and egg. Mix well.

In a separate bowl, combine flours, baking soda, and salt. Mix to combine. Add to creamed mixture and mix just until combined. Stir in pecans and coconut.

Cover and chill the dough overnight in the refrigerator.

Preheat oven to 350 degrees F.

Remove dough from refrigerator and form a log two to three inches in diameter. Cut into slices approximately ½ inch thick and place on cookie sheet spaced ½ inch apart. Bake 10–12 minutes, until lightly browned and set in the center.

Makes approximately three dozen cookies.

Quinn pulled the covers tight against her body and hoped Abby would think she was sleeping. She didn't feel like answering any questions and Abby seemed to think it was her right to know every little thing about Quinn's life.

Maybe once, that had been okay.

But it wasn't anymore.

She heard the key in the cabin door, and Abby's soft footsteps as she moved about, putting her purse away, hanging her jacket, refilling Tuxedo's food dish.

She'd been watching for signs that things were progressing between Abby and Jon, but if it had, the two of them were being sneaky about it.

Abby was twenty-eight. It was high time she had something to do besides worry about Quinn.

"Quinn?" Abby knocked gently on her bedroom door. "You awake?"

Quinn said nothing.

Abby pushed the door open and peeked inside. "Quinn?"

She held herself still for a moment, willing her sister to go away, to move on, to leave her alone for once. Anger bubbled in her veins and she felt herself trembling. It wasn't fair.

She wasn't a child and she wasn't stupid. But how could she prove it with Abby looking over her shoulder every damn minute of every damn day?

She threw back the covers and sat up. "What?" she demanded.

Abby jumped back. "Oh! I thought you were sleeping."

"Really?" Quinn flipped her legs over the side of the bed. "You were just staring at me sleeping, then? That's super-creepy, you know."

"No, it's not." Abby stepped aside as Quinn pushed past her. "It's affectionate."

Quinn groaned. "Please, love me less, I beg you."

She went to the small kitchen and poured herself a glass of milk. Wine would be better, but Abby wouldn't keep it in the house. Said they could drink wine with everyone else in the lodge, when they wanted.

She didn't trust Quinn with wine, is what she meant.

Because of their mother.

"I just came back from Roman's place," Abby said, taking a seat at the table. "He's pretty sick."

"He's been sick the whole time we've known him."

Abby was quiet.

"What?" Quinn said. "Are you crying?"

Abby shook her head.

"You are." Abby never cried, which meant she was pulling out all the stops. Did she know about the texts from Carly?

No, surely not. She steeled herself against another guilt trip. She'd always hated disappointing Abby, but sooner or later, she had to stop caring. Yes, she'd done some stupid things in the past, but how long did she have to pay for that? Would Abby ever trust her to look after herself?

Abby couldn't possibly know that she had been in touch with Carly again. Quinn missed her friend and had always felt awful about leaving without saying good-bye. Carly didn't blame her. She was so sweet and kind and Quinn had never found another friend like her.

She was becoming friendly with Sage, but she had a kid. Jamie was cool, but she was all about Gideon and Blake. Huck was nice. Some days she even thought he liked her. But he was a cowboy and probably closer to Abby's age than hers. Quinn just wanted to be a normal person, to go out and have normal fun, with normal people her own age.

And she wanted to fix things with Carly.

She wanted to do the right thing, something she should have done a long time ago. Abby would not approve but Abby had no right to make Quinn feel guilty about anything.

Abby couldn't read minds, Quinn reminded herself. She didn't know about her and Carly. So she leaned against the refrigerator and huffed out a sigh. "What did I do now?"

Abby looked up in surprise. "What do you mean?"

"Oh, come on, Abby. I must have done something. You never cry."

Except in L.A. She'd cried then.

Abby shook her head. "I'm fine."

"So am I."

"I know."

Quinn wanted to scream. Abby never wanted to face things. She always wanted to pretend everything was okay, she never let herself be angry or afraid or wish for anything. And she expected Quinn to be the same.

"Actually," Quinn amended, "I'm not fine. I'm bored to tears, but the second I try something the least bit different— even babysitting, for God's sake—you freak out."

"I didn't freak out."

"Then there's my birthday." A weighted silence fell between them. "You probably think it's going to trigger all sorts of memories, that I'll go off the rails again, run away, I don't know."

"You just admitted to being bored," Abby said in a tight voice, "and you expect me not to worry?"

Quinn tried another tactic. This wasn't going the way she thought it would.

"You don't have to worry about me anymore, Abs. I'm tougher than you think. I'm more mature now. I'm not that scared kid I was. I'm . . . not going to do anything dumb." She lifted her left hand, showing her tattooed wrist. "I promised, remember?"

Abby lifted hers in response. "I remember."

"Good," Quinn said.

Abby would definitely freak out if she knew what Quinn had really been thinking about.

Which is why she couldn't talk about it.

Abby lowered her arm. "You know, Quinn, this will come as a shock, but not everything is about you. I have other things going on in my life." Then she squeezed her eyes against another round of tears.

"I know that." She was torn between relief and jealousy. What else could make Abby react like this?

Abby rested her elbows on the table and dropped her face into her palms. "Roman's dying." Her voice was muffled.

That, again?

"Of course he's dying. He's a million years old. We're all dying."

"Yeah, well," Abby said, lifting her face, "you and I can expect many more years. He'll be lucky to see September."

September? That couldn't be. She'd just seen him. He looked exactly the same as always.

His hand shook when he used the currycomb on Apollo, but he'd always been a little shaky. He'd tripped over her name, but he said it was because Quinn was a weird name.

He was skinnier than usual.

She turned to the cupboard so Abby couldn't see her face. Roman was grumpy and demanding and sometimes rude, but she'd gotten used to seeing him around. He always had treats for Apollo and he was really nice to Chaos and the other dogs. And Jon loved him.

She grabbed the ceramic cookie jar and opened the lid. It was empty. "We're out of cookies."

She heard Abby get up and then felt her strong arms, holding her tightly. She turned around and returned the embrace.

"Jon doesn't know," Abby whispered. "Roman won't let me tell him. Please don't let on you know."

"Oh, Abs." Quinn's throat was on fire. She didn't want to think about people dying. She sure didn't want to think about her sister, burdened yet again with another secret that wasn't hers to tell. "Let's bake something," she said.

It's what Abby did to make herself feel better. They walked hand in hand to the lodge, quiet and dark at this time of night. Quinn got a soft playlist going on her smartphone and together they gathered the ingredients for Roman's favorite cookies. They couldn't stop him from dying, but they could do something to let him know that they cared.

When Daphne got up to find them washing dishes at two in the morning, it was because they'd awakened her with their laughter.

# Chapter Seventeen

From Abby's notebook:

*Allow the browning foliage of spring-flowering bulbs to die back before removing so all that good energy can return to the source.*

Midsummer was her favorite time in the garden. The work of planning and planting was done. Now it came down to fertile soil, warm sunshine, soft rain, and the magic of photosynthesis.

Rabbits had nibbled on a few edge plants but there were so many rows that they could afford to share.

Abby dug her hoe into the soft earth, turning over the dirt and breathing in the rich fecund scent. As much as she'd enjoyed the time with Jon, she'd missed this. The physical exertion helped dispel the stress that could so easily bring down her spirits at this time of year, when memories assailed her.

For a good thirty minutes she allowed her mind to go blank, letting the rhythmic motion and soft crunching sounds soothe her, feeling her muscles and joints grow warm and loose and strong.

When the rows were weed-free and the walking paths tidy again, she leaned the hoe up against the wheelbarrow and set off into the fields. A good walk always cleared her head. The day was unseasonably warm and clear for early July on the coast. Fluffy clouds high above promised rain later on, but for now, the fog had lifted and the sun warmed her back.

What was she doing with Jon? This wasn't like her. But she seemed powerless to stay away. She craved being with him. Felt like a different person, someone who might be normal, who might live the kind of life she imagined other women might live, with a future that might include permanence, intimacy. A man.

A future.

She owed it to him to be frank about her past, but she was a coward. It would change things between them and she was having fun right now. She didn't want things to change. Turned out she enjoyed having fun.

And oh, they were having a great time. Nothing had prepared her for the fire that Jon stirred in her blood. Every touch brought her alive and made her want more, made her want to laugh into the wind, to fling out her hands and fly, to risk everything and believe in the impossible.

She rounded a bend in the path and nearly stumbled upon Haylee, sitting on a fallen log.

Cleo, the terrier mix sitting next to Haylee, leaped up with a startled bark, then came pelting toward Abby.

"Hey there, cutie-pie." Abby squatted down to give the pup some love.

"Cleo," Haylee scolded. "Where are your manners?"

Instantly, the terrier backed off, plunked her butt in the soft loam, and lifted a front leg.

Abby shook the proffered paw and was rewarded with another round of face-licking. The whiskery muzzle tickled her chin, not as nice as Jon's stubble, but still sweet. She was a darling dog.

"A lovely day for a walk, isn't it?" Abby took a seat next to her friend and then looked at her more closely.

Haylee's blond curls were tucked up into a baseball cap but she couldn't hide the tears on her cheek.

"What's wrong?" Alarm heightened her voice.

Haylee shook her head and attempted a smile. "Nothing. I'm just pissed off. And when I get pissed off these days, I cry. Pisses me off even more." Her laugh turned into a fresh round of sobs. "It's the hormones. I swear I've cried more since Mattie was born than I have my entire life before that."

"Maybe you were due," Abby suggested. "Anything I can help with?"

"Nah. Just stuff with Sage." Haylee put her arm around Cleo and ruffled her ears. "Beverly wants her to come back to Portland."

Haylee's daughter Sage had spent her formative years with her adoptive parents, only seeking out her birth mother when she realized she was pregnant herself.

"Of course, Beverly's ex-husband got wind of it and decided he wants time with her, too, now that Sage is getting herself together. My poor girl. Her dad is overwhelmed with his own kids and Sage was never close with him anyway. Beverly's triplets are a one-room wrecking team. Sage and Sal get lost when she goes out there. And here am I, with Mattie and Aiden, so even I can't focus on her entirely."

Fresh sobs wracked her. "I want her to feel special, to know how much I treasure her, how much I missed her all those years, even if I pretended I didn't."

Haylee was a tough cookie. She didn't usually spend a lot of time worrying about things like this. Perhaps becoming a mother all over again with Matthew had brought it all forward in her mind.

"She knows how you feel about her, Haylee."

"Does she? I hope so. I don't know what to tell her. They're her family . . . but I want her here with me. They had her for all those years. Now it's my turn."

"What does Sage want?"

Haylee shrugged. "I don't know. I don't want to pressure her. It's her choice. A biological mother she's just getting to know or the adoptive parents she ran away from." She gave a little snort. "Some kids get all the luck, huh?"

Sage had been given away by an unprepared mother to two parents who wanted her very much. Then, when her life took a turn, she found her birth mother and discovered a whole new home.

In some ways, it was a heck of a lot more than Abby and Quinn had ever had. They'd gotten a father that had died before Quinn was even old enough to even remember him. A mother too grief-stricken and ill-prepared to look after two needy little girls alone, but too proud to admit it and seek help.

"I think Sage is very lucky." She said it without bitterness. Luck came in waves and what looked like good fortune one day might turn out to be the worst sort of luck the next. Having Rebecca as their mother had forced Abby to be strong. Losing her was devastating at the time, but as the years went on, she realized how much chaos their mother had brought into their lives.

"We're all lucky," she added. "You, me, all of us who've made our way here to the ranch. Things will work out. You'll see."

Haylee nodded. Then she sighed. "Olivia hasn't said anything but I think she and Gayle are going through a rough patch, too."

Abby remembered wondering about that herself. "I hope it isn't serious. They're really good together."

"I don't know." Haylee shook her head. "I think it's something bigger. I think having Sal and Mattie around has gotten to Gayle."

Abby turned to face Haylee. "Gotten to her? How?"

"She wants a baby. Apparently, she's talking about adopting again."

"Again? I didn't know she ever had been thinking about children."

"Yeah. Well. She's a bit younger than Olivia. I remember when they first met." Haylee's voice softened. "I'd never seen Liv so happy. Anyway. I guess Gayle had talked about adopting right off the bat but they never went any further with it. Liv and I were busy starting the ranch. Money, time, I'm not sure. Now they're both more settled in their careers, they've got money. Gayle wants to go to China, see the village where she was born, maybe find out who her birth parents were. I don't know how easy it is to get adoption records from Chinese orphanages, but she's going to try."

"Is Olivia going with her?"

Haylee sighed again. "She says she can't. Too much work here. I don't understand her. Gayle really wants her to come along. We can manage here without Liv. It sounds selfish to me. Selfish and stubborn. Guess that runs in the family."

"That's a little harsh. You and Olivia are two of the most generous people I've ever met. Kind and giving. You are this place. Look how many animals you've saved. Animals, people. You guys have brought a lot of happiness where there was sadness and pain. That's not selfish. And if you're stubborn, it's only so that you can achieve your goals."

"You're a good friend, Abby."

"Are you feeling better? Ready to go back to the house?"

"I think I'll sit here for a while yet. Thanks, Abby. I guess I needed to vent a little."

"Anytime. Want me to take Cleo back to the house?"

The little dog looked up at her name.

Haylee bent down and placed a kiss on the whiskered muzzle. "No." Her voice was husky. "I'll keep her with me."

Cleo had been a challenge for Haylee—until she started bringing the little dog with her on her pet therapy rounds. Once a week, Haylee took her to the hospital, a seniors' home and, the real winner, the local after-school facility for elementary students with learning disabilities. Playtime with Cleo motivated the kids to finish their homework, but they also took turns practicing their reading with her. It seemed that reading to a dog was less intimidating than reading to an adult. No one expected the energetic, headstrong terrier to succeed as well as easygoing Jewel, Haylee's elderly retriever, but all the teachers raved about Cleo.

Suddenly, Abby knew what was really bothering her friend.

She leaned against Haylee. "How is Jewel enjoying her retirement?"

Haylee lifted one shoulder and let it fall. "It's not the same without her. She's really slowing down and her appetite has fallen off lately. I took her to see Janice last week for her senior wellness exam. They found some abnormalities in her bloodwork. Janice took an ultrasound of Jewel's abdomen this morning." She paused and took a deep breath. "Abby, there's a mass on her spleen."

"Oh, Haylee."

"Janice says she might be able to remove it, but she doesn't recommend we try. At fourteen, with early kidney disease, the risks are too high." She swallowed, her throat making an audible click. "I'm not ready to lose her, Abby."

Abby's throat got hot and tears prickled her eyelids. "I'm so sorry. I know how much she means to you."

"Fourteen years she's been part of my life. Most Labs never make it this long. I'm lucky, I know that."

Abby was grateful that little Tux was just barely out of kittenhood. He was the first pet they'd ever had, adopted from a litter that Tyler and Duke had hand-reared last summer. The boys had found two batches of motherless kittens, the product of abandoned or feral cats that hadn't yet been trapped for neutering, and had ended up in the jaws of a coyote. Once Huck shot the coyote, a nursing mother herself, the predation ended.

Tux would be with them for many years but in the end, it would come to this. She'd be where Haylee was. Was it worth it?

"Jewel's been part of my life almost the entire time I've been here. Liv had dogs when I first came to stay with her in San Francisco. She got me started training. But Ju-Jube is the first dog I rescued myself. She's the one who taught me how therapeutic canine companionship can be. She's been with me through so much. She brought me and Aiden together, Abby. I can't imagine my life without her."

She was sobbing again and Abby pulled her close.

"I don't know what to say."

"I knew she was different, from the moment I first saw her. I knew she'd break my heart, but when it's off in the distance, you can ignore it. And it's worth it, you know? Love's always worth it. Even when you know it's going to hurt like nothing else you've ever felt."

Abby held her friend as she wept, wishing there was something she could do or say to comfort her. But there wasn't. That was the thing about loss. It happened, and there wasn't a damn thing you could do about it.

Jewel was dying. Roman was dying. Quinn would go away, eventually. Jon never intended to stay.

Quinn would probably take Tux with her. The cat loved her best.

She felt her own shoulders shake and she pulled Haylee closer.

Was love worth it?

She didn't know.


"Abby, Abby!"

Abby jumped hard enough to send her laptop shimmying sideways onto the couch. She caught it just in time, and ran to the door of their cabin to see Quinn running up the path, her hair streaming behind her like a wheat field in the wind.

She stopped in front of Abby with a triumphant hop.

"You'll never guess," she said, clapping her hands together. Her blue eyes were bright and shining and pink dots highlighted the tops of her cheeks.

"Give me a minute to restart my heart." Abby thumped a fist against her chest. "Okay. This better be good."

"Sorry, did I scare you?" Quinn laughed, then reached out and dragged her sister back into the cabin with her. "I've got great news. You'll never guess."

"Okay," she said cautiously. She went to the little kitchenette and filled the kettle. This sounded like a conversation that would go better with tea. Since the other night when she'd confided in Quinn about Roman's condition, the subtle tension she'd felt between them had lifted, and she was grateful. She still worried about Quinn's upcoming birthday, but knew that Daphne was planning something special. Hopefully, the good memories would one day outweigh the bad.

"Haylee asked if I want to start learning about dog handling." Quinn hugged herself.

"She did?" Abby turned the dial on the stove and got out their herbal tea collection.

"Yes. I'm going to be a dog handler, Abby! Me! She and Jamie are going to teach me."

"That's wonderful, sweetie. I'm so proud of you." She gave her sister a hug.

"I'm going to learn basic obedience along with one of the new rescue dogs." Quinn laughed, the sound tinkling in the small room. "It will be my responsibility to train the dog. That means, the dog will be staying with us in the cabin. Do you mind?"

"As long as Tux is okay with it, I'm okay with it."

The cat was pretty unflappable. Abby knew that learning to interact with a wide variety of people and other animals would be an important part of the dog's socialization.

"It gets better. Once Haylee and Jamie think I'm ready, they want me to start going along on therapy visits."

Abby turned in surprise. "They do?"

Haylee had founded her dog training program, Companions with Purpose, to partner talented shelter dogs with people who needed assistance but not to the level of certified service dogs. Many of her dogs had gone to the families of kids with autism. Some had gone to kids who were grieving the loss of a family member and needed someone to hug.

Most, if not all of her dogs, spent time in the Sanctuary Ranch pet therapy program as part of their socialization and to identify specific skills and traits that would help identify the best home for them. Haylee was both proud and possessive about her dog programs, but since giving birth to little Matthew, she'd been forced to share the responsibility with Jamie.

To everyone's surprise, what began as a grudging necessity had turned into a thriving partnership. Jamie lived for the dog training and there were more than enough requests for visits to go around.

"Haylee started with one dog, but now, when Jamie goes into the schools, she brings two. If I was with her," Quinn explained, "she could bring another one and that would mean more one-on-one dog time for the kids."

Abby wasn't surprised to hear that Jamie was ready to bring along another set of hands.

She never expected those hands to belong to her sister.

Quinn shimmied her shoulders. "I can't believe she asked me."

"I'm happy for you," Abby said, choosing her words carefully. "I didn't realize you were interested in doing that."

"I've been watching Jamie work with them while I clean the kennels. It's pretty interesting stuff." She looked down at her hands. "She's going to start me with the school visits."

Perhaps this is what Quinn needed to cure her restlessness.

Abby exhaled softly. "You'll do great."

"Do you think so?" Her eyes pleaded with Abby for reassurance. "I'm excited and nervous all at once."

"You love kids and dogs and you're a quick learner."

"Jamie says most of the kids we'll see have issues like learning disabilities, autism, anxiety. She's given me a bunch of material to study but I already know plenty about anxiety."

She gave a little self-deprecating laugh that tugged at Abby's heart. To joke about it like this showed how much confidence she'd gained, how much she'd grown.

How right Abby had been to come to this place.

"Maybe," Quinn continued, "I can become a dog trainer myself one day."

"One step at a time," Abby said, passing her a mug of tea. "If you start spending all your time in the kennels, Daphne will have something to say about that."

"Jamie warned me about that," Quinn said with a laugh. "Don't worry. I can handle the housekeeping and do this, too. Besides, Olivia says that Tyler is going to start helping with the cleaning during the busy season."

"He is, is he?"

"He's out of the system, which means he's staff now, like the rest of us."

Abby suspected the youth, who'd worked in the stables up until now, didn't expect to be placed on the cleaning roster. But Olivia believed in cross-training. She also believed in teaching headstrong young men that there was no such thing as women's work and men's work. There was only work, period.

"So," Abby said, "you've got two exciting things coming up. Dog training and Tyler training."

Quinn laughed. "I guess you're right. I think I know which one I'll enjoy more."

Abby thought about the way Tyler watched her pretty sister. Perhaps she'd have a conversation with Olivia about the wisdom of throwing these two young people together.


Jon couldn't stand being away from Abby. When she was too busy to come to the house, he went to the ranch. Today, she wasn't in the kitchen or the greenhouse or the garden and Daphne was too busy arguing with a supplier on the phone to talk to him. He remembered the place where she liked to go when she needed to think, the little area down from the gardens, where the blackberries grew, overlooking the water. He picked his way over the deer path, carefully avoiding the thorny vines this time, and found her sitting on the grass, her back against a large rock.

The greens and browns of before had turned into a pastel profusion of blooms. Little white flowers in low mounds, tall stalks with waving orange-tipped fronds, spiky purple swaths here, yellow bunches there.

"Hey," he said.

That slow smile he loved bloomed over her face as she turned to look at him. "Hey yourself." She motioned to the ground. "Pull up a seat. How's Roman?"

"Crabby. Sleeping. I'm hoping he wakes up in a better mood." He lowered himself to the fragrant carpet of green. "I sound like I'm talking about a toddler."

"And how are you?"

When Abby asked, it wasn't a perfunctory query. He got the sense that she really cared. The thought warmed him more than it should. He hadn't enjoyed a woman's company like this for a long time, if ever, but he told himself not to get his hopes up. After the kisses they'd exchanged, he'd felt her pull away from him, creating emotional distance, as if the earlier closeness was a regrettable lapse.

"I'm okay," he said. "A little worried about you, as a matter of fact."

"Me?" She looked at him in surprise. "Why?"

He shrugged. "We haven't really talked in a while. You seem preoccupied."

She gave a little laugh and looked off toward the water. "I'm fine."

He elbowed her gently in the side. "Does that mean I'm boring you again?"

Her posture softened. When she looked at him, there was anguish in her eyes. "I've had stuff on my mind, I guess."

"What stuff?"

She shook her head. Tears filled her eyes. "It's nothing. Forget I said anything."

"Oh, man, don't cry, Abby." He took her hand and brought it to his lips. "Makes me feel like I've done something wrong. Have I?"

"No, no." She squeezed the bridge of her nose, flicked the moisture off her cheeks and managed a shaky smile. "There. I'm okay. Is that better?"

Not really. But he'd take it.

"I'm so glad you're here this summer," she added.

He lifted his eyebrows. "Yeah? Why's that?"

She blushed and rolled her eyes. "For your dad, of course. You're more relaxed than you were when you arrived. I think Oregon agrees with you."

He gave her a quick side glance. "You might be right, though I'm not sure Oregon gets all the credit."

"Oh, come on. All this fresh air and open space. The quiet. The greenery."

"Is that why you stay at Sanctuary Ranch?" he asked.

She nodded. "That's part of it. It's a wonderful place for me and Quinn. Peaceful and secure."

Interesting answer, he thought. People valued the things they believed were at risk, or in short supply. Or things they'd never had but always wanted.

"Safety is important to you?"

"Of course." She reached down to a clump of glossy leaves at her boot, and came up with a long spike with several elongated buds at the end. "See this?"

"Yeah. What is it?"

"Monkshood. Wolfsbane. *Aconitum* is the proper name. It's about to bloom. It'll be a pretty blue-violet color."

"Nice. Does it smell good?" He didn't know much about flowers and had never really noticed them, other than as something that made the front of a house look nice.

She waved it gently in front of his face. "What do you think?"

A slightly acrid, bitter odor wafted over. "Ugh." He drew back. "That's a no."

"Used for color, not smell. Those regal blue spires make a lovely blue backdrop in a shady garden."

"Do you have some in yours?"

She shook her head and tossed the stem into the wilderness. "It's toxic enough to hurt a dog or a kid if they ate it. Poisonings are rare, but I won't take the risk."

"What kind of kid would eat something that smelled like that?"

She laughed. "I've read that it tastes even nastier than it smells, but there's always some kid who can't resist a dare. Not to mention golden retrievers. They'll eat anything. Mother Nature's quite something, isn't she? The flowers must be beautiful enough to attract pollinators, without attracting animals like deer and rabbits. Beautiful and lethal at the same time."

"How do you know all this stuff?"

"I read. In Ancient Rome, Livia, the wife of Emperor Augustus, poisoned several members of her family with monkshood. Now there's a recipe I'd love to see. How the heck did she cover up the taste, I wonder?"

Jon couldn't help but laugh. "You've got people to off, do you?"

She gave him an innocent look. "Academic interest only. I adore trivia. Here's another bit for you. Juice from monkshood root was commonly used to poison the tips of arrows before battles. The other name, wolfsbane, came about because ancient mythology claims that it repels werewolves." She frowned. "Or causes wolves to turn into werewolves. Reports are unclear. My guess is that some starving wolves once ate it in desperation and someone saw their death throes and thought they were turning into monsters. A quarter-inch piece would kill in about five minutes. What?"

She'd been so engrossed in her story that she hadn't realized how he'd been watching her.

A flush rose in her cheeks. "I go on a bit sometimes. Ignore me."

He hesitated before speaking. He could be way off base, but he had to know. "You seem happy here, Abby. But is this really what you want to do?"

"Of course. For now." She looked away again, to the horizon.

"But what would you do? If you could do whatever you wanted, and money was no object?"

She shrugged. "You're talking fantasyland. I'm a pragmatist. Brighten the corner where you are, and all. This is where I am, it's a beautiful place, with kind, trustworthy people. What more could I ask for?"

She wouldn't meet his eyes and he wondered what she was thinking about, what had happened to make her lose her ability to dream. "You like working at the ranch that much?"

"I like *this* ranch. I'm good at gardening. I love baking. It's great being surrounded by animals. Especially for Quinn. She's always wanted pets and we could never have one before."

His journalistic instincts told him to back off. But his male curiosity couldn't let it go. He wanted to know more about her. What made her the woman she was today? What did she want out of life? "But where do you see yourself ten years from now? Don't you ever think about that?"

She stiffened. "Maybe I'll still be here. Is there anything wrong with that?"

"Of course not."

He let the silence hang.

"Maybe I'll become famous for my garden design," she said eventually. "Maybe I'll become the Picasso of tulips, travel the world, following Quinn and the kids she's dying to have. I'll be the doting Aunt Abby who always has mints. Or, I'll stay in Sunset Bay and take over Goldie's bakery. Who knows, Jon? Ten years is a lifetime. I'm happy going season to season. That's a lot better than going day to day or hour to hour. I've lived that way, too. This way is better."

A tendril of hair had come loose, curling softly at her cheek. He touched it, caressing it lightly between thumb and forefinger, then tucked it behind her ear.

She didn't move.

"No special someone in that scenario?" He edged closer. "No kids of your own?"

If he leaned over right now, he could kiss her.

"Now we're really talking fantasyland." She pressed her hands into her thighs and got to her feet. "I better go. Those deer are probably eating my flowers right now."

# Chapter Eighteen

From Abby's notebook:

> *Weeds grow at precisely the rate you pull them out.*
> *Best to consider it meditation.*

"His name is Ziggy Bigelow," Jamie explained to Abby and Quinn, holding the leash firmly in her left hand. "He's a two-year-old retriever cross."

Quinn's eyes widened. "How much does he weigh?"

"Fifty-five pounds. He looks big but a lot of that is hair. And he's extremely gentle." Jamie fondled the soft black-tipped ears that offset his cinnamon-colored coat. "He was found last week at an abandoned building in Roseburg, tied up in the pouring rain."

"Oh, the poor thing."

"He was with his brother, Mr. Bean. We brought him back, too. Bean's a little smaller, only fifty pounds, and just as gentle. There was a note stuck to the wall, with their names on it and an apology. They couldn't afford them anymore, apparently." Jamie's face darkened. "So they just tied them to a door and drove off, hoping someone would find them."

"Poor boys," Quinn said.

Abby couldn't imagine living with a large dog in their little cabin. Tux might have something to say about that.

"You think he's got potential to be a therapy dog?" she asked.

Jamie tipped her head to one side. "I do. I can never be sure, of course. But Haylee's seen him and tested him. She agrees that his temperament is sound. The only thing is, we've discovered he's a chewer, so hide your shoes."

"He's a lot of dog for an inexperienced handler," Abby said.

Jamie smiled at Quinn. "He and his brother might have spent a lot of time scavenging for whatever they could find to eat. It'll take a while to teach him that he doesn't have to worry about meals anymore."

"You poor guy." Quinn approached him with her hand out, palm out. Ziggy sniffed it and wagged his tail.

"Your main job is socialization, as we discussed. Exposing him to a wide variety of people, places, and things, making sure he has positive experiences."

Abby wondered if her sister was ready for the responsibility.

But Quinn nodded. "I can do that."

"He'll be with you while you work, when you eat, when you sleep. If you go to town, bring him along. If you go to the beach, he comes, too."

"That's a lot," Abby said.

Quinn put her hand out for the leash. "I can do it. Hey, Ziggy, we're going to have fun together, aren't we?"

The dog lunged for her, his tail wagging and tongue lolling, but Quinn drew back sharply.

Jamie snapped the leash. "Ziggy, sit."

The dog whined, but sat, glancing anxiously between Jamie and Quinn.

"Is that a choke collar?" Quinn put a hand to her throat. "I thought those were cruel."

"They can be dangerous, if not used properly. That's why we prefer this kind. It's called a martingale." She ran her hand under the collar around Ziggy's trunklike neck. "It's half nylon, half slip chain. It doesn't hurt the dog but it does allow for a quick, sharp correction, accompanied by the sound of the metal clinking together. Believe it or not, that sound is just as much of a training tool as the physical check."

"I wonder if she should start with a smaller dog," Abby said.

Jamie's nostrils flared. She gave Abby a long look, then turned her attention to Quinn. "Is that what you want?"

Quinn bit her lip. "I don't know. Maybe. Do you think he's too much for me, Abby?"

Abby opened her mouth but Jamie stopped her.

"Quinn, you're the one who'll be doing the work, not your sister. I want your opinion, not hers. No offense, Abby."

Abby lifted her chin. "None taken," she lied.

When Haylee had first broached the subject of Quinn working with the dogs, Abby had assumed they'd have her start slowly. She hadn't expected Quinn to be tossed into the deep end.

"What will happen to him if I don't take him?"

Jamie shrugged one shoulder. "Then I'll do it. But I'm focusing on his brother, Bean. We're already pretty crowded, with Honey and Blake, when he's here. I can't have three big dogs."

Jamie's boyfriend Gideon had his son every other week and the boy had fallen in love with a standard poodle they'd rescued the previous year.

"He'd have to stay in the kennels, which is okay. It'll just take longer to get him prepared for serious training. They progress fastest with consistent, one-on-one attention from someone they trust."

Abby thought about the training Jamie had done with Roman and Chaos, and how hard it had been on Roman. But Jamie hadn't let up. It was no use, she always said, for Chaos to learn to obey her, when Roman was the one who needed him.

It had been a challenge to nurture the bond between Jon's father and the sweet dog, but Jamie never stopped badgering, and as Chaos learned to help his master, Roman came around.

She knew he still grieved for Sadie, though.

Suddenly she wondered what would happen to Chaos, when Roman was gone. Would Jon take him? He'd purchased the puppy in the first place, but only for his father.

She felt a sudden lump in her throat. Soon, not only would Roman be gone, but Jon and the dog, too. Roman's beautiful hideaway would be sold. Someone else would move in and just like that, a chapter in her life would be over.

She couldn't bear the thought.

She crossed her arms over her belly and hugged her elbows, wishing she'd never agreed to support Roman through his final days. It was going to hurt, more than she'd thought. Worse, she would be there to witness Jon's pain.

She had a feeling that she'd never be able to go back to the simple contentment she'd found at Sanctuary Ranch before becoming friends with the Byers men.

Is that what Jon was? A friend?

She didn't know. She cared about him. They spent a lot of time together and had grown increasingly comfortable in each other's presence. Roman made no secret of the fact that he wanted them to become a couple.

He wanted his son's future settled before he died.

It seemed like a lot of pressure to put on two people who

barely knew each other. But how did you deny an old man his dying wish?

She looked at Quinn, smiling now as she walked the big dog in a circle, keeping him neatly at heel. His stubby tail wagged and his tongue lolled out of gaping pink jaws. He looked like he was in love.

It would be good for Quinn to have this. She'd changed, grown, and Abby had to face that. She was finally blossoming out of the frightened stage she'd been stuck in for so long.

Changes, changes, everywhere. Quinn didn't need her anymore. Once Roman was gone, Jon wouldn't need her. Olivia and Haylee could hire anyone to do Abby's work. She wasn't indispensable anywhere.

She needed something to fill the void they would leave behind. She had to prepare herself, like a vaccine, for the emptiness that was coming.

She inhaled, uncrossed her arms, and turned back to Jamie and Quinn.

"I think you'll be fine, if you want to do this, Quinn. I'll help, too, Jamie. I assume I'm one of the people, places, and things that a dog like him needs to be comfortable with."

She squatted next to the big, panting dog.

"Hi, Ziggy," she said, letting him sniff her hand. "What do you think? You want to move in with us for a while?"

The smile Quinn gave her would have melted the sun.


Jon looked at the pages laid out on the table in front of him. So much research to sort through, so much information. He owed his dad for printer ink.

He took a cookie from the plastic container Abby had brought over earlier.

He had transcripts from six women who'd filed complaints against Richard Arondi, everything from grabbing buttocks to demanding sex from women who wanted roles. But one in particular stood out.

Typical story. Twenty-one-year-old Carly Cassidy worked in craft services while taking acting lessons, networking and hoping for the best. She got tapped for a bit part in an upcoming movie. Said she was told to go to the hotel where he was staying. She expected a conference room, so was surprised he answered the door in swimming trunks.

*He said he needed to relax. Asked me if I would join him in the hot tub, while we discuss the potential role. I told him I hadn't brought a suit, and he said it was okay, that I didn't need one. Eventually he realized I wasn't going to give in and we talked at the table on the deck outside. He sat next to me instead of across from me and kept touching my thigh, running his finger beneath the hem of my skirt. I kept edging away but he didn't stop.*

*I barely remember the conversation. There were people walking below us. If they'd have looked up, they would have seen us. I was scared but he was acting like this was all normal, so I pretended I didn't mind. I left as soon as I could get out of there. I figured I was lucky. I got the role and he didn't try anything creepy with me. Not really.*

But one night, after everyone had left, Carly was cleaning the coffee machines in preparation for the next day, when he found her.

*He trapped me in a corner and started kissing me, groping me. I was screaming, hitting, and kicking. But he's strong. He tore my blouse and was sticking his hand in my pants when a friend came looking for me. He stopped when he heard her voice and I instantly elbowed him in the nose and got away. I found my friend had called nine-one-one.*

The friend was identified only as Person X in the police report. Carly Cassidy refused to identify her. Arondi was furious. He'd heard the voice and seen a shadow, but didn't know who it belonged to.

The police took her statement. Carly hadn't been raped.

She had no bruises or scrapes. Other than the torn blouse, there was no physical evidence of assault. In the absence of an eyewitness, it would be her word against his. Richard Arondi was a powerful man with endless money for lawyers.

*He said if I didn't drop the charges, he'd dig up every little thing in my past, drag me through the mud, ruin me and my family.*

Carly Cassidy dropped the charges. She never identified her friend.

If Jon could talk to Carly, convince her to ask her friend to come forward, this story could result in Arondi being charged. If one woman could be brave, it would almost certainly bring others out of the woodwork. He'd be exposed in all his putrid glory and blacklisted in Hollywood. He'd never again prey on a hungry and desperately hopeful actor willing to do anything, almost anything, to get noticed.

He pushed aside his research and closed his laptop.

Yesterday, Abby and Roman had talked on the porch for a half hour, while the sun set over the hillside. He'd stayed inside, as instructed, but couldn't resist watching from the window.

Abby was leaning close, her expression urgent. But Roman's posture stayed stiff, shaking his head and at one point, slamming his hand on the armrest of his Adirondack chair.

Abby had come in with red-rimmed eyes and shiny cheeks, but she only said that if Jon had questions, he had to ask Roman.

Something was going on and whatever it was, it wasn't good.


Jon was in the kitchen, washing dishes, while his father watched hummingbirds battle at the feeders outside the big window in the room overlooking the yard.

"I've got two more reports of women who say they had

uncomfortable or inappropriate experiences with Richard Arondi," he said, over the sound of the faucet.

Roman had taken interest in the story, enough that Jon had started bouncing ideas off him. The old man was a surprisingly good sounding board, when he was in the right mood.

"All of them have been threatened," he continued. "Everyone is scared shitless of this guy. Nobody will go on record yet but I know if I keep digging, I'll find someone who will. It can't go on forever. He's reaching critical mass. His own hubris will take him down and when he falls, it'll be a crash unlike anything Hollywood has ever seen."

They'd been getting along remarkably well. Over the past few days, he and Roman had visited another round of restaurants and they'd had a great, if exhausting, time. The seafood place in town was fantastic. He reminded himself to take Abby there soon. According to Aiden, the oyster bar was the reason he and Haylee were together.

"You hungry, Dad? What do you want for supper?"

When he shut off the faucet, he heard the sound of a glass falling onto the hardwood floor.

"I hope that was empty." He was drying his hands on a towel when he heard strange clucking sounds coming from the other room.

"Is that dog puking?" he called out. "You've got to quit feeding him off your plate, Dad."

But Roman didn't reply. Instead, Jon heard Chaos whine, then bark, sharply.

"Dad?"

He threw the towel over his shoulder and went to his father's usual place in the chair by the window.

"Oh my God. Dad!"

Roman was slumped sideways, a thin string of drool coming from the side of his mouth. One hand gripped the armrest, the other rotated rhythmically at the elbow, palm up, palm down.

Chaos shoved his head under Roman's arm and whined loudly, but there was nothing he could do to help. His master was having a seizure.

Jon got his arm under his father and dragged him—how light he was now—onto the couch, where he placed him on his side. He unbuttoned his shirt and piled pillows around his head, between his knees, in the small of his back. The arm continued spasming.

Jon grabbed his phone and punched 9-1-1, taking note of the time. When had it started? Thirty seconds earlier? Maybe a minute? When had Roman last responded?

*Ring, ring.*

"Come on, Dad, you're going to be okay."

He spoke quietly and calmly, the way the articles said he was supposed to, but his heart thundered like wild horses in a canyon. Why weren't they answering?

Did he have epilepsy? Is that why he was on the valproic acid? Why wouldn't he warn Jon?

Flick, flick, went the hand.

Then, the hand went limp. Roman's body sagged.

"Dad!" Jon dug his fingers into the side of Roman's neck, feeling for a pulse, hardly able to believe it when he found it.

Roman's eyes fluttered open. "You tryin' to strangle me?"

"Hey." Jon's voice shook. "You're okay."

The 9-1-1 operator finally answered. "What is your emergency?"

"I need an ambulance," Jon said. "My father just had a seizure."

"No!" Roman grabbed for the device but only ended up knocking it out of Jon's hand.

"Dad, what the hell?" Jon found the phone, made contact with the operator.

"Please, Jon," Roman said, struggling to sit up. "No ambulance."

"Sir?" asked the operator. "Is everything all right?"

No, Jon wanted to scream. Things were not fucking all right.

With Roman batting at his arm, Jon described the incident. But upon learning that his father was breathing, conscious, unhurt, and begging to be put on the phone, the operator asked to speak to Roman directly.

"No ambulance." Roman's hand shook so hard that Jon had to hold the device to his ear, and his words, while slurred, were understandable and authoritative. He shot a glance at Jon. "I zoned out. I'm okay now."

# Chapter Nineteen

From Abby's notebook:

*Spittle bugs may appear on ornamental plants as foam on stems. In most cases, they don't require management. If they bother you, wash them off with water or insecticidal soap. You could also learn to accept them.*

Abby got there as quickly as she could. Jon had been adamant that she come help him convince Roman to go to the hospital.

Roman was equally adamant that he not go to the hospital.

She yanked up the emergency brake on her truck and ran up the porch steps.

"Roman?" she called, kicking off her boots.

"He's sleeping."

She followed Jon's voice to the couch by the window where Roman was lying, bolstered by cushions and his big yellow dog.

"I'm not sleeping." His voice was thin and weak, querulous like a sick child.

She touched his forehead. It was cold and damp. "How are you feeling?"

"How do you think?" He twitched away from her hand. "Tell Jon to quit fussing."

"He had a seizure. I'm guessing, since he's on this, that it's not the first time." Jon held up the medication vial. "Since when does he have epilepsy?"

His hair stood on end, as if he'd been tearing at it with his fists. His white T-shirt hung over the top of his jeans, which rode low on his hips. His feet were bare.

This was it, the moment she'd been dreading, and she found herself unable to look away from his feet, his long toes and their clean, tidily clipped nails.

"Abby!"

She shook her head. "Sorry, what?"

"What do you know," he said slowly and deliberately, "about my dad having epilepsy?"

Her shoulders tightened. She looked helplessly at Roman, willing him to answer for her, to explain, once and for all, what was going on inside him.

Roman's face was carved like stone, a sweaty, angry statue. "One little episode. No big deal. It happens."

She lifted her hands and let them fall with a smack against her thighs. "He's been having dizzy spells for a while now. Numbness in his hands and feet. He didn't want to bother you. The drugs keep it under control."

*Come on, Jon. Figure it out. Put it together.*

A muscle in Jon's jaw flickered. His blue eyes burned with icy fire. "We're going to the emergency room."

"The hell we are!" That brought Roman back to life. "I dropped a fucking glass, didn't even break it. So I'm on a boatload of pills. Do you think I know what each of them is for? I've been on pills of one kind or another for years. This is no big deal, Jon. Let it go."

But Jon already had his jacket on and his keys in his hand. "No way. I saw you. You were unresponsive. Drooling. Your hand was twitching."

"I'm old," Roman roared. "I dozed off. You were boring me."

"We were talking about Richard Arondi," Jon yelled back. "There's nobody you'd rather dish dirt on than him, so don't try to tell me you were bored."

He stopped. Blinked. Looked at Abby. "Maybe that's what triggered it. He's hated Arondi for a long time. Extreme emotions can trigger seizures, right?"

Abby stood up between them. She was done. Roman was being ridiculous and it was pissing her off and it was scaring the hell out of Jon.

"Roman, do you have something to tell your son?"

"Nope." He crossed his arms and looked out the window.

"Are you sure?"

She could feel Jon's gaze going back and forth between them, as if he was watching a tennis match.

"Roman!" She'd had enough. "If you don't tell him, I will."

"Tell me what?" Jon set down his keys and approached Roman's sofa. He squatted down beside it. "Tell me what, Dad?"

He looked up at Abby and those blue eyes had ice in them. "One of you better start talking, and soon."

"Aw, hell." Roman's lips twisted. He blew out a long, slow breath. At the same time, Abby held hers.

"Truth is, son," he said, "I'm dying."

Jon stared at him. "I've had a long, unpleasant day, Dad. I'm in no mood for hyperbole."

"I'm not giving you any." Roman turned his head on the pillow, as if looking for a comfortable spot and not finding one. "There's a tumor in my brain. That's why I fell in the bathroom. That's why I have seizures. That's why I get headaches."

"A tumor."

"Yes. In my brain."

There wasn't even a ghost of a smile on Roman's face.

Jon turned to Abby. "Where did he get this idea? If he's kidding me—"

"I wish he was." Her throat was so dry she could hardly get the words out. "But he's not."


Brain tumor. Brain tumor. The words bounced back and forth between Jon's ears, repeating endlessly until they lost all meaning.

What were they talking about? Roman had vertebral spurring, badly healed breaks, chronic arthritis, muscle degeneration, nerve impingement, the list went on. He had problems walking because of damage to his musculoskeletal system.

He didn't have a brain tumor.

He looked at Abby. She had tears in her eyes.

"Dad," he said, trying to ignore the panic rising up from his belly. "I came out here because you fell in the bathroom and hit your head. No one said anything about a brain tumor."

"That's because I told them not to."

Jon looked at Abby. "I don't understand. This doesn't make any sense. He's joking, right?"

Dad had to be joking. He didn't seem different. If someone had brain cancer, wouldn't they seem different?

Roman pushed himself upright on the couch. "You're not listening, son. Read my lips. Cancer. Of the brain. Of *my* brain. I didn't want to tell you. It's a fucking nuisance, is what it is."

Jon felt dizzy himself.

"Hang on. Go back. When . . . ? How?"

How could Dad be so sick without Jon knowing? Had he been that self-involved over the winter, immersed in work, that he'd missed the signs of a terminal illness in his own father?

Roman grimaced. "You and your questions. I got suspicious around Christmas. I started dropping stuff. One week, I smashed a bowl of soup all over my kitchen, followed by my best bottle of scotch. My hip was acting up and I thought it was making me clumsy. Then I got a kind of numbness all down the left side of my body."

"Oh my God," Jon said. "What if you'd been having a heart attack?"

Roman ignored that. "My doc said it was probably a pinched nerve—God knows I've got enough of those—but a few days later my head started aching, not the usual pain. Different. I can't describe it."

Jon fisted his hand and pressed his knuckle against his upper lip. "You have a tumor. And you didn't say a thing."

"I begged him, Jon." Abby stepped toward him, her eyes beseeching him. "I did everything I could to convince him to tell you, but he refused. He didn't want anyone to know."

"Anyone but you."

Her face fell at his tone, but he ignored it. "You should have told me anyway, Abby. I'm his son. His next of kin. I've got power of attorney, for God's sake."

"Exactly why I didn't want you to know." Roman shifted on the sofa and pointed at Jon. "I needed time to think, to plan, to decide what I wanted, before you barged in like a returning hero to save the day, deciding what's best for me without taking my opinion, my wishes, into account."

"I'm so sorry, Jon." Abby had her arms wrapped around her middle.

Against his will, he felt sympathy for her. Roman was a hard man to fight when he got his mind set on something.

"Let's remember the issue at hand, shall we?" Roman gave a bark of laughter. "I'm the one with the problem. A plum-size problem, you might say."

"Plum size." His dad picked a hell of a time for levity. "What does that mean? How big is it? What kind of cancer is it? Where's it located?"

"Does it matter?" Boredom and irritation spiked his tone.

"Of course it matters, Roman." Abby spoke from the corner. "Tell Jon what you know."

There were so many questions going through Jon's mind, he didn't know where to start. "What kind of tumor, exactly? What stage? Has it spread? What kind of treatment will you pursue? Do you need surgery? Chemo? Radiation?"

Then he stopped. Roman wasn't a reliable source. He probably didn't even know. A diagnosis like this wasn't confirmed without a lot of tests and appointments and consults. "We'll get you to a bigger hospital and figure out what's really going on."

"I've had enough of that, Jon-boy." He rubbed the back of his neck. "I went to Springfield a while back."

"Yeah?" Jon vaguely remembered hearing about that trip.

"I had a head CT." Roman shrugged a shoulder as if it was no big deal.

He'd thought his father was meeting an old friend, maybe a woman friend.

If he'd have spent a nanosecond analyzing that, he'd have realized how ridiculous that was.

"You went to Springfield for a head CT . . . alone?" Jon felt like he was about to explode.

"I went with him," Abby said quietly. "He was going to take the bus. I couldn't let him do that."

Jon dug his index fingers into his temples. "You knew he was having a head CT. And you still didn't call me."

His eyes met hers, trapped them, demanding an explanation.

"Focus, son," Roman broke in. "The scan revealed the tumor, neurologist confirmed it, end of story."

Again, the casual tone, as if he was mentioning an afterthought, rather than a life-altering, possibly life-ending news.

"Before you say it, I've already gotten a second opinion," Roman said. "I've seen all the specialists. It's a done deal."

"Not for me. Damn it, Dad." He stared helplessly at his father, who seemed suddenly so much older and more frail than he'd been ten minutes ago. "How is this happening?"

"It just is." Roman sighed. "Jon, I'm tired and my hip aches like my marrow's on fire. I'm sorry I didn't tell you when the headaches started, but it was such a little thing, I didn't want to bother you. The numbness in my hands raised some flags though, and that's when they started running tests. I didn't want to tell you then, because what if they were wrong? Then, when they found the cancer, I didn't know how to tell you."

He stopped then, like an old Cadillac that had just run out of gas.

"It's called a glioma tumor," Abby said, speaking quietly. "They can't remove it surgically. Chemo and radiation may or may not buy him some time."

"Time that'll make me wish I was already dead," Roman added.

Jon paced over to the window. Hummingbirds hovered and darted at the feeders, oblivious to the human drama nearby. Then he inhaled and opened his mouth. "There must be something they can do. There has to be."

He pulled out the spiral-bound notebook he always carried in his back pocket. "I want the names of your doctors, all of them. The tests you've had, the results, the drugs you're on. I want everything."

He'd put in a call to this neurologist, first thing in the morning. He didn't care that Roman had already gotten a second opinion. Jon would get him a third, or fourth, however many were necessary. Surely there were options.

Abby went into the other room, then returned with a stack of papers. "It's all here. They've given him anywhere from six weeks to six months." Abby swallowed. "I'm sorry, Jon."

He turned back and looked at her. She was sorry.

Roman turned over one shaking palm, like a shrug. "It'll take a while but you'll come to terms with it, son. I did. At least I'm not in pain. Well, no more than I was. Ha."

Roman's fingers fumbled at the side of the sofa for his cane. Chaos immediately scrambled to his feet, picked it up with his mouth, and put it into Roman's hand.

"Good boy," Roman muttered, fondling the dog's ears.

For a moment, Jon could not breathe.

With one hand on the cane and the other on the dog's harness, Roman got to his feet. "I'm tired of all this jabbering. I'm going to my room. The pain in my head is reading eight out of ten and I'm not interested in seeing it go any higher."

"Can I get you anything?" Abby asked.

"No, no. I'm sorry Jon called you from work for this," Roman said and waved her away. "Tempest in a teapot."

Jon followed his dad into the bedroom and straightened sheets that didn't need straightening. "We'll get this sorted out. Don't worry about a thing, okay?"

"Ah, my boy." Roman lifted one bony shoulder. "I knew this would be hard for you to accept. There's nothing to handle. Now go. We'll talk more later. If I'm still alive and kicking."

He gave a rough laugh that turned into a cough.

"Not funny, Dad." Jon took a step toward his father,

wavered, then pulled him into a gentle and completely awkward hug. "Not funny at all."

Roman absolutely, one hundred percent refused to see a new doctor. He did, after much badgering, give Jon permission to talk to the neurologist who'd provided the diagnosis.

Jon had called the office and left a detailed message.

Then, once Roman had gone to bed, he got out his laptop and began doing what he always did. Research.

He shook his head to rid himself of the anger. He had to think objectively. Big picture. Sketch out the broad strokes. Then get into the details.

It would all make sense then.

Treatment for glioma, he learned, depended on the type, size, grade, and location of the tumor, as well as the age and overall health of the patient.

Surgical removal was the first plan of attack, unless the tumor was located near sensitive areas of the brain, in which case surgery could be too risky.

Which portion of the brain was not sensitive? he wondered. Where was the best place to get a glioma tumor?

If Roman had undergone brain surgery, when would he have mentioned it to Jon? Or would he have left that to Abby?

He knew his anger toward Abby was out of proportion, but his father was dying and therefore not an appropriate target.

Surgery could result in a complete cure.

It could also damage the part of Roman's brain that controlled motor skills, speech, vision, and thinking. It could leave him blind, mute, paralyzed, in a persistent vegetative state, or he could die on the table.

The most important thing was timing. The earlier the tumor was caught, the better the chance of a good outcome.

"Damn it, Dad," he muttered. "If only you'd have told me sooner."

But there were other options. There was targeted radiation therapy, using computer-directed high-energy beams to kill the tumor cells, while leaving the healthy tissue untouched. He read about protons, X-rays, stereotactic radiation therapy, gamma knife targeting, intensity-modulated radiation therapy. He took note of side effects, including fatigue, headaches, and burns to the scalp.

Then there was chemotherapy. Poisons taken either orally, or intravenously, all of which was likely to produce nausea, vomiting, hair loss, headaches, fever, weakness, and none of which was guaranteed to add any quality time.

Jon could read between the lines. He knew all about subtext. When someone talked about quality time, it usually meant that quantity time wasn't an option.

He closed his laptop, folded his arms on the table, and rested his head on them, too exhausted and overwhelmed to read anymore.

The next morning, the neurologist returned his call. He confirmed everything Jon had read during the night and very kindly answered all of Jon's questions.

No, surgery was not a viable option.

No, chemo and radiation were not likely to affect survival time.

Yes, he'd urged Roman to tell him earlier.

Finally, he was very sorry about the news.

Everyone was sorry.

The first time Quinn and Abby accompanied Jamie to the school, they brought three dogs, a white standard poodle named Honey, Haylee's terrier Cleo, and a young Cavalier King Charles spaniel named Lily that recently arrived at the shelter. Haylee stayed at the ranch to spend time with Jewel, who was fading quickly. Abby was there to provide an extra pair of hands if needed, and otherwise to stay out of the way. This was Quinn's thing, not hers.

Honey actually belonged to Gideon's son, Blake, but when Blake was with his mother, the dog stayed on the ranch. Blake graciously allowed Jamie to let Honey visit other kids who might need her special brand of love.

Blake was a cute kid.

Jamie and Gideon were a cute couple.

Abby and Jon were—

"Hey, Abby!" Jamie broke into her thoughts. "I'd like you to supervise the one-on-one time with Lily. Quinn, you can take Honey to the reading corner while Cleo and I do some tricks over here."

Quinn's eyes widened and flew to Abby's.

"Go ahead," Abby said. "Honey knows what she's doing. You'll be fine." She focused her attention on the little spaniel and the child who was eagerly awaiting a turn with the dog. Quinn was having first-time jitters, that's all.

The teacher, Mrs. Hill, took out a notepad she used while observing the children interacting with the dogs. "The kids look forward to this all week," she said to Abby. "They earn time with the dogs by meeting the goals of their individualized learning plans. You should see them work!"

Abby smiled. "I'm happy it helps." She chucked little Lily under her feathery chin. Lily had soft, silky chestnut-and-white fur and big eyes that drew children to her like magnets. She was the gentlest creature Abby had ever known.

On her first wellness visit, the veterinarian had discovered congenital heart disease so severe that she warned the breeder the pup likely wouldn't live to see her first birthday. The breeder couldn't in good conscience place her with a loving family, nor could she bear to euthanize a puppy that was, to all outward appearances, completely healthy. So she called the ranch. Haylee, unable to say no to such a sweet face, had agreed to let her live out whatever time she had with them.

That had been eight months ago and while the heart murmur was as ghastly as ever, the puppy showed no signs of illness. So Haylee decided to include her in the dog visitation program. Lily had proven to be especially effective with children who weren't comfortable around animals and had even won over some who'd been truly frightened of dogs.

"She's a little wonder, isn't she?" Abby whispered to Mrs. Hill. A little girl named Farrah sat cross-legged on the floor, enjoying her ten scheduled minutes of Lily's undivided attention. Lily wiggled and licked her face, then settled down in the girl's lap to listen to her read.

"She's started participating in class," Mrs. Hill whispered back. "Farrah never raised her hand until Lily started coming. Never spoke unless I called on her, and even then, rarely more than a word or two. It's wonderful, Abby."

Abby looked at the notepad in Mrs. Hill's lap. She'd sketched out the room, with circles and initials and numbers scrawled in various spots.

"That looks interesting," she said, nodding toward the paper. She didn't want to pry but Mrs. Hill was watching so intently and the indecipherable notations had piqued her interest.

"This?" The teacher smiled. "I got a degree in mathematics before I went into teaching. Math and psychology, in fact. When I first started teaching remedial language arts, I never thought I'd be putting those early skills to use."

"And you are?" Abby replied, confused.

"Oh, I am." Mrs. Hill pulled open her desk drawer and handed another notepad to Abby. "See this? This is from last week."

The names of the students were all listed, with check marks, circles, and numbers beside them.

"What does it mean?" Abby asked.

"At the end of every Friday," she explained, "I ask my students to write down the names of the student or students they would like to sit with next week. No more than four, but at least one. Only I can see the lists and they know that I may or may not implement their requests. I also ask them to nominate one student whom they think deserves special recognition for being an especially good class citizen. Then, I put my math brain to work and I look for patterns."

Mrs. Hill looked fondly over her group of children, all with something or other that made learning more difficult than usual for them. These were a challenging, and challenged, group. But she seemed to have genuine affection for them.

"And what do you learn from that?" Abby asked. She wished Quinn would have had one teacher who'd have noticed her challenges. She wondered if having access to dogs in the classroom would have helped ease her sister's anxiety.

"I learn which children get requested often, and which ones never get requested." The teacher's eyes stopped on one small boy who sat slightly apart from the rest. "I learn which names never come up for nomination. I notice who had everyone wanting to sit with them one week, and no one the next. I don't care who wants to sit where, Abby. What I want to know is which kids are being ostracized, which kids are being overlooked, which ones seem to be invisible to their peers."

Abby put a hand to her heart. She'd never forget the day Quinn had come home, shaken and scraped up because two mean girls decided to pick on her during recess. She'd gone all afternoon with bleeding knees and no one had noticed. Ten years old and not a single friend to come to her assistance.

And no mother to console her at home.

*Was I enough for her? Or was I too busy mired in my own misery to help a little girl who needed so much?*

Which one thing had been the last straw for Quinn, that had shifted her from a quiet child to a young woman who kept herself apart from everyone, whose eyes were so empty some days that Abby feared asking what terrors lay behind them?

Perhaps teachers had tried with Quinn.

Social workers certainly had, but by then, it was too late.

"I used to teach high school," Mrs. Hill went on. "In Colorado. Math, biology, chemistry. A student came in one day with a gun."

Abby went cold. She looked at the little boy by the window.

"I'd taught him," the woman said. "I knew he was deeply, deeply troubled. We were lucky. He was disarmed before hurting anyone."

"Oh thank God," said Abby.

Mrs. Hill made a small humorless laugh. "He went home and shot himself in the head."

Abby swallowed.

"I finished the year, but that was it for high school, for me. The damage to that poor young man had started years earlier. The signs were all there. I knew it, Abby. If someone had asked me which student is most likely to want to blow up the building, I'd have named him. We all saw it coming. And we did nothing. I'll never forgive myself for that."

"It wasn't your fault."

"No. It's no one's fault, of course." She shook her head. "That's how we comfort ourselves, but I couldn't live with it. So I switched to children. Kids at risk. Kids in trouble. And I went back to my math roots. Every child wants attention, community, safety. Humans are pack animals. We all crave connection, and being alone, especially when surrounded by those who are not, can break a soul. Kids who are routinely left out, pushed to the sidelines, picked on, made fun of, or simply made to feel invisible and unworthy of love, will develop problems. I want to know which kids those are, before it gets to that stage. I'm with these kids twenty-five hours each week. There's only one of me and eighteen of them, but by God, I will make sure that in this room, for the time we have together, they will know that they are all worthy. I will find the good in them and shine a spotlight on it so their peers see it. I will do what I can."

"You are amazing," Abby said. "Have you told other teachers about this?"

"Ah, you are idealistic, aren't you? There are already so many rules and regulations in place about classroom behavior. Mandating something like this would instantly ruin it. It works for me because I believe in it and I want to do it."

She pointed to where the little girl was giving Lily a good-bye hug.

"Do you see that? Farrah has been in three different foster homes this year alone. She has learned not to bond, not to care because she knows that it never lasts. But here, with Lily, she allows herself to care."

Abby pressed a knuckle against her lip and fought back tears. This is why Haylee started the program. This is what the ranch was about. What everyone on the ranch was about.

"Love is about connection, Abby." Mrs. Hill's wise eyes evaluated her. "You and your sister are lucky to have each other."

"I know."

"Don't put me on a pedestal. This is how I've made peace with what happened, that's all."

She glanced at the clock and clapped her hands. "Students, it's time to switch circles. Everyone gets their turn."

# Chapter Twenty

Jon guessed that Roman had been using all his energy to hide his symptoms. Now that he no longer had to do that, he was at ease, and the full extent of his illness roared to the forefront.

One week ago, he had been able to walk, with help, through his garden, admiring the vegetables even if he could no longer eat them, and checking on apple sets that wouldn't mature until after he was gone.

Then, overnight it seemed, he wasn't able to leave his chair. He was down to a semi-liquid diet of applesauce, juice, and pudding and even eating that exhausted him. His skin was loose and gray, his eyes sunken, and the tremor in his hands had worsened.

The end was coming, and as much as Jon thought he was prepared, he found himself panicking at odd moments. He found it difficult to be inside the house, crowded as it was with the rented hospital bed, the oxygen bottles, the bottles of pills and bags of fluids, the extra pillows and towels and sheets.

Abby tiptoed around them both. He was angry with her for not telling him the truth earlier. He'd lost time with his father, time he'd never get back. Now, all that was left was the dying time.

Some of his anger was toward himself, he admitted. The signs had been there, had he chosen to see them.

Everything changed once he learned about his father's condition. His feelings toward Abby weren't simple anymore. He wanted to trust her. He knew that Roman had put her in an impossible position, that it wasn't her fault.

But she was here and his anger had to go somewhere, though he did his best not to show it.

Abby was doing everything she could now to help. She'd convinced Roman to hire a palliative care nurse and, since he steadfastly refused to go to the hospital, Jon was grateful.

When Roman was sleeping or Abby or the nurse was with him, Jon escaped to the outdoors. He'd developed an appreciation for the work Abby had done in the yard and garden. It was truly an oasis and he was grateful that Roman's last view would be of the place where he'd found joy, peace, and purpose.

He wished he'd realized sooner how much this place meant to Roman and deeply regretted pushing so hard for him to move. He could barely remember why it had seemed so important. His job was just a job and not even a particularly good one. He'd enjoyed freelancing far more than he had reporting on town hall meetings and whether or not rezoning proposals had been voted in.

He'd been thinking of his own needs, thinking that he had years and years of guilt-ridden trips down the coast highway to visit his father when in fact, they were almost over.

"I'm sorry," he whispered to a big tree swishing softly in the breeze. His chest felt like it wasn't big enough to contain everything he was feeling, not if he wanted to keep breathing.

He hadn't expected grief to feel so odd, he thought, bracing his palm against the rough trunk as his head spun. He'd be walking outside and suddenly the green grass zoomed in and became more vivid while the sky grew paler and more distant. He could pick out individual voices of birds, see a ray of sunshine refract into a rainbow off a bead of dew. He could hear the rush of blood through his body and feel the pulse of life in his fingertips.

He stood still, waiting for his balance to return, feeling the raw heat inside his rib cage.

Roman's spark was growing dimmer. His spirit was ebbing away and soon he would disappear, leaving nothing but a shell. How was that possible? Where did that energy go?

Perhaps in those moments when nature twisted into a macabre fun-house carnival, Jon was being given a glimpse behind the curtain between this world and the next. Maybe the universe was preparing him for that which the human mind cannot accept.

Footsteps sounded behind him and he pushed himself away from the tree.

"Abby," he said.

Her face was white, her eyes huge, stricken. She stopped six feet away from him and simply stood there, her hands hanging loosely at her side, as if she didn't know what to do with them.

"What is it? Is he—?"

"Your father's fine." Abby's voice shook. "I mean . . . you know."

Jon nodded, exhaling slowly. Every day, every interaction was fraught with dread. One of these days his father would not be fine.

"What is it?" he asked.

They hadn't been alone together since the seizure. She came early each morning to tend to Chaos and spell the night nurse. Jon looked after the house, kept food in the re-frigerator, and made himself available for whatever his father wanted.

They took turns keeping Roman company. Cribbage had been big at first. Yahtzee for a while. Jigsaw puzzles. But as his fine motor skills deteriorated, the effort it took for Roman to shake dice or pick up a puzzle piece became too distressing, and Jon chose to watch TV with him or read aloud from the newspaper. Watching his father fail at such basic tasks was intolerable.

It hadn't bothered Abby, though. She shook the dice for Roman and asked him what to save and what to re-throw. He spied puzzle pieces and she put them where he told her. Jon guessed that being a woman, and a friend, simplified the relationship. Roman's fatherly pride wasn't on the line as it was with his son.

Now he saw, though, what it was costing her to be present for Roman.

"Jon." Her voice cracked and she reached for him. "I'm sorry. I'm sorry for everything. Please believe me."

Before he even knew what he was doing, he had her crushed against his chest. The sensation of her body in his arms stopped the spinning around him, grounded him, connected him, made him feel like he could actually get through this, that with her help, he could make sense of life once again.

"He's your dad, not mine," she said, her face muffled by his shirt. "If I'm intruding, you'll tell me, right?"

"Intruding? Never." If anything, she wasn't here enough. If he had his way, she'd never leave his side, and they'd be together forever. But that had to be her choice. Only she could slay the demons that haunted her.

"I don't want to co-opt your loss." Her shoulders shook and hot tears dampened his neck.

He pushed her back and looked into her face. When he could trust his voice, he said, "I'm so grateful that you've been part of this, Abby. I can see how much you care for him and I know he loves you. You have a right to grieve."

She took a deep, shuddering breath and looked away.

"Abby." He squeezed her upper arms gently until she met his eyes again. "What is it?"

Helplessly, she shook her head. "I don't know. I don't know. I've only known him a short time. How can you survive it? How can anyone survive it?"

Through his pain, a spark of hope flared to life.

"Love is worth it, Abby."

"People keep telling me that. But is it?" She seemed to be genuinely asking. "I've missed you, Jon. You've been here but we've hardly talked. Even that hurts like hell. What if . . . what if it was more?"

He pulled her close and lowered his lips to hers. She clung to him as if he was a life preserver and she was drowning. She tasted of berries and fresh, clean water. Knowledge he'd long refused to admit flooded into his mind.

"It's already more, Abby," he murmured against her mouth. "The timing sucks, but I'm in love with you."

She looked panicked, but she didn't pull away. "I don't know how to do this!"

"Listen to your heart," he said, and kissed her again.


Abby picked her way over the stone-and-mulch path to the timber-framed two-bedroom cabin she shared with Quinn at the far end of the workers' row. Stars peeked and twinkled overhead, brilliant in the dark of the new moon. The pause between breaths, Jamie called it. Time to rest, regenerate, prepare for the next cycle.

What would the next cycle contain for her? She hugged her elbows, partly against the chilly night air, partly from nerves. Jon, in love with her.

She wanted to believe it.

She was afraid to believe it.

He belonged in the bright lights and gridlock of Los

Angeles, not out here in ranch country, where a traffic jam meant someone was moving a herd of cattle across the road. Other than sharing the same ocean, the tiny windswept community of Sunset Bay and its long lonely stretches of pristine sand had nothing in common with bustling Santa Monica or Venice Beach.

Jon liked to be where the action was, where the stories were.

Abby relished the peace here and her story was not meant for telling.

She lifted her face to the starlight again and breathed deeply. For the first time in her adult life, things were stable. They had enough money. They had a roof over their heads, food, friends, work.

But Abby wondered if she or Quinn would ever be truly free of the scars those early years of insecurity had left on them. If Abby would ever be able to accept Jon's love and return it.

She passed the last of the cabins and turned on the path to her own. Her heart lifted at the sight, as it always did. With two windows framing the wooden door and a half-width porch on the front, it always looked to her like the cabin was waiting for her with a smile of invitation.

It was all quiet inside but a light was burning over the kitchen sink. Abby was surprised that Quinn had gone to bed early. Maybe she was taking the new moon to heart as well.

Abby tiptoed across the creaky floorboards, shedding her light jacket and hanging it on the back of a chair. With a soft *mmmrrt,* Tux jumped down lightly from the windowsill where he loved to sit and watch the night-flying insects and bats that came out in warmer weather.

"Hello, handsome," she whispered, bending down to stroke the sleek black and white fur that had inspired his name. He alternated his nights between the two bedrooms on a schedule that only he understood and Abby was ridiculously pleased that he'd passed up snuggling with Quinn to wait for her.

Quinn had wept for the orphaned coyote pups as much as she'd wept for Tux's mother, and Abby had been helpless to comfort her. There was no explaining the randomness of life. One predator is accepted, another rejected. Some babies saved, others left to starve unseen.

Despite being motherless, the kittens had all grown into excellent hunters, thereby earning their keep by controlling the mouse population in the barns.

Tyler and Duke too, had thrived with the responsibility, showing themselves to have developed nurturing skills that no one would have expected when they'd first arrived. On the cusp of adulthood, according to the state, they were no longer entitled to mandated care, though they were even less prepared than most to live independently.

Had it been Olivia's tough love that had saved them? Would they have ended up on the streets? In prison? Dead? Or would they have finished school, sidestepped the lure of gangs and drugs, discovered dreams, made something of themselves, without Sanctuary Ranch?

Nature, nurture, instinct, education . . . who knew what was most important in helping a creature become the best it could be?

Was it a roll of the dice? A bad deal that just left some with losing hands, no matter how they played their cards?

She poured fresh kibble into Tux's bowl and listened to him purr for a moment. His white-tipped tail curled at the end as he settled down to crunch on his meal.

"Okay, sweet-face." When she was sure he'd finished his meal, she gathered him into her arms and carried him to her room. "Time for bed."

After she'd finished washing her face and brushing her teeth, she nudged the door to Quinn's room and peeked inside.

A soft *woof* came from the foot of the bed. Ziggy Bigelow

lifted his shaggy head and blinked at her. His socialization was going well. If he continued to progress, Quinn would soon be bringing him along to the schools.

"Shh," Abby said.

The dim glow of the hallway light, Abby could see the outline of her sister's slender body beneath the quilt. Quinn slept with a pillow over her head, as if hearing echoes of the sounds that had once kept her awake and now bounced around inside her sleeping mind like pinballs in a machine.

Ziggy Bigelow padded to the head of the bed, turned a circle, and flopped down.

Right on top of Quinn.

Except Quinn wasn't there.

As soon as the night nurse arrived, Jon got into his car. He needed to clear his head, to be away from Dad and the dog and the house and the dread that overwhelmed him.

He was falling in love, while his father was dying. It seemed so wrong.

He parked near the beach on the outskirts of town, then got out to walk. The wind held enough strength to make him hunker his shoulders against it, and enough salt to make his eyes sting. He was tired of feeling inadequate and guilty at the same time. It would almost be easier, he thought with still more guilt, if his father had died while Jon was still in L.A.

The waiting was horrible.

Even as he thought it, he realized how selfish and petty he was being. If it was hard on Jon, how much harder was it on Roman? He wasn't even seventy, but chronic health issues made him seem older. He should have been looking at many more years of life but that's not the hand he'd been dealt.

He stopped and stared out at the horizon, listening to the

rhythmic shift and flow of the waves. The steel-gray water was touched with whitecaps that glowed pink in the setting sun and white-wing gulls flipped and soared overhead, their piercing cries a perfect accompaniment to the wordless ballad underscoring his life.

Abby was afraid; he got that. Would she learn to trust him?

He shoved his hands deeper into his jacket pockets and continued walking. Up ahead, he spied a seafood restaurant with twinkling lights strung along the upper deck railings that were just becoming visible in the growing darkness.

Music drifted down and he could see people dancing inside.

A beer at the bar might make him feel better. He wasn't in the mood to talk to anyone but he knew he shouldn't be alone right now.

The wide-plank wood steps were grayed from the elements and years of foot traffic, though peeling white paint still showed in the corners. He opened the door to a waft of air fragrant with bacon grease and fries and his stomach growled, reminding him that it had been hours since he'd last eaten, days since he'd eaten properly.

He found a seat at the bar and ordered dark beer, then sat back and looked over the menu. Besides the usual pub fare, they featured fresh oysters, a market-price catch-of-the-day item Aiden said sold out quickly. He'd have to come back another day with Abby.

"Here you go, love." The waitress was a young woman named Amina who wore her black hair in an enormous ponytail made up of dozens of tiny braids. When she leaned forward to set his glass onto a cardboard coaster, the beads at the ends of her braids clicked like tap dancers. "Kitchen's closed but I could get you a sandwich if you're hungry."

Jon thumbed away the caramel-colored froth that slipped down the edge of his frosted glass. "I'm good."

He took a deep drink of his beer, relishing the smooth

slide down his throat. He watched the servers moving back and forth behind the bar, pulling drinks, sending in orders, chatting with customers, deftly riding that line between friendly and flirtatious. Amina had just enough sternness in her expression to indicate that she was not to be messed with and her athletic build suggested that if someone required more assertive handling, she would happily provide it.

Physically, she couldn't have been more different from Abby. Skin color, bone structure, hair, eyes. Amina's edges were hard where Abby's were soft, the planes of her muscles flat and solid, where Abby had the lean strength of a dancer. Yet Jon sensed, without being able to put his finger on exactly why, that Abby could deal with anything Amina could. That maybe, like those tai chi practitioners who could disable an opponent by turning his own power against him, Abby had discovered powers of self-defense far beyond the purely physical.

He finished his drink and was about to signal Amina for the bill, when he noticed her watching a group near the window.

Several young men and women that had been laughing together the whole time Jon had been at the bar, had been joined by a larger group. Tables were pushed together, chairs rearranged and now they'd opened up an area of the parquet floor for dancing.

The volume of their laughter and the loose limbs of the dancers indicated that they'd been drinking for some time. Women tossed their hair, adjusted their thin-strapped tank tops, men slapped each other on the back, looped arms over the backs of chairs, glanced at cleavage.

Then he saw a flash of shiny wheat-gold hair.

Quinn?

He straightened up to get a better look. Yes, Abby's little sister was out and having a great time, by the look of it.

She was sitting on the lap of one man, laughing loudly at

something he said, leaning her chest near his face. His hand rested on her thigh, just below the frayed edge of her short denim cutoffs.

Quinn, who'd barely talked to him, who'd been afraid of her own shadow.

He paid his bill but asked Amina if he could stay a while longer. Something wasn't right about the situation with Quinn and he didn't want to leave until he'd figured out what.

When he saw the man stand up, and half carry, half lead Quinn toward the door, Jon moved quickly to follow them. He caught up to them in the parking lot, where the guy was attempting to pour Quinn into the passenger seat of his pickup truck.

"Excuse me," he said. "Quinn, what are you doing?"

"Back off, buddy," said the cowboy. "She's with me."

"What's her last name?" Jon asked. "What's her first name?"

The man looked blank.

"That's what I thought." He reached around the man and pulled Quinn out. Her head lolled against his shoulder. "Come on, honey. I'm taking you home."

"I bought the drinks," the cowboy snarled. "She owes me."

White heat flared behind Jon's eyelids. "If you touch her again," he said, "I will fuck you up. Do you understand?"

He grabbed the man's keys from his hand and hurled them onto the beach. "Maybe by the time you find them, you'll be sober enough to drive."

Then he carried Quinn to his car.

"You're not s'posed to know I'm here," she complained. "Nobody's s'posed to know. Abby'll have a fit."

"Yeah, for good reason. What's the matter with you? Do you have any idea how much this will scare her?"

Quinn fell into a sullen silence.

"Don't puke in my car, okay?" he said. "I can't believe

this. After everything she's done for you, this is how you repay her."

"Man," cried Quinn. "Enough with the guilt trip. I already feel bad enough, okay? I tried to make things better for Carly and she wouldn't let me. Now we're stuck out here and Abby won't have any fun because she thinks she doesn't deserve it."

"Wait," Jon said, thinking quickly. "Who's Carly? What do you mean, she wouldn't let you? Wouldn't let you do what?"

Quinn turned her head to the window. "They won't listen to me until I'm twenty-one but you know what? I'm almost there. Then they have to. Then I'll do the right thing, and Abby can't stop me. She thinks I'm not tough enough but I am. I am."

She sniffled the rest of the way home and refused to say anything more.

But Jon had a feeling he already knew.

# Chapter Twenty-One

"Come on, Quinn, pick up." Abby punched the redial button on her phone for the tenth time, willing her sister to answer, but with no luck. She had her car keys in her hand and was about to pull the door open when she heard the sound of tires on the gravel driveway.

She ran outside to see Jon, carrying a sleeping Quinn in his arms.

"Oh my God," she cried. "What happened?"

"She's fine," he said. "She's extremely drunk, but otherwise unharmed. I found her in town with a bunch of tourists who thought they'd have some fun with the locals."

Abby held the door open for him and led the way to Quinn's room. When he entered the bedroom door, Ziggy looked up and growled.

Jon stopped. "What's with the welcoming committee?"

"Ziggy," Abby scolded. "Off."

She pointed to the crate in the corner and he slunk inside, tail down.

"Quinn's socializing one of the latest rescues."

"He looks a little iffy to me."

"Yeah. Well. She's no shining example herself right now."

She tucked Quinn in, put a couple of aspirin and a big glass of water on the night table, and turned out the light.

Her heart was still hammering in her chest. Not again. Not again.

"Has she done this before?" Jon asked.

She nodded. "A few times. But she's doing better out here. I thought she was, anyway."

"She mentioned something about wanting to fix something. To do the right thing. Something you didn't want her to do. What was she talking about?"

Abby's blood turned to ice. "I don't know."

Jon looked quizzically at her. "Really?"

She steeled herself not to react. "She's drunk, like you said. Who knows what she's saying?"

"She mentioned someone named Carly."

Abby swallowed. "Did she?"

"Come on, Abby. Talk to me."

Quinn's birthday couldn't come soon enough. Her stomach churned as she lay in bed listening to Jon and Abby. Yeah, she was drunk. But she still knew what she was doing. She'd finally convinced Carly that she wanted to come forward with her information. Between her and Carly, surely they could find someone who would listen and do something. No one wanted the report of a minor, but the second she was twenty-one, she was going to step up.

She'd been running from this for a long time. Abby didn't understand. She hadn't seen what Quinn had seen. She didn't live with the guilt of watching a good friend be hurt and humiliated and staying quiet.

Quinn had just been a kid at the time. She understood why Abby wanted to protect her. And Carly was generous and kind, like Abby. Neither one of them wanted to pit quiet little Quinn against the monster Richard Arondi.

Only, she wasn't quiet little Quinn anymore. She was tougher and smarter now.

Okay, so maybe the booze wasn't smart. It made her feel brave and strong but it didn't last. And this swirly feeling sucked, big time. She hadn't been interested in that cowboy and was kind of glad that Jon had shown up when he did.

But was it any worse than what had happened to Carly? No. She deserved to be punished, for hiding out here while Carly and those other girls lived with what Arondi did to them.

She sat up, then quickly changed her mind.

She was going to puke eventually, and she hated that.

But then she was going back to Los Angeles. She was going to find Carly and they were going to go to a police officer and make him or her listen.

Then she could stop running.


On the day of Quinn's party, the table on the deck was laden with the usual summer fare: salads of every kind, cold meat, fried chicken, pickles, buns, cheese, fruit and vegetable platters. All the staff were here, plus significant others, kids, dogs, and their current guests.

It was like a huge family gathering, or what Abby guessed such an event would be like.

Quinn looked a little overwhelmed at being the center of attention, but Abby could tell she was soaking it in.

Roman rallied enough to join them. In fact, he'd vehemently refused to be left out. News of his condition was common knowledge now. Jamie had driven out to see him as soon as she found out, tore a strip off him, and then fell into his arms, weeping.

Roman said he'd been quite entertained by the spectacle.

He was in a wheelchair now, for safety's sake. He could still walk around his own home but navigating elsewhere exhausted him. A portable oxygen tank rolled with him now, too. The poor dog kept having his feet run over, but it didn't deter him. If anything, Chaos stayed closer than ever to Roman's side, as if aware on some level that his time was drawing near.

Haylee and Sage were with him now, letting him hold the babies. He was making macabre faces but seemed to be enjoying it. He seemed to be enjoying everything now, though Abby sensed an air of desperation about him. He touched people more, clutching at hands, patting and stroking.

He wanted to hold on, to not be alone, left behind while the world kept moving.

Grief, sweet-sharp like the Jonagold apples, hit her and she looked away, breathing deeply.

Roman vowed that if she cried, he'd leave. Today was about Quinn and he refused to get in the way of her celebration.

She hoped it gave Quinn what she needed. The drinking last weekend had terrified her. What she'd said to Jon terrified her even more. He was a smart guy. He would soon put two and two together and then what? Quinn would be in Richard Arondi's crosshairs.

She couldn't let that happen.

A *whoop* of approval went up and Abby looked toward the sliding door, where Daphne appeared, holding an enormous layered sheet cake. Someone struck up a round of "Happy Birthday," the candles were lit and blown out. Slices were cut and handed around.

Quinn came up to Abby and grabbed her hand, grinning. "This is the biggest party I've ever had. I'm now an adult, officially, legally."

Abby hugged her. "You'll always be my kid sister."

"But you can't boss me around anymore. You're free and so am I." Quinn wrinkled her nose, flipped her hair over her shoulder, kissed Abby's cheek, and went to accept more good wishes.

We've always been free, she wanted to say. Please stay, Quinn.

Another turning point, another fork in the road.

"Cake?" said a voice at her elbow. It was Jon, carrying two plates.

Abby accepted one. They moved to the porch railing and stood at it, looking out over the yard. It was easier than looking at each other, though she was viscerally aware of Jon's proximity. It was as if her skin was tuned to his frequency. All the little hairs on her arms lifted in his direction when he was near.

She thought she'd feel lighter once Jon knew about Roman's illness, once she was no longer carrying that secret, but instead, a new awkwardness had set in. The kind of emotional rawness they'd witnessed in each other didn't translate to ordinary social interactions.

"Quinn's having a good time," Jon said. He sounded hesitant, too.

"She is. Looks like your dad is enjoying himself, too."

Silence descended. Sweet chocolate frosting coated the back of her throat and she set her plate aside, half eaten.

"Poor Chaos," Jon said. She followed his gaze. Little Matthew was tugging on his ear while Sal was attempting to climb on his back.

"He'd leave if it really bothered him."

"He's a good dog." Jon swallowed and she heard his throat click. "He'll be lost without Dad."

Abby couldn't speak. She'd grown to love the big, goofy dog and would miss him dreadfully. She hoped Jon would keep him, though she couldn't imagine Chaos enjoying life in the city, after all the freedom he'd enjoyed here. Maybe Jon would bring him back to visit.

Although Jon hadn't said he was going back, he hadn't said he wasn't, either, and she refused to ask. She also refused to take his declaration of love seriously. He was grieving. He deserved some slack.

The sound of a spoon clinking against glass caught their attention.

Quinn was standing on a chair.

Abby blinked in surprise. A speech? That wasn't like her sister.

"Hi, everybody. Thank you for the party. This is awesome." She cleared her throat. "I have something to say and I wanted to say it in front of you all, because it's important. My big sister, Abby, as you know, has been kind of a mom to me, too. She's done a lot for me, sacrificed a lot so we could stay together."

Abby pressed her fingertips against her lips. She felt Jon move closer and put his hand around her waist.

"I haven't made things easy for Abby." Quinn looked down. "But she's always protected me, no matter what, even when I didn't want her to."

She lifted her head then, smiled at Jon, and met Abby's eyes. "Thank you, Abby. For everything."

A cheer went up then and everyone clinked glasses.

"I'm not done!" Quinn yelled, waving her arms. Laughter sounded. "Abby, I want you to know that you don't have to protect me anymore. I can handle myself. I'm twenty-one. It's time I did the right thing."

A block of ice formed in the pit of Abby's stomach. No, she thought.

Quinn bit her lip, then shrugged. "That's it," she said. "I'm done. Now you can clap."

"That was cryptic," Jon said. "Do you know what she's talking about?"

"Oh, God," Abby said, faintly. She gripped Jon's hand.

"Abby? Are you okay?"

She shook her head. She whirled around, speaking low and fast. "Promise me, Jon, that if she comes to you about the Arondi story, that you won't let her do something stupid."

He stared at her. "What are you talking about?"

She pulled him away from the crowd, in the direction of her cabin. She had a feeling Quinn would be following soon and she had a lot to tell Jon, first.


She pulled him inside the small cabin, closed the door, and stood with her back against it, breathing hard. The soft swell of her breasts rose and fell above the neckline of her yellow sundress.

"I think I know what Quinn wants to do," she began. "She knows you're writing about Arondi."

A sick feeling came over him. Not this. Anything but this.

"Abby." He pulled her toward the couch and pushed her gently onto it. "What happened? Who's Carly? Is she Carly Cassidy?"

"You know her?"

Jon nodded. "Quinn is Person X, isn't she?"

She pressed her face into her hands. "It was never supposed to come out."

"What does she know? What happened?"

"At first, I wasn't sure. One day she came home from the set saying she wanted to quit. She wouldn't say why, just that she hated the whole scene. She was angry and sometimes I heard her crying in her room at night."

Jon knew. Quinn had witnessed her friend being assaulted. No wonder she was freaked and acting out.

"She just said she was sick of everyone, sick of Los Angeles, sick of being broke and alone. I knew the rumors. Arondi was a total creep. But I couldn't believe that something like that had happened to her. And she promised me she wasn't hurt, just scared. But she wasn't just scared. She was angry, too. It was too much."

He stroked her back. She was cold and shaking.

"Finally, Carly contacted me. She . . . told me what happened. No details, but I didn't need her to draw me a picture. I was sick about it, Jon. My sister's testimony could have—maybe—been used to nail Arondi. But he could also have turned it around on her, ruined her life. He'd done it before. A lot of people listened to him."

"I know." Excitement simmered in him, though he tried to keep it in. Abby was terrified for her sister. But this could be the thing that would finally turn the tide against Arondi.

It wasn't the story, he told himself. It was about justice.

"That's when I decided we needed to get out of the city," Abby continued. "We bounced around a bit after that. She got into some trouble. It was . . . it got a little scary for a while. I thought . . . I thought I might lose her."

She twisted her arm, showing Jon her wrist. A semicolon, tattooed on smooth skin, a match to the one that covered the thin, slicing scars on Quinn's forearm.

"I figured," he said softly. "I'm so sorry."

"Then I heard about the ranch. It saved us."

Abby had gone to great lengths to keep her sister safe.

"And she never talked to you about the incident with Carly herself?"

Abby shook her head. "Pressing her about it only upset her, so I stopped asking. She promised me over and over that she hadn't been hurt, just that she'd seen things she wasn't comfortable with and didn't want to be there anymore."

Jon hated what he was about to do. "Abby, I've talked with six women while building my story on Arondi. All aspiring actors who'd auditioned for parts in his productions. All young, pretty, and desperate. They all tell similar stories, but in every case, it's her word against his. They know that he controls Hollywood and he can ruin them if he wants. There's never been a witness. Until now."

The color leached from Abby's face as she listened. "You can't ask her to do this. Do you know what he does to people? You said it yourself: he destroys them. I won't let that happen to her. Oh, Jon." She buried her face in her hands. "What was I thinking, getting her involved in that world? I should have known better."

His heart ached. He understood completely how she felt.

"Please," she whispered. "Please don't ask Quinn to do this."

"I won't," he said. He swallowed. "But if she wants to do this, Abby, you can't stop her. You can't protect her anymore. You have to let her make her own choices."

Abby lifted her head. "This is what you've been waiting for, isn't it?"

He couldn't deny it. "I want to write this story, Abby. With Quinn's help, we can bring him to justice. We can right a terrible wrong for many women."

"And resurrect your career in the meantime."

"It's not about that anymore, Abby. I don't care about *Diversion.* I don't want to go back to Hollywood. I love it here, with Dad." He hesitated. "With you."

She got up. "I'm tired, Jon. You're going to do what you're going to do. You and Quinn both. It doesn't matter what I say."

"What about us, Abby?"

She gave him a sad smile. "Let's face it, Jon. There never was much chance for us. I'm a bad bargain with too much baggage."

"You still think I'll disappear on you, the way your mom did. You think I'll break your heart."

"Jon," she said. "You've already broken my heart."

# Chapter Twenty-Two

From Abby's notebook:

*Prune spring-flowering shrubs after blossoms
fade. Next year's blooms depend on the cuts you
make now.*

Abandonment issues were such a cliché, thought Abby. Couldn't she come up with a more interesting reason for breaking up with Jon?

"Why aren't you angry?" she said to him. "Why can't you see that I'm too broken, too damaged to have a normal relationship?"

"You think that you need to end things now, while it's still easy, so neither of us gets hurt, is that it?"

"Come on, Jon. The statistics don't lie. Happily ever after is barely batting fifty percent. For people like us, like me," she corrected, "it's a losing proposition. I do care about you, though. And that's why I'm doing this. So you can move on to someone better. So you can have a future."

Jon was always looking to the future. Planning a season in advance was a big step for Abby. There hadn't been much point, before. Keeping Quinn safe and happy had been her only goal. It had taken all her time and energy to make that happen.

"Quinn's just an excuse," Jon said. "You don't know how to handle what's happening between us. Your sister has her own goals. She's an adult now. She's making good choices mostly. She's looking after herself. She wants to go to school. She wants a life of her own. She's setting you free, Abs, and you don't know how to handle that."

She yanked away from Jon's grip, hating the truth of his words.

She'd done a damn fine job. And now it was over.

Since she was a kid, forever it seemed, Abby had been pedaling madly to keep ahead of the slavering jaws snapping at their heels. Suddenly the beast was gone and she was coasting on a road without a map, or brakes or armor for when she crashed.

The imagery displeased her. Quinn wasn't a beast. Caring for her hadn't been a burden. She loved her sister. She was the oldest, so the responsibility fell to her to keep things together.

"What did you tell me? You put on your big girl panties and did the hard work because you had no choice." Jon's voice was kind, his touch gentle. "You had to be the adult because there was nobody else to do it. You took over the role of mother, Abby, but Quinn's not your child. She's your sister. If you don't let her go, let her make her own decision about this, you'll lose her. And if you don't find a life of your own, you'll end up resenting her."

Yes, she loved Quinn.

But now she allowed herself to remember other times. When she hadn't been able to go to her own prom because Mom was gone and there was no money for a sitter, so Abby had to stay home. When Quinn whined and argued and pestered her until she thought she'd lose her mind. When she spent precious grocery money on ice cream and cake only to have Quinn get sick in the night because she'd eaten too much.

When she wanted to hang out with friends, or accept the movie invitation from that cute guy at the coffee shop but she couldn't because what nineteen-year-old brings her kid sister along on date night?

And the guilt. Oh, the guilt had been overwhelming. Every time she'd heard Quinn crying into her pillow at night, it was a twist of the knife.

So, she'd quit being resentful. She'd become an adult, done what was necessary.

"We were okay," she said softly. "I did my best and we were okay. We are okay."

"You did an amazing job," Jon said. "I can't believe you got through what you did. But surviving is different from thriving. You've got the chance to be better than okay now, Abby. You're done raising Quinn. You've got friends. You have people who"—he hesitated—"people who love you. If you'll let them. We have a good thing, Abby. Why can't you believe it could work between us? Why can't you let yourself be happy?"

He made it sound so easy.


At her request, Jon drove Quinn to L.A. Also at Quinn's request, Abby remained at the ranch, her eyes empty, her arms folded over her chest, fear written in every line of her body. He knew it must feel like betrayal to Abby, but he also knew that getting this out into the open was the only chance he had at moving forward with Abby. He had to take the risk.

He and Quinn met with Carly. The girls told their story, over and over. They answered Jon's questions, they talked to investigators, lawyers, other women who'd been harassed and assaulted.

Finally, Jon had everything he needed for his exposé.

He didn't care.

He couldn't get back to Oregon fast enough, to his father. To Abby.

Roman was holding his own, but as the summer flowers faded and the grasses went from green to gold, he stayed in the house more, spent more time in his wheelchair for fear of falling.

Time was running out quickly for him.

"What do you need, Dad?" Jon asked, over and over. "What can I get you? What do you want to do?"

The haunted look in Roman's eyes broke his heart. It was so hard, watching someone fade away, being able to do nothing.

"Son, everything I need is right here. I've got you. I've got a good dog. I've got fresh air, sunshine, flowers, and a pretty girl comes around from time to time to flirt with me. I'm the luckiest bastard in the world."

Jon didn't know how much more he could bear.

Eventually, Roman could no longer keep anything but fluids down, and a mere cup a day at that. But he was on enough medication to manage his pain, without making him sleepy and confused.

"I'm going out exactly as I wanted to, Jon," Roman said. Chaos lay on a quilted blanket at his side. The dog, normally so energetic, had taken to lying as close as possible to his master, no matter where they were. Roman rarely asked anything of Chaos but the dog seemed to understand how much his presence was valued. He left Roman's side only to eat or drink, or answer the call of nature, but always did so quickly, eager to return to his post.

They were sitting on the porch, overlooking the yard as they often did on clear evenings. Sunset streamed through the willow tree that drooped graceful limbs down toward the creek, and cast a golden glow over the tidy flower beds.

Abby had built up the berm next to the fence, to close off the space where Chaos used to escape as a pup. She'd cut soft curves into the front side and planted a variety of foliage in different heights and textures, giving a restful effect best viewed from exactly where he and Roman were sitting.

She'd known before he had, Jon remembered. The twist of betrayal had long ago disappeared. Jon's distance, both physical and emotional, had caused Roman to seek out someone else. Abby had been what Roman needed at the time.

She still was.

Roman loved him, Jon knew that. But one person isn't always enough, and with her calm acceptance, Abby gave Roman something Jon could not.

"Dad?" Jon said. The backs of his eyes felt hot. "You know I love you, right?"

Roman sighed. "My boy. I've never doubted it. Not for a second. It's me who should be asking you that."

"I wasted so much time trying to get justice for you, trying to make a name for myself in the process. I failed you."

"*Pfft*. I never needed justice."

Jon smiled. It might be true now, but getting there had been a journey.

"They say living well is the best revenge," Roman added. "So I'm good."

He spoke as if the lonely, painful years had never happened. As if he'd forgiven the people who'd turned against him, the industry that had thrown him to the wolves and forgotten him, and gone on to venerate men who were true predators and villains.

"Is that how it works? When you come to the end, you choose what to remember and what to let go of?"

Roman shrugged. "If you're smart, you'll do it long before the end. I've had a good summer. A good year, in fact. A few good years. This is a good place, Jon."

Jon nodded. Sunset Bay had been a true refuge and he was grateful his father had found it when he did. He only wished he'd been there more to share it with him.

"Knock that shit off now." Roman smiled and nudged him gently. "I know what you're doing. No regrets, hmm?"

Jon sighed. "That's a tough order but I'll try."

As the light faded, bats came out to hunt insects, darting here and there in their random, jerky flight paths. Now and then, they felt the little rush of air as one flew past, barely but always, missing them.

"How do they do it again?" Roman asked. "Radar? Sonar?"

He sounded tired.

"Echolocation," Jon replied. "Do you want to go inside?"

"No. I like watching them." His voice was faint, his words meandering in the dark, as if he was recalling a dream. "I like knowing that there's another way of traveling through the night. That the way we see isn't the only way. I like thinking about worlds beyond this one, time that isn't linear, language we don't know we understand, until we find ourselves speaking it."

Jon couldn't respond. Instead, he reached out and took Roman's thin hand in his and held it.

They stayed that way, connected, watching bats and pondering the universe until Abby came out a half hour later.

"It's late," she said softly, reaching for the handles of Roman's chair. "We should get you to bed."

Roman grunted. "No. Sit with us, Abby."

She glanced at Jon and he nodded. She pulled a seat up to Roman's other side. He reached for her hand and tugged it into his lap, next to Jon's.

"You two," he said, with a sigh.

Chaos shifted on the blanket at Roman's feet and thumped his tail.

In the time they'd been sitting there, it had grown chilly, yet Roman didn't seem to feel it. Warmth and strength radiated off him, despite his frail, slumped body.

"Dad?" Jon said.

"Look after each other." Roman squeezed their hands, pressing them together between his. The tremor that had bothered him was gone. "Promise me."

Jon looked across at Abby. Her eyes were wide, cautious, but she nodded. "Of course, Roman."

"Jon?"

"Sure, Dad."

He exhaled and seemed to fold in on himself, like a spent bloom, shriveling on the stem.

"Good," he murmured. "That's good."

After a long moment, he added. "And look after the mutt, will you? He's a good boy."

Chaos, hearing the coveted words, got to his feet and wiggled his head under Roman's arm.

Roman released his grip on their hands and reached down to stroke his beloved dog's ears.

Then he sighed, long and slow. His hand dropped away from the silken fur, his head slipped forward, and he was gone.

From Abby's notebook:

> *Stake tall-growing flowering plants such as delphinium, hollyhocks, and lupine before they bloom. It's at the height of beauty that they are the heaviest and need help to stay upright.*

Roman's memorial was held in the Sunset Bay funeral home. It was a small affair, announced to a select list prepared by Roman himself before his death. Jon had said a few words, as had Olivia and Jamie. Haylee, who'd lost Jewel the previous week, clung to Aiden and little Mattie, barely able to speak.

Abby read a poem and provided the fresh flowers. Roman hadn't wanted anything from the hothouse. Only things that could be planted in his garden after.

Daphne baked all his favorites for the refreshment table.

Abby baked the cake she'd created for him, made with his favorite Jonagold apples. He'd managed a tiny taste of it in the week before his death, enough to pronounce it better than any apple pie, certainly better than the one he and Jon had made under her guidance.

She called it Roman's Apple Cake. It was her favorite recipe so far.

Photographs were displayed on poster boards of Roman in his heyday. He and Jon had picked them out weeks ago. Abby was happy to see that Roman had, at the end, been able to remember his career achievements with pleasure and pride.

He'd had more friends than he realized. At least he'd re-connected with most of them while he still had time.

Time. It's all there really is, she thought.

To Abby's surprise, Lydia, their quiet repeat guest, had traveled out to pay her respects. She was even more surprised by the woman's firm, warm hug.

"I'm so sorry for your loss," Lydia said. "I know he was your friend."

"Thank you," Abby said. "Roman had many friends here."

"He was a good man. And where is his son?"

Abby gestured discreetly to where Jon was standing in a receiving line. He'd remained for the memorial but she knew he was heading to Los Angeles shortly. He insisted he was coming back and she let him think she believed him.

"Shouldn't you be with him?"

"Oh," Abby said. "I'm not family."

Lydia gave her a sharp look. "Abby. What happened?"

This wasn't the sort of conversation she expected to have at a funeral. Certainly not with a ranch guest she barely knew.

"Jon and I are friends." How often had she said that?

"Surely you were more than that."

Abby crossed one arm over her stomach. The Arondi

story was breaking wide open and she had no doubt that his career drought was over. Some things just didn't work out. There were too many strikes against you, the timing was wrong, obligations didn't allow for emotional involvement.

Excuses, all of them.

"It's been a difficult time," she said.

"I was married, you know." Lydia looped her arm through Abby's and walked with her to the tea-and-coffee station set out in the hall.

"Oh." Lydia was clearly here for a purpose but Abby couldn't divine what it was.

"Next month is our anniversary. It would have been, I should say. Thirty-five years."

"Oh my. Congratulations. I mean . . . oh dear." Abby floundered. *Would have been* implied something had happened.

"Don't worry about it," Lydia replied. "You couldn't know. I've taken pains not to talk about it. That's why I keep coming back, you see. Sanctuary Ranch is a place where I'm not . . . the person I am at home."

"And . . . who's that?"

Lydia was quiet for a beat. "The widow. The woman who lost her husband." She gave a little laugh. "It's a funny term, isn't it? *Lost.* Like I misplaced him or something. Like I might come across him again if I look in the back of the closet or maybe the garage."

Abby understood. She kept expecting Roman to be in the next room, or on the porch or with Jon.

Whenever she saw Chaos, going from room to room searching for his missing master, she had to look away.

Abby touched the woman's arm. "I'm so sorry, Lydia."

"I know. Everyone's sorry. But the fact is, it doesn't matter. Henry is gone. He's not lost. I know exactly where he is. He's buried beneath a purple buddleia bush."

"Thirty-five years is a long time."

"Yes. It is."

"You must have loved him very much."

"I did." Another little laugh. "Of course, I hated him at times, too. At the funeral, I gave a short eulogy. I hadn't had a lot of time to prepare. His death was unexpected. A massive heart attack on the golf course. I think he'd be quite horrified at going in such a clichéd manner, but we don't get to choose, do we?"

"No, I guess we don't." Lydia obviously had much to say, now that she'd begun, and Abby didn't want to distract her.

"I said all the right things, things that made people feel good. We were soul mates. He was a good man, lived life to the fullest, we shared dreams, were very blessed with our children, our home, our travel plans. People said it was a lovely service. At the memorial, people got up to share memories of Henry. Everyone loved him. He was everyone's best friend. It's amazing at funerals how suddenly a person has a million best friends."

Her face clouded over. "But the truth is, that's not really what love is about."

Abby looked at her, unsure of how to respond.

Lydia turned then and skewered her with a look of such intensity that Abby actually pulled away.

"You think that love is like the way I spoke of Henry at the funeral. How his friends and acquaintances remembered him at the open mic. And that's part of it. But there's another part, that we don't like to talk about but I think we should."

She took a deep breath but the only thing that indicated the level of emotional intensity was a quiver in her voice.

"I loved Henry. But like I said, I hated him too sometimes. We hurt each other, never intentionally, but there were times . . . well." She shook her head. "Being together for that long, we went through a lot of change, together and separately. It's hard. After a certain point, you realize that you're not married to the same person anymore. And that he isn't either. The kicker is, can you live with the change? That's what the vows are about, after all. Better, worse. Richer, poorer. Sickness, health, all that. You don't think, when you're standing at the altar, with stars in your eyes and roses in your sweaty hands, that you'll ever feel differently, but of course you will."

"I've never been married," Abby said. "I don't think I have what it takes." She thought of Jon and how he'd looked at her, how he'd tried to convince her that they could be good together, that he would never hurt her, that he loved her no matter what. She'd hurt him, badly, with her response. Or lack of response.

"No one has what it takes, Abby," Lydia said, looking at her tenderly. "That's my point. We all think it should be roses and wine and sunsets but in fact, it's trusting someone with the real you. I was petty and selfish and forgetful and Henry ignored my needs sometimes and lost his temper and never did learn how to load the dishwasher properly, which drove me nuts, I tell you."

Abby's laugh caught in her throat.

"Henry also brought me coffee in bed every single Sunday. That's more than sixteen hundred Sundays, give or take. With a kiss and a smile, regardless of if we were at odds with each other or not. It didn't matter, you see. I thanked him every time, but I wonder, if I'd have known that they were ticking down, this is the last twenty, the last ten, the second last, the very last, would I have appreciated it more?"

Yes, Abby thought. When time is all there is, every second mattered.

"You're in love with that nice young man, Jonathan. Aren't you?"

Abby opened her mouth to deny it, but the words didn't come. She lifted her hands and shrugged helplessly.

"Well, whatever you feel, he's definitely in love with you.

He's scared and I don't blame him. He's opened himself up to a world of hurt, and right now, you're letting him swing in the wind. Is that what you intended?"

"No, of course not." Abby's chest was shuddering, like she couldn't coordinate her breathing anymore. Her vision blurred and her throat was tight. "Why are you doing this? This is Roman's memorial. It's not about me and Jon."

"But you see," Lydia said, "it is. Roman asked me to come. He asked me to talk to you. He saw how the two of you were struggling. He believes in you."

"He . . . he does? He did?"

"He loved you, Abby. He wanted nothing more than for you to be his daughter. He knew it wouldn't happen while he was alive, but he died hoping that you and Jon would make it."

### HOLLYWOOD POWERHOUSE ARRESTED ON MULTIPLE COUNTS OF SEXUAL MISCONDUCT. MEDIA GIANT FALLS SOON AFTER

by: Jonathan Byers,
special to the *Los Angeles Times*

More than two dozen women have come forward so far to accuse Richard Arondi, of Arondi Productions, of assault and harassment dating back more than a decade. Charges are pending as the investigation goes on and more victims tell their stories.

The exposure of Hollywood's most open of open secrets has led Arondi's accusers—as well as their loved ones, journalists, and those working in the industry—to ask why, exactly, media giant Whitey Irving of *Diversion* magazine preferred to champion Arondi instead of investigating him.

Former *Diversion* staffers describe a classic you-scratch-my-back-I'll-scratch-yours situation, with editorial slanted to put the best light on Arondi and his activities, in exchange for Arondi maintaining a massive advertising budget with *Diversion*.

"You were neutered as a reporter," said one former *Diversion* writer. "Any pieces that didn't paint Arondi in a good light got tweaked before going to press. I quit to go freelance."

Irving even let Arondi and other favorite sources vet stories that mentioned them, letting them make adjustments.

If a reporter or an editor at a major daily newspaper flouted the basic rules of journalism the way Whitey Irving did, they'd have been sanctioned, or have their press passes revoked.

Meanwhile, Arondi treated the female actors that came to him with callous disregard. Women report interviews in which he invited them to join him in the hot tub, auditions in which they were ordered to remove items of clothing, meetings that were unexpectedly changed from public to private locations, unwelcome physical advances, inappropriate conversations, and several instances of unwanted intimate contact. Women who complained did not receive roles and were never hired by Arondi Productions. Women who acquiesced found a modicum of success, but at a price too high.

The tide finally turned against Richard Arondi when a previously protected witness came forward to corroborate the accusations of one of Arondi's victims. This brave person has given courage to many other women who've until now felt powerless against a monster.

Defamation suits are also being brought against Arondi, who was found to have waged numerous smear campaigns against competing production companies, including the late Roman Byers, whom Arondi claimed was negligent in the Vasquez Rocks accident that killed one young actor and injured several others.

Numerous settlements of undisclosed amounts have been awarded. Whether Arondi receives a prison sentence for his crimes remains to be seen, but what's clear is this: the king of Hollywood has been dethroned.

Lawyers for Arondi declined to comment.

# Chapter Twenty-Three

From Abby's notebook:

*Cover fruiting berry bushes with netting to keep
birds from eating all the crop. You've done the work.
You deserve to enjoy the result.*

Jon walked up the steps of the main house porch and made
his way to the kitchen. He'd already looked for Abby in the
garden, the stables, the kennels, the little cove of blackberry
bushes by the beach, where she went to think. If she was
here, she'd most likely be helping Daphne.

If not, Daphne might know where to find her.

"Jon." The moment the cook saw him, she ran to him,
wiping her hands on a towel. He hadn't realized how much
he needed the touch of a friend until he felt her firm, warm
embrace.

"Daphne," he said, with a tear-thickened voice, "where's
Abby?"

She cleared her throat, stepped back, and motioned for
him to take a seat at the island. "Out. She'll be back. Sit

down. I've been worried about you, my boy. You shouldn't have left the way you did. This is when you need your friends around you, people who care about you. People who remember your father and have an idea what you're going through."

"I know," he said. "I had some things to take care of."

She reached into the cupboard and came out with a plate of cookies, which she plunked onto the countertop in front of him.

"Oatmeal-raisin, peanut-butter, chocolate-chip, and coconut-pecan. Pick your poison."

Then she poured two tall glasses of milk and sat down opposite him.

"Tell Daffy what's on your mind, honey. Don't pretend it's nothing because I can see it's something. And don't make me guess because I already know."

The cookies smelled fresh and his stomach rumbled. He realized that, despite the numerous casseroles and baked goods dropped off by well-meaning acquaintances, he hadn't eaten much lately. He'd packaged the food up and put it all in Roman's freezer, unsure if it would ever get eaten.

He took a cookie from the plate.

"I thought I knew what I wanted. I became a journalist to fix things that were wrong in the world. To shine a light in the dark areas."

"And you did that."

"Did I? I might have gotten the ball rolling but there's so much more to do."

The legal machinations would take years. Arondi's behavior had been exposed, which meant he wouldn't be able to prey on women like Carly Cassidy anymore. Whitey Irving had taken a massive hit, too. *Diversion* was circling the drain, its reputation shot, its advertising gutted.

Jon had offers from every entertainment magazine in

the business. He could write his own ticket, thanks to the Arondi exposé.

But somehow, the victory was hollow.

There were a million causes, he thought. Somewhere along the way, he'd gotten so focused on one pile of manure that he'd stopped seeing the big wide world around it, filled with lots of other shit that could be cleaned up, or, better, turned into acres of beauty. Sanctuary Ranch was making the world a better place, far more effectively than he ever had.

He didn't want to live in Los Angeles anymore. And now, he didn't have to. His condo had sold the week after the funeral. He'd packed up what little he couldn't live without, giving away the rest, and now it sat in a trailer in front of Roman's house, waiting to be unloaded.

He had a home here in Sunset Bay, thanks to his father. He had friends, a dog who needed him.

"You know, your father was pretty smart." Daphne took a bite of her cookie. "He picked Abby out for you long before either of you had a clue. Of course, he was also thick as a brick. He should have told you the truth about his cancer when he found out. But I guess better late than never. I'm going to miss that man."

"Yeah," said Jon. "Me, too. Are you going to tell me where Abby is?"

"Depends. What are your intentions toward her?"

Jamie's face peeked from around the corner of the door. Below it was Sage. Above was Haylee.

"I can see you," Jon said.

The three women practically tumbled into the room.

"She's our friend," Jamie said. "We have a right to know."

"If you hurt her," Sage warned.

"Sage!" Haylee said. Then she turned to Jon and smiled. "You weren't planning on hurting her, were you? Because we would have to kill you, then."

Jon couldn't help but laugh. The strength of these

friendships went past anything he'd ever experienced. This place was a family, in every sense of the word.

"She's the best thing that's ever happened to me," he said. "I want to be with her for the rest of my life. I'd tell her, but I don't know where she is."

The women looked at each other.

"I don't know," Haylee said. "Do we trust him?"

"He's a man," Sage replied. "I thought that meant an automatic no."

"You have much to learn, young one," Daphne said. "Not all men are scum. Some can be taught. I believe this one has potential."

"I do," Jon said.

"Practice those words," Daphne said. "I'll be expecting to hear them said properly, very soon."

Abby hiked the wheelbarrow up and began carting it to the compost heap. She was tired. She wanted to work on her recipes, but this was the growing season.

She missed Jon. She missed Roman. She missed Chaos. She'd missed the routine of going up to the house, playing games, and having quiet cups of tea on the porch.

The house was empty now. Jon was in Los Angeles. Chaos was probably becoming familiar with doggy daycare and forgetting all about his human friends here in Oregon.

As Jon predicted, Quinn's testimony had been the lynchpin in the case against Richard Arondi. She'd spent some time with Carly while she'd been there but had returned as soon as she could.

Quinn appeared . . . settled. As if something that had been bothering her was now put to rest. She was working hard with Ziggy, her rescue dog. She spent time every week with Jamie and the therapy dogs. She had begun studying canine behavior via an online course.

She was talking about going to college, possibly becoming a teacher. Or a psychologist.

She insisted that Abby no longer had to worry about her, that she could just be an ordinary sister now, but Abby had no idea what that meant.

She was floating without an anchor.

Lost and alone, exactly as she'd always expected.

But letting Jon go was the right thing to do. He deserved a chance to achieve his dreams, and in a small town like Sunset Bay, that wasn't going to happen.

All the time she and Quinn had been alone and struggling, she'd never felt as lonely as she did right now. Her sister had plans but Abby didn't.

She'd never looked toward the future. She'd never imagined a life of possibility and hope, despite what Jon had told her. He'd been wrong about a lot of things.

She certainly never dreamed she'd fall in love.

All those things had happened, but they'd happened out of order, and now her reasoning no longer applied. Jon had been right. She was a coward. She had been using Quinn as an excuse.

But it was too late now.

She straightened up and wiped her forearm across her brow. Somewhere beyond the trees, she heard the sound of tires on gravel, followed by a car door. The dogs in the kennel set up their usual racket when someone came on the yard.

Life would go on, as Roman said. She'd recover, find a new way to be. It would be fine.

The barking grew louder and then, a dog burst through the leafy green screen beyond the garden.

He raced toward her, a yellow Labrador with a red tongue lolling out of his grinning mouth.

"Chaos?" she said, dropping her gloves.

The dog leaped and cavorted at her side, licking and howling and leaning against her in an overflow of affection.

But if Chaos was here . . .

Against the setting sun she saw a figure approaching. A tall, lean man with a distinctive lanky gait.

It couldn't be. She pressed a hand to her mouth, unable to move.

Jon.

"Settle down, Chaos," he said. "It's my turn."

He strode up to her and took her in his arms without missing a beat.

"You . . . you left."

"You think you can get rid of me that easily?" he said into her hair. "Think again."

She burst into tears. "You came back?"

"Of course I came back."

"I've missed you so much." She hung on to him like he was a life preserver and she was drowning.

She took a step back, peered into his face. "But what about your job? Your condo? Your . . . life?"

"I sold my condo. I turned down the offers in L.A. My life is wherever you are. I'm moving into Dad's place. I told Elliott that I'd be happy to contribute remotely, until he can find a replacement, but I'll be freelancing while we decide what the future holds. I'm thinking of writing a book."

She couldn't make sense of his words. "Freelancing? A book?"

"I'm back, Abby. Not just for a visit, but for good. I love you. You're here, so this is where I have to be."

His expression was so earnest, so full of love, she could barely say what she needed to. "I love you too, Jon. I do. I can't help it. But I'll always be Quinn's big sister and if she needs me, I have to be there for her. I'm sorry."

He pushed her back so he could look at her. "Don't be sorry. Of course we'll be there for her. She'll always have a place with us, if she wants. To live, to visit, to look after our babies, whatever."

Abby's jaw dropped.

He raised his eyebrows. "Oh yes. There will be babies. Puppies and kittens for sure. Probably human babies, too. I suspect Quinn won't want to live with a couple of lovebirds like us, but that's totally up to her."

"And you want to live here, in Sunset Bay, at Roman's place?"

He shrugged. "It's grown on me. I don't think I slept properly for a single night in California. The air is different out here. You told me it was a healing place and I think you're right. I healed my relationship with my dad before he died. Now I want to heal my relationship with you."

The dog had plopped himself into the warm earth and was watching them, panting happily.

"Chaos missed this place. He missed you, too. I missed you. You have no idea how much."

"I have more of an idea than you know. But Jon, you can't further your career from a remote location like this."

He lifted his eyebrows. "You'd be surprised. Plus, you know the old saying about how if you keep doing what you've always done, you'll keep getting what you've always gotten?"

She nodded.

"I wasn't reaching my goals in Hollywood. I thought I was. Dad made me see that I'd been focused on revenge, when I should have been focused on making the world a better place. So, I'm changing my goals."

"That's wonderful, Jon."

"And I want you to think about yours, too. You can keep working here at the ranch, of course. I know how much you love it. But what about horticulture school? Or opening your own landscaping business or flower shop? As long as we're together, Abby, we'll come up with bigger and better dreams than we ever imagined. And whether we succeed or fail, it won't matter because we'll have each other."

His dreams for her were bigger than anything she'd dared hope for herself, and he wasn't done.

"I love you," he said. Then he spread his hands out at his sides, helplessly. "I love you. Wherever you go, whatever you want to do, if you'll have me, I'll be there. The only thing that matters is that we're together. I want to spend the rest of our lives taking care of each other. So, Abby, I'm asking. Do you love me, too?"

"Yes, Jon," she whispered in his ear. "I love you. I think I always have."

He dropped to his knees and she gasped.

"Abby Warren," he said. "Will you marry me? I can't live without you. I know, because I tried."

She couldn't speak. She wanted to, but the words wouldn't come out. Her voice failed her. Jon was a man who lived by words and she had none to give him. She'd kept her words tucked inside her, where they were safe, where no one could steal them or twist them or use them against her.

But he'd understood her anyway. Jon said Roman had talked about a language that we didn't know we understood, until we found ourselves speaking it. He meant love, she realized. It had always been there, waiting for her to be ready.

She nodded. Up and down, again and again, until the words came back.

"Yes." The word came out in a squeak. "Yes! Of course I'll marry you."

Chaos leaped to his feet and ran circles around them, barking with joy.

Behind them, their friends high-fived and laughed and hugged each other.

"About time," Daphne called.

In her mind's eye, Abby imagined that she could see, somewhere beyond the garden, past the stables and the kennels, up the wooded hillside and on the other side of the creek, a gray-haired man with wise, satisfied eyes peering between the silvered clouds at them, smiling.

Abby gaped uncomprehendingly. "What?"

"The terms of Dad's will are clear." Jon squeezed her hand. "It's a done deal. It's in your name. Goldie's bakery, although she said she'd be happy for you to rename it whatever you like."

Luckily for her she was already seated because she couldn't feel her legs. Roman had left her a business? With waterfront property?

"This is like a soap opera," she said. "The penniless young woman wiggles her way into the affections of an older man with a terminal illness, so she can get her hands on his money."

"He probably got a kick out of it, too," Jon said.

She shook her head. "What am I going to do with a bakery?"

"Abby." Jon took her hand. "Don't panic. There's no rush. No need to make any decisions. The mortgage and taxes are paid. The property is yours to do with as you like. Dad wanted to do this for you. He understood how much you've sacrificed in your life, how much you've had to fight and claw for everything you've got, how hard you work, how much you love your sister."

Hearing all those things brought tears to her eyes. Roman, for all his gruff mannerisms and sometimes harsh words, had seen the truth of her. And yes, he'd loved her.

"He also wanted to make sure that Roman's Apple Cake became famous. He made me promise to write about it in the *Sunset Bay Chronicle*'s annual restaurant round-up. The apple cake, the cookies, all of his favorites. You're to bake to your heart's content. You were the daughter he'd always wanted. He wanted to give you this chance. What you do with it is up to you."

"Jon, did he give me your inheritance?" She pressed her palms over her mouth. She'd sign the deed over to Jon, in that case, no matter what Roman's final wishes had been.

But he squeezed her hands and bent forward, peering at her from around the curtain of hair.

"Abby," he said, "my father was a very wealthy man. He received a generous insurance settlement following the accident in L.A. He invested it wisely and he lived simply, out here with his dogs and his birds and his garden. He never let on that he had money, probably because he didn't want people to think there was anything to get from him. I suspect he included me in that group."

"Well." Abby gave a hiccupping laugh. "He certainly had us all fooled. I'm happy for him but I still can't take the money."

"He thought that's how you'd feel. So here's the other part. He's set up a fund for Quinn, so she can go to school."

Another shock. He'd thought of Quinn, too?

"Enough for four years, tuition and housing. She can become a teacher if that's still what she wants. Or do something else with the money, it's up to her. But if you don't accept yours, she doesn't get hers."

Quinn, a teacher. Abby's mind boggled. She had a gift for children, especially those with needs over and above those met in a typical classroom. Quinn recognized the outliers, the watchers, the not-included. She recognized them because she'd been one herself, and knew, instinctively, what they needed.

"He thought of everything, didn't he?"

Roman knew exactly how to play her. He knew that if there was a chance to help Quinn, she'd take it, no matter how difficult it was for her.

"He gave a lot of gifts, not all money," Jon said. "He made

a donation to help start up the equine therapy program—and to keep Apollo in oats for the rest of his life."

Abby laughed. "He certainly loved that horse."

"Apollo was good for him."

And not just that horse. Roman had become a favorite with many of the rescues: horses, dogs, even the barn cats. For someone who'd once been a recluse, he'd ended up touching so many lives.

"He was a wonderful man."

Jon's face grew distant for a moment. "You gave him the gift of one last summer, staying in his house, where he wanted to be. I didn't know it at the time," he said, turning back to her with the smile she loved so well, "but it turned out to be the best gift for me, too."

## ROMAN'S APPLE CAKE

Preheat oven to 350 degrees F.

Combine in mixing bowl:
    1 cup brown sugar
    1 cup all-purpose flour
    1¼ cup whole wheat flour
    ¼ teaspoon salt
    ½ teaspoon baking powder
    1½ teaspoon baking soda
    ½ teaspoon cloves
    1 teaspoon cinnamon

Beat in:
    ⅔ cup canola oil
    2 eggs
    ⅔ cup buttermilk
    1½ teaspoon vanilla

Add:
    3 cups Jonagold apples, peeled and chopped

    Mix well. Pour into greased and floured 9 x 13 inch pan.

Crumble together:
    1 tablespoon melted butter
    2 teaspoons cinnamon
    ⅓ cup brown sugar
    2 teaspoons flour
    ½ cup coconut
    ½ cup rolled oats

    Cover cake batter with streusel topping and bake uncovered for 30–35 minutes. Let cool completely before serving.

If you enjoyed BLACKBERRY COVE,
be sure not to miss the book where it all started,

# SUNSET BAY SANCTUARY

by
Roxanne Snopek!

Available in your favorite bookstore or e-retailer.

*Turn the page for a peek at Haylee and Aiden's story!*

*"Two thumbs up for Sanctuary Ranch: go for the horses.
Stay for the food. Best week ever."*

—DanandJan

There was a lot to love about ranch life, and as Haylee
Hansen breathed in the aromas coming through the open
sliding doors to the main house, and listened to the cook and
her assistant bantering in the kitchen, she agreed with Dan
and Jan's Trip Advisor review.

Horses, *dogs* and food, she amended.

Best *life* ever.

"Come on, Ju-Jube," she said to the elderly dog at her
side. "Let's see what Daphne's got for us tonight."

The dog, who was actually called Jewel but responded to
a variety of names including *Jay, Sweetie-bear, treat, walkies,
car-ride*, and anything to do with food—perked her ears and
wagged her beaver-fat tail, her tongue lolling sideways from
her grinning jaw. Jewel was the unwanted product of a classic
princess/stable boy romance between a champion pedigreed
Labrador retriever and an unknown opportunist, but her ac-
cidental life had brought immeasurable joy to dozens of
people over the years.

Haylee loved her like a child.

"I hope that animal's feet are clean." Daphne took one hand off a generous hip and pointed at Jewel. "You know where your bed is, Miss Ju-Jube-Bear. No getting in the way, you hear me?"

Jewel ambled to the large pillow in the corner and flopped onto it with a grunt, wagging her tail the whole time. She knew the drill.

Haylee stood on her tiptoes and peeked at the oven. "Is that pot roast I smell?"

"It's the smell of murder." Jamie, the kitchen assistant, stood at the prep station, her pierced eyebrows furrowed, up to her elbows in greens. She'd gone vegetarian three weeks ago and considered it her sacred duty to convert everyone else, as well. A month before that, she'd been all about coconut oil, which Daphne had been surprisingly open to. This, however, was a battle doomed to failure.

"It's pork shoulder and root vegetables roasted in pan drippings." Daphne donned oven mitts, opened the door and lifted the enormous roasting pan onto the stovetop. "Kale salad, too. If Jamie can chop and complain at the same time."

Haylee's stomach growled at the rich, fragrant steam that wafted into the room.

"It smells amazing," she said. "Where are the guys? Still out on the trail?"

The wranglers had taken the foster boys plus a group of horseback riders out that morning.

Daphne nodded. "Olivia suggested they might want to top the day off with a wiener roast at the lookout, so I packed them a basket."

Haylee busied herself pouring a drink, grateful for Olivia's thoughtfulness. Of course, her aunt would be doing it for herself, as much as Haylee. It was a tough day for both of them.

"It's just you, me, Liv, and Gayle tonight," Daphne said. "And plenty of leftovers for tomorrow's lunch."

Haylee looked at Jamie. "You're not eating with us?"

The girl lifted her chin with a martyred air. "I'll be enjoying my salad in my quarters."

Jamie Vaughn was twenty-five, with the life experience of a forty-year-old and the attitude of a teen. She had arrived on Olivia's doorstep from Los Angeles several years ago like an oil-slicked seabird, all gawky limbs and tufted, greasy black hair, only tolerating their kindness because exhaustion and misery outweighed her ability to fight it off.

She'd been back and forth a few times but this time she seemed to want to stay. Haylee hoped she would. The ranch was good for Jamie. There was something healing about the Oregon coast. The air had a fresh, stinging bite. Food tasted better. With all the quiet, sound seemed purer, clearer, especially after busy city streets.

The ranch was good for all of them, in different ways.

"Your choice," Daphne said pitilessly. "Everyone's welcome at my table, but I set the menu. Take it or leave it."

"I choose life." Jamie plunked the enormous wooden bowl onto the long wooden dining room table. The salad was gorgeous, fresh curly leaves of kale mixed with sliced red cabbage, shaved brussels sprouts, slivered almonds and chewy cranberries, all covered with a sweet, tangy poppyseed dressing.

She served herself a large portion and then looked at Daphne. "Enjoy your flesh."

Daphne gave a low chuckle. "I've always enjoyed my flesh, honey."

Jamie made a face. "Gross. I'm outta here. Oh!" She stopped and turned to Haylee. "Before I forget, there's someone I want you to meet at the shelter. You have time in the next day or two to come with me?"

Haylee winced. Jamie's probation included community service at a variety of animal shelters, and Haylee's intake of potential service dogs had gone up dramatically since Jamie's arrival. She loved the young woman's enthusiasm, and had to admit she had great natural ability with dogs, but Sanctuary Ranch had only so much space.

She sighed. "Sure. Let's talk tomorrow, okay?"

Jamie grinned and bounced out with her plate, the argument with Daphne forgotten.

Olivia and Gayle arrived in time to hold the screen door for Jamie, and managed to hold back their laughter until they got into the kitchen.

"I understand we've arrived at the scene of a crime," Gayle said, giving Haylee a one-armed side hug.

"That girl." Olivia took her usual seat nearest the window, her long, gray-blond braid slipping over her wiry shoulder. "I can't wait until she finds herself. But she's entertaining, no doubt about that."

Daphne glanced out the window. "Don't tell her, but I'm experimenting with some meatless dishes."

Haylee gave a bark of laughter and nearly dropped her water glass. "Seriously? This is going to be awesome." Then she thought for a moment. "The guys are going to hate that."

"So what? We could all do with a little less cholesterol. It's not like I'm going to quit cooking meat entirely." Daphne set the platter of sliced meat and crispy skinned vegetables onto the table. "I was already thinking about it before she went all Tibetan monk on us. Now, she's going to think it was all her idea. She'll never let me hear the end of it."

She surveyed the table. "What am I forgetting? Oh yes, applesauce."

Daphne went back to the kitchen and Haylee watched from the corner of her eye as the cook casually glanced over her shoulder, then set a small plate in front of Jewel. Haylee pretended not to notice.

No one went hungry in Daphne's kitchen. Period. It was an inarguable precept. If Jewel came in, she got fed. Haylee didn't believe Daphne would enforce the ban, but she also didn't want to test it. The compromise was lean meat, vegetables and equivocation. Jewel certainly wasn't complaining.

"Applesauce?" Haylee said.

Daphne laughed. "Behind the bread basket. I guess we're both blind today."

They passed the dishes around family style, laughing and chatting in a way they couldn't quite do when the whole motley staff was present.

Yes, besides the animals, the best part of life on the ranch was the joy of coming together at the end of the day to share food, stories, news, gossip, the little things that make up a day, a week, a life.

Meat or no meat.

"Have you heard?" Gayle was saying. "There's a new doctor in town. I met him today at the department meeting. He comes from Portland with a rock-star reputation. He's also single, gorgeous and let's just say, if I wasn't batting for the other team, I'd be checking him out."

"Hey," Olivia protested. "I've got feelings, you know."

"Your feelings are as fragile as a bull moose," Gayle said with an affectionate smile.

Olivia tilted her head and looked at the ceiling. "True. So tell us more."

"Maybe we could set him up with Haylee," Daphne said, her eyes alight.

"Ooh, good idea," Olivia said. "It's high time."

"They'd look good together," Gayle said. "He's got dark hair and eyes, almost Mediterranean-looking."

Daphne put a hand to her chest and sighed. "With Haylee's fair coloring and curls."

"Hello." Haylee waved her fork at them. "I'm right here."

"He's heading up the emergency room," Gayle continued, ignoring her. "Maybe she'll get kicked by a steer again."

"She's awful clumsy," Daphne added thoughtfully. "Just yesterday she stumbled bringing in a bagful of groceries. She could have fallen off the porch and broken her arm."

"I am not clumsy," Haylee said. No one even looked at her.

"Gideon's got that new skittish horse," Olivia said. "Maybe she could help him. That's an accident waiting to happen."

"While I appreciate your good wishes," Haylee broke in, "I'm not in the market for a rock-star boyfriend and have no intention of injuring myself for an introduction."

"Oh, honey," Daphne said with a laugh, "you stick to your animals and leave matters of the heart to the experts."

She lifted a palm and Olivia and Gayle returned air high-fives to her from across the table.

"A lesbian couple and a happily divorced middle-age cook?" Haylee said. "I question your credentials."

"Evil child. I'm in my prime." She got to her feet, her smile gone. "Who wants pie?"

Too late Haylee remembered that Daphne referred to herself as a divorcée but was, in fact, happily *widowed*, the end of her marriage and the end of her husband occurring around the same time, under circumstances that would have felled a lesser woman.

Haylee carried her plate to the sink, and gave the cook a hug. "Sorry, Daffy," she whispered. Then she straightened and raised her voice. "Dinner was great. I'll have pie later. Right now, Jewel and I need a walk. Come on, baby-girl."

The dog lurched to her feet, casting a longing glance at the plate beside her, licked glistening white, as if nothing had ever besmirched the pristine surface.

Not many people were on the beach, which suited Haylee's mood perfectly. She walked near the shining edge where the sand was surf-hardened and damp, enjoying the solid crunching shift of each footstep and the briny bite of ocean air. Occasionally she landed on a soft spot and her feet sank an inch or two but she didn't care. There were worse things than wet feet.

A lot worse.

There was no point lingering in the past, but memory was cyclical and the calendar didn't lie, so one day a year, she allowed herself to test the heaviness, like a tongue seeking a sore tooth, to see if it was still there, if it still hurt.

It was, and it did.

But a little better each year. And she'd feel better tomorrow.

Jewel gave a muffled woof and Haylee jumped. She lifted her gaze to see the dog loping awkwardly on dysplastic hips to greet a man approaching from the opposite direction.

"Jewel," she called, but the dog ignored her.

By sight, or by the dog they were with, she knew most of the people who frequented the stretch of sand between the town and the ranch property. But this man, she'd never seen before.

He lifted his head and pulled his hands from his pockets as Jewel came nearer, and reached out to pat her. He was tall and broad, his dark hair a fiery halo in the waning light.

"Hey there. This your dog?" His voice was espresso rich, deep and smooth as cream. "She's a real sweetheart."

If this was the rock-star doctor, Gayle hadn't been kidding.

"Yeah." She cleared her throat and swallowed. "Sorry about that. Jewel, come on back. She's very friendly."

"So I see. It's nice." The man squatted on his haunches to give Jewel a good scrubbing on her ribs. The dog groaned, her entire body wagging in delight.

A rock-star doctor who liked dogs.

"Sorry to interrupt your walk," she said, coming close enough to clip the leash onto Jewel's collar. He stood up as she did and she felt the full force of his presence.

There were lines around his eyes and mouth, laugh lines, she guessed, though the shadows dancing across his sculpted features suggested he hadn't been laughing much lately. Her stomach gave a little flip.

Maybe he was just tired.

"Don't apologize." His gaze was direct and appreciative. "A friendly face is just what I needed today."

Haylee looked away, fumbling with the leash. "Good. I'm glad. Well. See you around, I guess."

She tugged gently and led the dog away. He may or may not be the person Gayle described but she had enough sense to know that chatting with a strange man on a nearly deserted beach as the sun went down was a bad idea. Dog lover or not.

Even though she really wanted to stay.

Especially since she wanted to stay.

She angled her path upward so she could keep an eye on him as he walked away and before long, he'd disappeared around a rise of black rock.

"He seemed nice," she told Jewel. "Though I could be biased by pretty packaging and a very nice voice. I'd ask your opinion but you're as subtle as a freight train. You'd snuggle up to Jeffrey Dahmer if you thought he'd feed you."

The dog kept looking behind them, as if hoping the man would reappear. And he hadn't given Jewel any food whatsoever.

"I don't have time for a man," she said. "Or interest."

She'd blown through her share of relationships—if you could call them that—years ago and wasn't interested in revisiting that minefield.

Fine. She was a coward.

"On the off chance I read the vibe correctly," she continued, "I'm doing him a favor by shutting this down before it gets started. Trust me."

Jewel wagged her tail, panted and licked her lips.

"Enough arguing," she said. "Time to head on home."

As they retraced their steps to the area where she'd last seen the man, a sound wafted over the water. A voice, calling out. Calling *her*?

"Did you hear something?"

Haylee squinted against the last rays of gold and scarlet painting the smooth ripples of the bay, in the universal human belief that by straining her eyes she'd be able to hear better.

She glanced at her dog, ambling across the vast, lonely stretch of sand ahead of her.

Of course the dog had heard it. The lapping Pacific surf that muffled sound to human ears was nothing to a dog.

*His* voice?

She was probably imagining the distress.

Most likely, she was hearing some kids horsing around up by the cabins, in which case, they'd say hello and call it a night.

But what if it was someone in trouble?

"Find it, Jewel."

Immediately, the dog put her nose to the ground.

Haylee picked up her pace, watching Jewel's tail sweep back and forth, a flesh-and-blood metronome, the *tick-tick-tick* measuring out a life lived in the moment, anticipation unmarred by dimming vision and arthritic hips, joy untarnished by worry or regret.

She thought of her current fosters: the little terrier cross, so full of attitude. Another Lab–pit bull, who was almost ready to move to his forever home. The border collie with the thousand-yard stare. None of them compared to Jewel.

She pulled salt air deep into her lungs following as the dog moved upward, scrambling over the surf-scoured rocks gleaming against the fading citrus sky, absorbed, Haylee imagined, not so much in the object at the end of the search, as the search itself. The journey, not the destination.

Jewel glanced back as if to say *Pay attention!*

"Right behind you, girl."

She'd heard no more calls, but the old dog's zeal was a joy to see. And you never knew.

Like freshwater pearls on a loose string, the Oregon coastline was dotted with beaches, each one a glowing gem nestled against the velvety silhouette of black rock. The wind-and-surf-pounded outcroppings, with their hidden caves and mussel-laden tide pools, all gloriously inviting in the light of day, told a different story when darkness fell.

It wouldn't be the first time an unsuspecting beachcomber or sunbather had miscalculated the tides and spent a chilly night waiting for the ocean to recede.

Newcomers and visitors were especially vulnerable.

She cupped her hands around her mouth. "Hello? Is someone there?"

In the silent suspension between waves, Haylee listened for the voice, but caught only the *pad-pad-swish* of foot and paw on sand, empty nothingness.

Not the tall stranger then, with his piercing eyes and soft dog-patting hands who may or may not be Gayle's handsome doctor.

"Ju-Jube, honey, I think we're SOL on this one."

But Jewel bunched her shoulders and clambered ahead. Haylee knew when she was being ignored. She ought to be firmer. She ought to reassert her position as alpha.

Being and doing as she ought to got old. It wasn't as if Jewel sought domination of their little pack, after all. She knew on which side of the pantry door her kibble was buttered.

Just then the ocean paused its breathing and the sound came again, a voice, certainly, *his* voice, maybe, carried gently over the evening air, but landing not so much like distress as . . . the sounds you made when you banged your head getting into your car, cussing yourself out for stupidity. *Dumb-ass noises,* she thought.

"Woof," said Jewel, breaking into a stiff old lady's run.

"Please don't throw yourself at him this time," she cautioned. "He could be hurt." More likely a loss of dignity, which did not preclude the need for assistance; however, she knew from experience that where dignity was concerned, the need for assistance was often inversely proportional to its welcome.

"Hello?" she called again. "Is everything okay?"

No answer.

Haylee pulled herself up onto a ledge of rock, the top still dry, but not for long, as evidenced by growing splotches of foam where the incoming tide marked it. Already across, the dog splashed through a tide pool still warm from the sun, and disappeared around a corner. Haylee hissed as her knee grazed a section of mussel-encrusted rock, glad she'd switched her flip-flops for sturdy-soled ankle boots after supper. She'd have to check Jewel's paws carefully when they got back.

A watery crash sounded, large-dog loud.

"Jewel!" Haylee hauled herself over boulders slippery with algae and bits of kelp. The Labrador retriever in Jewel gave her a great love of the water, but the Y chromosome could have come from a hippo, for all the grace she had.

Another splash, then a storm of sloshing and splattering, and then the voice again, clearer now. Her pulse sped up a notch.

It was definitely him. Didn't sound like he was in trouble. Though he could certainly *be* trouble. And now, there wasn't a single other soul to be seen on the peaceful beach.

"Are you okay? Be careful with my dog. She's old."

More squelching slips, accompanied by grunts and indeterminate half shouts. Haylee wide-stepped over a shallow pool and clambered around another section of rock, peering frantically for Jewel's form among the shadows beneath her.

"It's the friendly dog," came the voice. "That's a relief."

She looked down onto the rocky landing from where she heard the voice and saw a figure sitting on the dark slab of rock next to a glittering pool, the sharp edges worn smooth by surf and wind. A white T-shirt clung to his upper body, cargo shorts below, both darkened by water. Jewel draped over him like a bad fur coat, half-on, half-off, her tail slapping wetly on the rock.

The man sounded neither surprised nor irritated but, since Jewel's sudden appearance would most certainly be cause for such reaction, this in itself was disconcerting.

"We heard you calling," she said. "Thought you might need help."

"Way better than an amorous sea lion, at least, which was my first impression," continued the man, as if she hadn't spoken.

That nice crisp voice had a note of desperate calm running through it now.

Haylee half climbed, half slid down the rock separating them.

There he was, the same handsome stranger, in the flesh.

"So, you're okay, then?" she asked, slipping down the last bit, until she was standing just above where he sat with Jewel.

"Oh, absolutely. I'm more than okay. I'm fantastic." He gestured to the dog. "I can't feel my legs, though. Do you mind?"

"Right." Haylee motioned for Jewel to climb off.

He winced as the dog's nails dug into his thighs. "You sure she's not a sea lion? Ow! Or possibly a walrus? Wait. No tusks."

Haylee gave Jewel a hug. "Good girl, you found him. What

a smart girl you are." The dog was wet, happy, and whole. She'd definitely earned her cookies tonight.

The guy rubbed his legs and got to his feet, keeping a hand on the rock. Yes, still tall. Still big. And all muscle, despite the unsteadiness.

Her pulse jumped another notch. The vibe coming off him was clangy, discordant, like an orchestra in warm-up, after the long summer break. The scattered light reflecting off waves and wet rock cast stark shadows across the rugged planes of his face. No laugh lines now.

"She was looking for me? Not to appear ungrateful, but I can't imagine why. If she's a sniffer dog, the cigarettes are oregano, I swear. I'm holding them for a friend. I've never even inhaled."

She took a step back and put a hand on Jewel's warm back.

There was no scent of tobacco, let alone weed, but he was speaking too quickly. Something definitely had him rattled and it was more than indignity.

"I'm joking. Badly, I see. Don't worry, I'll keep my distance. I bet you wish you'd taken a different path tonight."

"What are you doing out here?" Someone needed to get this conversation on track.

He wiped his face with his forearm. A tattoo ran along the underside but she couldn't make out details. His strong jaw was liberally covered in a two-day growth of dark whiskers.

You expected such a man to growl or roar or paw the ground, yet he talked like he had a beer in one hand and a pair of aces in the other.

Bluffing?

"It went something like this. I was watching the sunset, minding my own business, when a large, sea lion-esque creature"—he indicated the dog nudging her pocket—"belly-flopped into the tide pool at my feet. She seemed to not want to be there, so I helped haul her out. That's when she took our relationship to the next level. You arrived. The end."

"*You* hauled *her* out?"

"What can I say?" he answered. "I'm a helper."

"In that case . . . thanks." She hesitated, then thought what the hell. "I'm Haylee Hansen. I work at Sanctuary Ranch, about a mile inland. You're the new doctor, aren't you?"

He looked a little taken aback but then he caught himself and said, "Guilty as charged. Aiden McCall. Nice to meet you, Haylee. And Jewel, the friendly dog."

"Why were you yelling?" Haylee asked. "I thought you were hurt."

"Would you believe I was practicing for an audition?"

"No."

"Right. My stand-up routine sucks. Oh well, worth a try."

He kept both hands on the rocky outcropping at his hip, as if he expected the earth to fall out from beneath his feet.

"You're going to be trapped," she said. "The tide's coming in."

He glanced down, as if only now noticing that his once-dry perch had an inch of water covering it.

"Huh. What do you know? I guess we'll be trapped together, then."

"Nah, that's a rookie mistake." She hesitated a moment, then sighed and held out her hand. "Come on. I'll help you out."

But just then, a chunk of mussel-shell broke under her boot. She stumbled forward and would have slipped into the water below, but he caught her, one hand on her arm, the other around her waist, and pulled her away from the edge.

His hands were cold from the water, his grip like icy steel but instead of a chill, heat rushed across her skin where he touched her. His scent enveloped her, a light, woodsy cologne overlaid with kelp and brine and wind and sweat.

She'd misinterpreted his body language, she realized. Tight, tense, alert, this man was *on*, the same way she remembered her father and brother being, as all firefighters, soldiers, and surgeons were, even on weekends. Life-and-death situations demanded and honed a kind of raw energy, a costly undercurrent that didn't disappear at the end of a shift.

"God, I'm so sorry," she said with a gasp. Daphne would love this story, if she ever got wind of it.

"Don't be." His breath was warm on her neck. "My male ego is vastly improved."

He stepped away the second she found her feet, then slapped wet sand from his thighs and butt.

Lean. Muscled. Nice.

*Oh dear.*

"Follow me," she told him, hoping it was too dark for him to see the blush she felt on her cheeks.

"What about your sea lion?"

"Jewel?" Haylee gave a little laugh. The dog had given up on extra treats and was now trotting down the rocks back to the sandy beach above the waterline. "She's way ahead of us. You okay to get back to . . . to get back?"

He lifted his chin and looked at the horizon, his eyes narrow, his full lips set tight with thin lines slicing deep on both sides, as if in pain.

"You bet," he said. "I'm great."

Sunset colors splashed over the stark planes of his face, warmth meeting chill, light and shadow flickering and dancing. Haylee shivered.

He looked, she thought, like a man walking through fire.

As the last of the light faded, Aiden McCall walked the half hour across the beach, angling upward until the smooth sand became interspersed with the rough brush and tall, spiky grasses growing roadside. How much of his rant, he wondered, had that dog-walker caught?

A million miles of empty beach and he had to pick the one spot where someone could hear him.

And not just anyone.

A cute blonde with long curly hair, toned arms, and the kind of no-nonsense attitude that belonged behind a triage desk.

Had she really thought he'd been stranded? Her dog—Jewel?—seemed to consider him the prize at the bottom of the Cracker Jack box. How long had he been sitting there? Surely not that long. But he wasn't the most reliable witness, was he?

One second he'd been watching the sun move down toward the sea and the next he was wrestling a dog in the semi-dark, up to his ass in seawater.

He swiped at his face, recalling the animal's warm tongue, ripe with the stink of life. Bacteria too numerous to count, certainly. Nothing dangerous, hopefully. Pet lovers always told him that living with animals strengthened the immune system; he preferred the soap-and-water method himself.

Still, the creature had shocked him with its fleshy closeness. The heavy body leaning against him without boundaries, judgment, awkward courtesy, or worst of all, sympathy, had been oddly intimate.

If only the woman hadn't been there to witness it all.

He kicked at a piece of driftwood. With his luck, she'd turn out to be pals with the head ER nurse, and before he'd even set foot in the hospital, everyone would know that the new trauma doc spent his evenings yelling into the sunset.

*Let it out. Yell. Scream. Be angry. Find a place where no one can hear you and get it all out.* Psychobabble bullshit.

What a load. Letting it out wasn't his style, but good old-fashioned denial wasn't working, so he had to try, didn't he?

Aiden preferred joking. He teased. He laughed. He

prattled in true idiot savant fashion. Because, contrary to the board-mandated therapist's belief, he was already plenty angry and well aware of it. But open that can of worms? Let it out? Who would that serve?

Still, he'd tried, as he'd tried everything. He'd yelled into the setting sun and not only did he not feel better, but by to-morrow, they'd be calling him Crazy Eyes and monitoring his scalpel blades.

If he had the energy, he'd feel mortified. Or at least, em-barrassed. But once you've self-diagnosed a heart attack in your own ER and been convinced you were dying, only to be informed that you were one hundred percent A-Okay, just suffering from anxiety, well, it was tough to beat that low.

His ward clerk finding him hyperventilating in the mop closet had done it, though.

That's when he knew he had to leave Portland. Two hun-dred and ten pounds of raw, quivering panic caused by a little car accident? He'd faced down whacked out meth-heads, calmed an armed man in full paranoid delusion, leaped into codes, led his team, handled everything, seen everything.

But the memories intruded, as they always did.

Tires squealing, metal screeching against metal, *"Mommy-Mommy-Mommy . . ."*

Then, silence.

The silence was the worst.

Aiden could hear his breath over the soft sounds of night. Slow down. Don't think about it.

Don't think at all.

But like avalanches, thoughts once started aren't easily stopped. They tumbled in, over, through, gaining momentum until now, after thirteen years running a Level 1 emergency facility in one of the biggest hospitals in the Pacific North-west, he was falling apart.

It was the damnedest thing.

His chest hurt. He couldn't catch his breath. He needed to get inside. To sit down. To lie down.

It was almost full dark now as he wound through the rabbit warren of Beachside Villas, looking for the one he'd rented for the summer, trying not to violate the privacy of those who hadn't drawn their curtains.

But the eye naturally follows light and every window seemed to frame people sitting around tables or moving about kitchens. Ordinary people. Ordinary meals. Not take-out in soggy cardboard containers, eaten alone in front of the TV, but real food. Eaten on dishes, at tables. Families. Friends. Husbands and wives.

Children.

Babies.

He couldn't resist looking, even though the sight of one towheaded youngster in a high chair brought Garret to mind so clearly his knees nearly buckled and he had to stop walking. This, years after the memory of his young son's face had faded, after making peace with Michelle's remarriage, being happy for her, even.

The vise grip banding his ribs tightened but he stumbled on, tearing his gaze away from the window frames.

Almost there. You can make it.

Rich smells spiked the air, piercing his mind, giving his fragmented concentration something to grab on to but it made things worse: spicy tomato sauce spilled thick and red, garlic bit like acid, grill-seared flesh smoked, choking him.

He gripped the back of his neck, then brought his hand up over his head, crushing his cap, as if he could physically squeeze the negative thoughts from his brain.

He was over this! He was strong, fine, great. So why was he gasping like an asthmatic in a dust storm?

He bent over, bracing his hands on his knees.

He'd probably forgotten to eat again. That was a mistake.

There was a bagel left in the cabin, he thought. In a bag on the counter. He'd eat that. That would help.

*Right. A bagel. That'll fix everything.*

He half straightened, stumbling Quasimodo-style to the small playground adjacent to his unit. He grabbed at the lamppost that cast a soft light over the swings and teeter-totter, swallowed hard, then forced his ribs to expand and contract.

Garret was gone. It was no one's fault. But that little boy six months ago, well. Aiden, of all people, should have known to check.

The lights from the windows started to dance in pairs, then triplets. He couldn't get enough air.

Rough gasps tore raggedly from his throat, littering the serene night air.

*In-one-two-three. Out-one-two-three.*

Nope. The lights stopped dancing and coalesced into one small pinpoint, disappearing down a long tunnel, far away, like a subway train.

*You're catastrophizing again,* called a little voice from way off on the subway train. Mountains, molehills. Tempests, teacups. Crazy eyes, yes, a result of adrenal overload caused by living in the worst-case scenario, of which he had endless templates.

It was entirely possible that he'd pull himself together, get a full night's sleep, and walk into the office tomorrow morning bright and competent, prepared to become the new emergency physician in the smallest trauma center he'd ever seen. It would be perfect. Bug bites. Food poisoning. Cuts and scrapes.

Yeah. He could do that.

Except that he was going to die first. His heart was exploding. The roar of the ocean pulsated all around him, thump-thump-rushing like blood from an aortic dissection.

Just because he hadn't been having a cardiac event last month didn't mean he wasn't having one now.

He pushed his back against the lamppost and slid down until he plopped hard into the dirt. He was fine. He just couldn't breathe, that's all. No one died of panic. Of course not. That was silly.

They died of cardiac arrest. Which followed respiratory arrest. Which was happening to him.

Right. Goddamn. Now.

He pushed his head between his knees, hoping to hell that he'd get over this spell before someone came by and found him. He imagined that big friendly dog leaping on him, body-slamming him to the ground, knocking the dead air out and resetting his lungs.

He remembered the woman, Haylee, when she'd fallen into him, her warmth bleeding into his cold flesh, hearing the steady, normal rhythm of her heart, the weight of her slender body like a blanket on a cold night, or a brick on a sheaf of papers, keeping them from flying away in the wind.

Slowly, slowly, the tunnel shortened.

The steel band around his chest loosened and he gulped in desperate lungfuls of cool night air. He was drenched all over again with icy sweat, as if he really had been trapped by the tide, like Haylee, the pretty dog-walker had warned. His limbs quaked and he couldn't have gotten to his feet for anything, but he could breathe again.

"You all right there, young man?"

Aiden lifted his head with a jerk. A figure stood in the lane beneath a large oak tree, her hair glowing white in the lamplight. Thin, knobby fingers gripped the slack leash attached to an equally small and elderly terrier.

"It's just, you look a little frayed around the edges," she added. "I recognize the signs, being a little frayed at times myself. Only you being young and strong, well. Seems a little out of place."

He got to his feet, keeping his back to the post in case the dizziness returned. It was too late for anonymity anyway, if such a thing was even possible in a small town.

"I'm . . . fine, thank you," he managed. "It's been a . . . fraying . . . kind of day."

"Ah, yes. Those happen, don't they? Is there anything I can do to help?"

Her gentle smile eased the embarrassment that welled up in him at being caught. "You already have." He glanced around the deserted play area. "It's late. Would you like an escort home?"

She hesitated and he realized he'd overstepped. She was right to be cautious. He started to speak, but she interrupted him with a laugh, a crinkly, tinkling sound that danced over the night air. "My name is Elsie. My husband—Anton—and I are in cabin three. You're the new doctor, I believe, yes? In cabin four?"

He held out his hand. "I see word's gotten around. Aiden McCall. I'm very pleased to meet you, Elsie."

Her small bones felt like twigs. The dog eyed him suspiciously and took a couple of steps sideways.

"Be nice," Elsie said to the dog. "Her name's Bette Davis. She'll be fine once she gets to know you. I've got apple pie in the cabin. Would you care for a piece?"

A short stand of shrubs blocked his view of the cabins on either side, a factor that had played into his decision to rent here. He wanted privacy, not company. Still, her easy generosity drew him.

"I appreciate the offer, Elsie. But I've got an early morning tomorrow."

"Young people, always so busy," she said with a sigh. "We'll be off, then. But the offer stands if you find yourself at loose ends another time. I love to bake and pies are my specialty. We're here year-round and always enjoy meeting the summer people."

He waved at her. His hands were steadier now, his vision clearer.

"See you, Bette Davis," he called.

The dog glanced over her shoulder and gave a low *woof*.

Elsie waved again and disappeared around the corner.

Aiden leaned against the lamppost. Elsie and Anton, he thought. They sounded nice. He hoped they had a dozen pie-loving grandchildren.

He waited a minute or two to let his new friends get a head start, then followed the trail back to his cabin. What would he do if a dozen children suddenly showed up next door?

He'd have to find a new place.

No. He couldn't keep running. He had to be okay. He *was* okay.

He could breathe.

Some days, that was the best you could get.